the

making

of

her

Anna Aysgarth

To my husband who believed in me and made me believe in myself.

one

The flowers were already wilting as she crammed them into the jam jar, but she couldn't help it. That was the trouble with bluebells; they had looked stunning earlier that morning as she had walked through the woods. They had stretched before her like a living blue carpet. She had breathed in the scent, surprised something could smell so sweet so close to town, where the smell of smoke and dirt were dominant. Part of her wanted the moment to last forever, because she knew that from today, her life would change.

"What lovely flowers! Bluebells are my favourite," a voice said softly. Lily had not heard the classroom door open.

"Yes, Miss Hodgeson. I only picked them this mornin', but they're already dyin'."

The teacher walked further into the room, her movements, though efficient, caused her petticoats to rustle beneath the long, black skirt.

"No," her teacher agreed, "they don't last long, but they are very beautiful."

"They're for you, miss."

Miss Hodgeson smiled, her rather stern features softening. "Well, that's very kind of you, Lily. Thank you."

Lily took a deep breath. She did not return the smile. "I wanted to give you something, miss. Only I didn't have no money."

"Any money," Miss Hodgeson corrected automatically.

"Any money," Lily repeated. "Anyway, I wanted to get you somethin'."

Miss Hodgeson leaned forward to catch the scent of the flowers. "That's very thoughtful of you, Lily." It was not surprising seeing Lily in the classroom so early. Although teachers were not supposed to have favourites, Lily had been difficult to resist. She loved learning, soaking up as much knowledge as she could. She was always the first child to arrive in the barren playground and the last to leave.

If things were different, the teacher thought, *Lily would possibly have gone to university.*

She and Lily's mother had persuaded her father to let her stay on for three years or so as a pupil teacher. But things were as they were. Lily lived in a small Yorkshire mining town on the edge of poverty; her parents could neither afford her education nor had her father any interest in doing so. They needed the money she would bring in to help feed the rest of the family. Like most of the girls in the school, when she left at the end of the year, Lily would end up at the factory making shirts.

"The thing is, miss, it's my last day today. My dad has got me a job. I'm to start tomorrow."

The teacher took a step back and looked at Lily in surprise. "What do you mean your father has found you a job? You're a bright girl, Lily. You passed the scholarship. You should have gone to the grammar school. I had hoped that with the help of the tutoring you might be the first girl from this school to go on to university."

"My dad don't hold with schoolin' for girls. Says it's a waste of time. In any case, we couldn't afford it, and that's that." Lily wiped her nose with her sleeve. She had promised herself she would not cry, but the thought of leaving school filled her with a sadness she couldn't explain. Miss Hodgeson had opened Lily's eyes to a world beyond the grimy, crowded, mean streets of the misnamed town of Hope in which they lived.

Miss Hodgeson could have wept with her, but she had learned she could not interfere. The lives of the children in her care were often precarious. Mining communities were close-knit; they looked after each other. But many parents struggled to feed their children and put shoes on their feet, so who was she to judge what was for the best? She knew Lily's father had been injured in an accident, and that meant that the little money Lily could earn would be needed now more than ever before. She also knew that if Lily's father wanted to take her out of school, that is what he would do. In fact, it was a wonder he hadn't done so sooner. With almost any other parents, she would have gone to their home and tried to change their minds, but with the Russells, she knew Lily would suffer if she interfered.

Lily looked at her teacher with eyes wiser than they should be for a child of sixteen. "It's no use, miss. My dad's made up 'is mind. I'm to go into service at Mr. Grove's. It's a good position. I shall be a 'ousemaid. Who knows? One day, I may be a lady's maid or a 'ousekeeper."

"I'm sure you will, Lily. You work hard and be ambitious."

"Well, anyway, I just wanted you to have the flowers as a thank-you, like for the books you lent me and all the other things you taught me." Lily stopped, knowing that if she continued, she would cry. The long experience of being the daughter of Joey Russell taught her that crying, especially over something she could do nothing about, changed nothing. And it usually meant an extra beating.

Miss Hodgeson nodded and, to spare them both the risk of further embarrassment, said briskly, "I have to go out and ring the bell now. Check the inkwells, please, and fill them. Each pupil will also need a sheet of lined paper and blotting paper for our composition lesson."

Lily looked around the classroom, savouring the brief moment of silence before the other children came tumbling in: the windows that were too high for even the tallest child to be distracted from their work, the cream-and-green walls, the tall teacher's desk and chair overlooking the rows of desks, the slates neatly stacked on the shelves, and the rows of well-thumbed history books that had captured her imagination as she had learned about the Ancient Egyptians, Boudicca and The Romans, and the Anglo-Saxons and the Normans. She breathed in. More than anything, she would remember the smell of chalk, cabbage, and children. After today, she would no longer be part of this world. Her childhood, such as it had been, would be over.

Although Lily wanted time to slow down so she could savour her last day at school, it seemed to speed up. English, mathematics, history, geography, music, and art flew by at twice the speed they normally did. At the end of the day, Miss Hodgeson handed her a small, brown, paper package tied with string.

"It's nothing much. I know how much you enjoyed it when I read them to the class. I thought you might like to have your own."

Lily's eyes shone as she hugged the books close to her chest. "Thank you, miss. I won't forget you."

Her teacher smiled. "Nor I you, Lily. Now off you go, and remember that whatever you do in life, do it in the best way that you can."

Lily smiled to herself as she walked down the hill. She had never owned a book before, and now she had two. Her smile turned to a frown. She would have to be careful when she got home, or her precious possessions would be taken from her. There were no books in the house. Her father said books were a waste of time and they had more important things to spend their money on. If he found them, they would no doubt end up at Uncle Joe's at the end of the street. He would claim he had to pawn them to buy food for the family, but she knew from experience, they would see little of the money. And if her father didn't find them, her brothers would, and they would take the books just to torment her.

Lily had wondered on more than one occasion whether she really belonged to the same family. She was the only one who had any interest in learning, but a look in the small square of mirror in the kitchen had confirmed that she was. Her auburn curls, green eyes, heart-shaped face, and small nose were exactly like her mother's. She did not know how she came to be tall, but it was yet another thing for her brothers to pick on.

She quickly looked up and down the street as she turned the corner. There was a small gang of lads kicking a can around, but her brothers were not among them. Tucking her parcel down her skirt and wrapping her arms around it, she walked quickly towards her house. It was one of the shabbiest on the narrow street amidst a long terrace of brick houses that were broken only by the entrance to a backyard or other equally rundown streets. No blade of grass or tree was evident as far as the eye could see. Front doors opened directly onto the street, while the back doors led to small yards that held communal washhouses and toilets.

Her mother looked up from the range as Lily entered the house. The baby sat on her hip sucking the end of a wooden spoon. "Here, take Emily a minute. Your dad'll be back in a minute an' you know what he's like if food's not on the table by the time he's taken his boots off. If you think she'll settle, put her down, and then come down. I need the potatoes peeling." She thrust the child at Lily and turned back to the smoke-blackened pan.

Lily took the child without comment and carried her up to the bedroom she shared with her brothers and sisters. She lay her youngest sister in the drawer that served as her crib before taking her precious package out from her skirt and quietly opening it, careful to keep the brown paper from crackling. The walls of these houses were thin enough to hear a conversation going on in the next house. She caught her breath when she saw the titles: *David Copperfield* and *Oliver Twist*. Miss Hodgeson had read the stories to the class, but now she would be able to read them for herself. Carefully, she wrapped her books and placed them under the mattress of the bed she shared with her sister.

"Lily, what are you doing up there?" Her mother's irritated voice was shrill. "These potatoes won't peel themselves."

"Just settling Emily," she shouted back. She then ran down the stairs before her mother came looking for her.

As usual, the meal consisted mostly of potatoes, carrots, and onions. Mrs. Russell did the best she could with the money they had, but even when her father had been able to secure work of skilled roofing jobs, there never seemed to be enough. Now that her father could no longer earn a full wage and her brothers were getting bigger, they all knew the constant pangs of hunger. She reflected on her conversation with Miss Hodgeson, who encouraged her to pursue her education. Lily knew that in reality, it was not for the likes of her. Her wages would make the difference between the family managing to survive until her brothers could go down the pit or going to the workhouse. It wasn't called that now, but a workhouse was a workhouse, however they chose to say it.

She picked up the knife and began to peel. "Mum, what will it be like? At the big 'ouse?" Her mother paused and looked up from the range. "You're to be a house parlourmaid. Mrs. Grove's housekeeper will instruct you. It's mostly dusting, tidying, serving meals, washing up, and looking after the things the family needs. There'll be a lady's maid as well who looks after Mrs. Grove. Perhaps you could do that one day, though you've never shown any great talent for sewing. But it's better than being a housemaid. That's what most girls from around here do if they don't go to the factory, and that's hard work, believe you me. If it wasn't for your father, that's what you'd be doing."

"Why? What did Dad do to make me get a better job?" Lily asked, making the most of the chance to talk. Her mother rarely had the time or the energy to have a conversation; there were too many clamouring hands and mouths taking up her attention.

Her mother gave the pan another stir before turning and sitting on the wooden stool next to Lily. "When that scaffolding collapsed and your father fell from the roof, it was because the foreman had told the apprentice to put it up while he did something else. The apprentice had never done it before, and the foreman didn't check the work. The lad hadn't tightened the bolts properly, and when your dad was climbing up with the slates, the whole thing collapsed. The foreman tried to blame the apprentice, but the men went to Mr. Grove and told him the foreman was always cutting corners. Not only that, when Mr. Grove investigated, he found out that the foreman was cutting corners so he could steal materials as well."

"I still don't see why he would offer me a job because of that," Lily said, taking the peeled potatoes over to the sink and emptying them into a pan of water.

"He didn't. It was only when your dad went to see him and demanded compensation that Mr. Grove offered him anything at all. Your father threatened to go to the papers about the foreman; Grove didn't want the scandal of people thinking his buildings weren't safe, so he offered your dad a job for life at the yard. Your dad tried to get jobs for the two oldest lads, but Mr. Grove said that the only other work he had was at his house, and that's how you got the job. Now, we haven't time for chattering. Set the table. And remember that when you're working, they won't be paying you to talk."

As she finished setting the table, a thought occurred to Lily. "Mum, how do you know about housemaids and parlourmaids and ladies' maids?"

Her mother turned once more, tucking the wisps of hair that had escaped from the tightly drawn bun she habitually wore. "I wasn't always married to your father."

Lily expected her to go on, but she didn't. "But—" she began.

"That's all, Lily. You ask too many questions. Now go and call the others. Your dad will be here in no time."

Lily collected the tin plates and mugs from the shelf and started to put them on the table. She stole a glance at her mother, who was pulling loaves out of the oven. They were not close, not like some of her friends were with their mothers. When she stopped to think about it, she knew more about some of their mothers than she did of her own. Her mother was not from Hope, that she knew. There were no grandparents or aunts or uncles. That was why, as soon as she was able, she was expected to help with the house and her younger brothers and sisters. But she only recently noticed that her mother didn't speak like everyone else in Hope. She sighed as she placed the last of the spoons. She could ask, but if her mother had wanted her to know, she would have told her.

As ever, her brothers and sisters appeared in the street when the food was on the table. Their father came through the door just as his wife was spooning the watery stew onto plates. Lily cut the bread into thin slices while her father took off his boots and washed at the kitchen sink. The other children stood behind their chairs until they were told to sit down. When everyone was served, there was silence, broken only by the sounds of cutlery scraping across plates. There would not be any left over, but no one complained about the meagre portions or lack of a scraping of butter for their bread. They knew there were others in the street who had even less.

two

Her bundle of belongings was very small: her "best" clothes, some underwear, and her books. She had packed her things and made the fire in the range before her mother got up, as it was still early. Her brothers and sisters were still in bed, and she could hear the distant sounds of the knocker-up, but he wasn't in their street yet. The first streaks of dawn were still an hour or so away. Lily had been up early. She wanted to wash before the others came into the scullery. She had even washed and dried her hair, trying to bring some order to her curls. If this was to be the start of her new life, she wanted to make a good impression. As she put the kettle on the hob and started to cut the bread her mother had made yesterday, she heard the thin wail of her baby sister and heard the bed creak as her mother went to her. A few minutes later, her mother appeared.

"You're up, then," her mother commented as she accepted a cup of weak tea. "And packed, I see." Her mother nodded to the small bundle on the table. "Your father will walk you to the Groves' house on the way to work."

"Mum, what if—" Lily began.

"What? Spit it out, lass."

As usual, Lily was discouraged by her mother's harsh tone. It was as though Lily's birth had annoyed her and continued to do so. However, on this rare occasion when she had her mother's undivided attention, Lily decided to risk it. "What if they don't like me? What if I break something? If I 'ave to leave school, I could go to the shirt factory and still live here. The money's better anyway. I don't want to leave you and Dad and Betty, Vera, Nora, Emily, John, and Tommy."

Her mother's face softened. "Lily, you're bound to feel a bit at sea to begin with, but they'll teach you the things you need to know. This is your chance to make something of yourself, to get out of here, to escape. In no time, you'll be able to apply for a job in a big house. You'll get to see something of the world and meet different people. Girls working at the shirt factory will earn a bit more, but that's where they'll stay. They'll marry a lad from down the pit, and they'll end up in Hope all their lives. I want something better for you, Lily. I know you wanted to go to the grammar school, but even with the scholarship, we couldn't afford it. So this is your second chance. Take it. Don't let anything hold you back. Learn as much as you can, work hard, and speak properly." In a move that slightly surprised Lily, her usually undemonstrative mother pulled her close and hugged her tight. "A chance like this won't come again, so take it, Lily. I know I haven't been the mother you wanted, and one day, I'll explain. But never doubt that I love you." She stepped back, her usual brisk self. "Now pour your dad his tea. He'll be down in a minute."

Grove House was at the other end of town, but it might as well have been at the other side of the world. Her father put his snap tin in his pocket, and they set off in silence. Lily could see that walking was now a trial for her father. The once fit, invincible Joey Russell started to breathe heavily after only a few yards. The strain around his mouth told her that every step caused him pain.

As she walked, Lily noticed how the narrow, terraced streets led onto larger terraces with pocket-handkerchief gardens in the front. Up the hill, the houses were bigger with neat gardens. She smelled the foundry before they approached it and crossed over the railway.

"Your grandfather helped to build that," her father commented as they passed. "You never met him. He was a navvy. Met your grandma and stayed, went down the pit, and was killed when the shaft flooded just after I was born. Your grandma died soon after."

Lily looked at her father. "I didn't know."

He looked straight ahead. "No reason why you should. Miners risk their lives every time they go to work. It was a long time ago. No point talking about it. Talking won't change 'owt."

They continued to walk in silence. Lily had plenty to think about. She knew her father had been brought up by his aunt. Now she knew why. She had never heard her father speak of his childhood. He had never shared fond memories. Perhaps because he didn't have any. She remembered once visiting Aunt Mary, a gaunt, gimlet-eyed woman with white hair and few teeth. The aunt had barked instructions to her mother, and the children were not allowed to sit down at her table. Her father had sat red-faced in his stiff collar. It had been an uncomfortable visit, and they had not seen her again. The woman had terrified her, and she began to understand why her father, who had been shown little affection as a child, had shown little affection to his own children. His whole life had been a battle to overcome the death of his parents and an upbringing by people who saw him as a burden on their own meagre resources.

On the other side of the railway, the houses were much bigger, large villas that were built in the middle of the last century. The shop owners' businesses had flourished as mining, iron works, and factories had grown up. Butchers' and bakers' wives and daughters worked at being ladies. Further up the hill were the houses of the families with the real wealth in the town: the mill and mine owners. They finally approached what looked to Lily to be a park with grand wrought-iron gates announcing Grove House.

"Now then, lass," her father said as they walked down the drive. Though at this point, the house was not visible. "Mr. Grove's given yer this job. He didn't want to, but he 'ad to. And every time he sees yer, he's going to remember that 'e lost that battle, and 'e doesn't like losing, doesn't Mr. Grove, so they'll look for any excuse to get rid of yer. Don't give them a reason. A working man 'as few rights and little power, but just remember this, Lily. You're as good as any of t' folk you're going to meet in that house, master or servant." Lily looked at her father in surprise. In all her sixteen years, she had never heard him say so much.

Lily's green eyes widened when the house came into view. It had been built by Mr. Grove's father only a few decades before. The turret reminded her of the castles she had seen in books. All it needed was a moat. In the spring sunshine, the windows shone, and the stone reflected the light, unlike the smoke-blackened stone on the houses in town. As they walked towards the house, they saw a man pushing a wheelbarrow.

"What do you want?" he demanded. "They don't buy nothing from tinkers."

Lily could feel her father bristle, but he said, "I'm bringing my daughter. She's to be the new parlourmaid for the 'ouse."

"Go round t' back then. Ask for Mrs. Cadeby. She'll see to you." He resumed his journey with the barrow.

A few moments later, they were shown into the house-keeper's sitting room. Mrs. Cadeby sat writing in a ledger but closed it with a snap when they entered. Although her features were severe, her eyes were a piercing blue, and her nose was a little too long. Her features relaxed when she smiled, and Lily felt she would be fair. It was clear Mrs. Cadeby enjoyed neatness. Not a thing was out of place in her sitting room, not a hair was out of place on her head, her black skirt was uncreased, and her white blouse was spotless. The only splash of colour was the blue of the cameo at her throat.

"Well, Lily, welcome to Grove House. I hope you will be happy here. As soon as your father has said goodbye, I will explain to you what your duties are. Later, I will present you to Mrs. Grove. She likes to meet all the servants when they begin. Now I suggest you say your goodbyes quickly. There's no point lingering over these things." She stood up and left the sitting room, leaving them to their goodbyes.

Lily's father cleared his throat and ran his hand round the inside of his collar. "Right, lass. I'll be off. Look after yerself. Remember what I said." For a brief moment, Lily thought he was going to kiss her, but he didn't. He looked at her as if trying to memorise her features. Then, without another word, he took his cap out of his pocket, put it on, turned, and walked out. It was only later that Lily realised she had said nothing to him.

Mrs. Cadeby returned, holding a pile of clothes. "This is your uniform." Lily took the clothing. "You will wear the grey dress in the mornings and the black one in the afternoons. There are four sets of aprons. Mrs. Grove is very particular, so make sure they are always spotless. And here are two caps. Are they your only shoes?" She looked at Lily's sturdy black boots. Lily nodded. "They will make far too much noise. You will need to get some softer ones. There may be an old pair of Miss Eleanor's that will do."

They were interrupted by the arrival of a young woman with a tray. "Ah, come in, Lottie. This is Lily. She is to be the new parlourmaid. Set the tray on the table."

Lottie placed the tray carefully on the table but, at the last minute, wobbled slightly and a cup rolled off. Automatically, Lily stepped forward and caught it.

"Well done, Lily." Mrs. Cadeby smiled. Lily was surprised when she turned to the other girl and said, "Much better, Lottie. Now back to the kitchen with you. I'm sure Cook has plenty for you to do." Lottie turned to go, giving Lily a shy smile as she left.

"Now, Lily, here is a list of your duties." Mrs. Cadeby's voice had become businesslike again. She handed Lily a sheet of paper. "That is for you to study. If there is anything on it you do not understand, you need to ask. Now we shall have a cup of tea, and you can tell me about yourself. Afterwards, I will take you to your room so you can unpack and change into your uniform. Then I shall take you to meet Mrs. Grove in the morning room at ten o'clock sharp, and you can make a start."

———

The rest of the morning passed in a blur. Lily found she was to share a room with the housemaid, Aggie. She didn't care. After sharing a room with her brothers and sisters, sharing a large room with only one other person was a luxury. She didn't even mind the uniform, though it was a little small, hugging her waist. But it was better than any of her other clothes. She liked the crisp white pinafore and found the hat useful in keeping her hair in some sort of order.

Lily had read and reread the list of duties. The list was long, but when she thought about it, she had been helping her mother in the house since she could remember, and most of the things she was expected to do were either similar or just common sense. The only thing that had dented her natural optimism was the meeting with Mrs. Grove.

"Now, you address Mrs. Grove as ma'am, Mr. Grove is sir, young Mr. Grove—who is, at present, at university—as Master Jonathon, and Miss Grove as Miss Eleanor. Mrs. Grove expects good manners at all times. And try to speak properly. Mrs. Grove does not care to hear broad Yorkshire," Mrs. Cadeby warned as she pushed Lily into the morning room.

A tall, dark-haired woman in a grey dress sat writing letters at a bureau. The sun streamed in through the large, mullioned windows. She turned as Mrs. Cadeby announced, "The new parlourmaid, ma'am. Lily Russell."

As she turned, Lily could see there were streaks of grey in her hair, which was drawn from her face in a loose bun. The dress fell in soft, grey folds to her feet as she stood and beckoned Lily to come further into the room. Her eyes were a piercing blue, and Lily could see she had once been beautiful. She was still striking, but her expression suggested that for all her wealth, she was a disappointed woman.

"So, Lily Russell, you're to be our parlourmaid." Her voice was low, but there was no mistaking an undertone of disapproval. "Has Mrs. Cadeby explained your duties?"

"Yes, ma'am."

"I expect everyone who works at Grove House to live by the highest standards, Lily. I will not tolerate idleness or slovenliness in work, appearance, or the way you speak. It goes without saying that your morals must be equally high. There will be no entertaining of young men in this house, and should I hear of any behaviour that does not meet my high standards when you are about the town on your afternoon off, you will be dismissed. You will have one half day off per week and one Sunday per month. Is that clear?"

"Perfectly, ma'am."

"Do you have any questions?"

"About my wages, ma'am," Lily began.

"I believe my husband and your father have reached an agreement regarding that. Half of your wages will be paid to your father along with his own. Now, if you have no further questions, you may go." She sat down and continued her correspondence.

It was at that moment Lily decided she would one day have her own money and she would control it. She would become an independent woman. She didn't know how, and she didn't know when, but it would happen. She would make it happen. Of that, she was sure.

three

The first week, all Lily wanted to do was go home. Each night, she fell into bed exhausted from rising at six to lay out Mr. Grove's clothes when he was there, lay the breakfast things, have the morning papers ready, wait on those at breakfast, and then clear the things away for Lottie, the scullery maid, to wash. Then she had to ensure that the library and morning room were readied with sufficient ink and other writing materials. When she finished that, she went to dust the drawing room. Mrs. Grove was most particular about the castors, skirting boards, and silver. All the time, she kept her ears open and ready to answer the front door to callers. A week ago, she had known nothing about arranging flowers, but she was learning fast to deadhead the old ones and replace them with fresh ones from the gardener.

At twelve-thirty sharp, she had to change into her black uniform. Fortunately, Aggie attended to the fires while Lily served luncheon. She and Aggie had just enough time to dust the sitting room and eat a hasty lunch while Mrs. Grove and any guests she had were having coffee. Then there was time to sit and do some mending of clothes or table linens before it was time to serve afternoon tea. Their own tea was served half an hour later.

On her way to lay out Mr. Grove's clothes, she lit the gaslights. On her way down to lay the dinner table, she rang the dressing gong and did another quick tidy. After waiting on those at dinner, serving coffee, and clearing, her day was coming to a welcome close. All that remained for her to do was turn off the gaslights.

At ten o'clock—if they were lucky—she and Aggie made their way up to the room they shared in the attic. It was a large room, and from the window, she could look right down into Hope. If she craned her neck the other way, she could see the woods where she had picked the bluebells for Miss Hodgeson. Even farther in the distance was Ober Stand. It was a place she had always desired to visit but had never been able to. Perhaps, on one of her days off, she would walk there.

For the first couple of days, Aggie had seemed a little resentful as housemaid; she had hoped to be promoted to parlourmaid. Even still, Lily was grateful for the advice Aggie often gave her. Within four days, the two were on the way to becoming friends. During the day, they had little time to talk, but for a few minutes before they went to sleep, they quickly began to share confidences. Aggie had worked for the Groves for two years, ever since leaving school. Like Lily, she came from a large family; there were eleven brothers and her.

"Enough for a football team." She had laughed, but like Lily, the family needed her money to survive.

Aggie was also able to tell Lily the things she needed to know about her employers, things Mrs. Cadeby would never tell and would sack Aggie for if the housekeeper ever found out she had repeated them. Mrs. Grove was the grand-daughter of an earl.

"That's 'ow she comes by those 'igh and mighty manners." Aggie grinned. " 'Er mother was the daughter, I think, so there was no money. Mr. Grove 'ad money but no class. She 'ad class but no money."

"It was a marriage made in heaven, then?" Lily asked.

Aggie had laughed. "I don't think so. Mr. Grove got a society wife with useful connections, and she taught him how to speak and use the right cutlery. She got to live the lifestyle she was brought up to expect, but you'll notice 'e's not 'ere some nights. That's 'cause 'e's staying with his fancy woman in Danton as 'e's done for years. 'E thought Danton was far enough away, but everyone knows about 'er."

"Does Mrs. Grove know?"

"I should think so, but she ignores it. She's busy with 'er charity works for the 'ospital. Truth to tell, I don't think she cares."

"I think my mum would chase my dad with the bread knife." Lily laughed. Her father was not an easy man. He had enough faults connected with drink and his temper, but he remained faithful to her mother; Lily was sure of it. She had seen the looks they exchanged some nights and heard the bed creaking many times.

"Mine too," Aggie agreed, adding, "She'd catch him too and give him a good skelping."

They both giggled at the thought of their respective fathers—one a builder and the other a miner—being chased, caught, and punished by women half their size.

"What about Miss Eleanor and Master Jonathon?" Lily asked. "If it's common knowledge, do they know?"

During her first week, she had not seen Jonathon Grove, being informed that he was at Oxford University and would not return until Christmas. She had only seen Miss Eleanor at mealtimes, during which she had looked through Lily as though she wasn't there.

Aggie paused thoughtfully for a moment. "I don't think Miss Eleanor knows. 'E dotes on 'er. Spoils 'er something rotten, if you want my opinion. And she worships 'im. I think 'e would try to keep 'er away from any tales about 'imself that might make 'er see 'im in a bad light. Both of them act like there's nothing wrong around 'er. As for Master Jonathon, 'e's very much a chip off the old block."

"What does that mean?"

"You ask too many questions, Lily Russell." Aggie yawned. "I'm too tired now, and it'll be 'alf past five afore we know it. I'm going to sleep now. I'll tell you about Mr. Jonathon tomorrow." Aggie's voice became muffled as she drifted off to sleep.

Lily was curious, but Aggie was now sound asleep. Punching the pillow to try to disperse some of the lumps, Lily closed her eyes.

The following morning, she met Miss Eleanor. As she was passing her room, there was a resounding crash, followed by someone crying. She stood for a second before knocking on the door and entering, wondering whether there had been an accident. Eleanor Grove sat on the floor surrounded by the remains of what had once been a Wedgwood vase standing on the mantelpiece and what Lily took to be the pieces of a letter she had received moments before.

"What is it, Miss Eleanor? Can I help?" she blurted out.

Apart from the damage to the vase, the rest of the room was tidy. The bed was made up with the white cover she and Aggie had changed earlier that morning, the perfumes and creams were in neat order on the white dressing table in front of the window, and the cushions on the chair and the window seat had not been touched.

Eleanor looked up with tear-stained eyes. "Who are you?"

"I'm Lily, miss. Lily Russell, the new house parlourmaid," Lily replied, already busying herself picking up the pieces of vase off the floor and dropping them into the coal scuttle. "I heard a crash, and you were crying. I thought you might be hurt."

Eleanor gave a harsh laugh. "Hurt? Well, I'm furious, if that's any help."

"That would explain the vase, then," Lily said drily. "But don't worry. It won't bother you again. I think you killed it."

To her surprise, Eleanor Grove grinned. "My mother is going to be angry. It came from her grandfather's castle. Do you think there's any way it can be mended?"

"I don't think so, miss. The top half is almost all right, but the bottom half is in too many pieces. Even if someone could stick it back together, the lines would show."

"That's it, Lily! You're a genius! I'll balance the top half on my dressing table and surround it with other things so that when Mother comes in, it will seem normal." Her eyes wandered to the torn fragments on the floor. "Or perhaps I'll admit to the vase being broken when I tell Mother that the young man she thought I was going to marry has now decided to marry an American heiress he met in New York. Believe me, the vase will pale into insignificance when she hears that news."

"I'm sorry, miss. My mum would say there's plenty of other fish in the sea." Lily smiled at the older girl.

"And what would your father say?" The older girl looked with interest at the new maid, who until that moment had not interested her at all.

Lily's smile became a grin. "He'd say bugger 'im." Then she clapped her hand over her mouth. Mrs. Grove did not like to hear her servants speaking with a Yorkshire accent. Swearing was probably enough to get her sacked. "Begging your pardon, miss," she added hastily.

She was amazed when Eleanor laughed. It was not the harsh, mirthless laugh of minutes ago but a genuine laugh. "I think I am in agreement with your father's sentiments." She gasped. "Now we are even, Lily. You know about my vase, and I know about your colourful language."

Lily nodded warily. Although she was aware she had gone

too far, she sensed for the first time that rich people were not so different from poor people after all.

"Now Lily, if you could only dress hair as well, I would say that you were the perfect maid." Eleanor sighed, getting up and reaching for the hairbrush that had obviously been the weapon she had used so effectively on the vase.

"I used to do my mum's hair sometimes, miss. I could have a go, if you like."

Eleanor Grove handed her the brush and sat down in front of the dressing table. As she did at home, Lily started by brushing the older girl's hair with long, smooth strokes. It had always seemed to calm her mother, and it seemed to be having the same effect on Miss Eleanor. She could see her visibly relaxing with each stroke.

"That feels wonderful, Lily. I am already beginning to feel that Archie's American is welcome to him. Father will be furious. He is determined for me to marry someone with a title," Eleanor mused.

Lily began to twist Eleanor's hair into a loose knot at the back of her neck, threading a white ribbon through it and teasing some tendrils free to frame her delicate face. "Perhaps it's for the best, miss," she ventured. "Better to find out that you don't suit before the wedding than after."

Eleanor opened her eyes. "I think you're right, Lily. Archie was fun and all that, but truth to tell, I think he would have bored me within a month of the wedding. Having been brought up to be a gentleman, the only thing he has any idea of doing is hunting, playing stupid tricks, and gambling. I don't think Archie has ever had a serious thought in his life."

"In that case, my mum would say it was a blessing in disguise. There, miss." Lily stepped back and held her breath.

There was a slight pause while Eleanor turned her head from one side to the other. Then she smiled through the mirror. "Thank you, Lily. When Croft does my hair, I think she is trying to make me look like my mother. I shall speak to Mother and ask her if you can be spared to do my hair."

"I'd like that, miss." Lily smiled back. "Now I'll just finish setting the room to order while you go and give your mother the news." She swept up the remnants of the vase. "Best to get these things over with," she added.

four

The fire in the grate in Mrs. Cadeby's parlour lent a cheerful glow to the dark evening. The green damask curtains were drawn and the gas lamps lit. The day's work was done, and Lily was ready to fall into bed. She had been surprised to be summoned and even more surprised to be offered tea. Mrs. Cadeby was not one to fraternise with her staff.

"I will come to the point, Miss Russell. Miss Eleanor has requested that you are to be trained as her lady's maid."

Lily's mouth formed a surprised "Oh." Since the incident with the vase, she had barely seen Miss Eleanor and had been too busy to think any more of it.

"The question that remains is, is that what you want, Miss Russell? To be a lady's maid?"

Lily could not form an answer immediately. It was not that she was short of opinions; it was that no one usually bothered to ask her for them. "I haven't really given the matter much thought, Mrs. Cadeby," she replied, stalling for time.

"Then I suggest you think about it—and quickly," the older woman shot back. "Neither Mrs. Grove nor Miss Eleanor are women of patience."

This surprised Lily. She had never heard Mrs. Cadeby

express an opinion on their employers before, let alone one that could be considered in the slightest bit critical. Such thoughts were not unknown. Lily and Aggie had shared many whispered conversations after long days when they had been on the receiving end of Mrs. Grove's tongue. These secret conversations would have been enough to send them packing had they been overheard.

Mrs. Cadeby poured tea into two plain china cups and set one before Lily. "I should like to give you some advice, Miss Russell, and you will choose to take it or you will not, but that will be up to you."

Lily nodded, unsure of how else to respond.

"The first thing to consider is whether or not you in fact wish to be a lady's maid. There are benefits, of course. The work is lighter. I cannot deny that. You would be responsible only for Miss Eleanor's wardrobe, her jewellery, her toilette, and her hair. There would be an end to the cleaning and what might be termed 'heavy work.' It is likely she would take you with her when she travels. A lady's maid does get to see more of the world than a housemaid. That's for sure."

"It does sound tempting," Lily replied. "I have always wanted to see more of the world than Hope."

"I have no doubt you would make a very good lady's maid, Lily. I have watched you. You are both a quick learner and a hard worker." Mrs. Cadeby smiled and took a sip of tea. "A lady's maid also enjoys significant perks. Any clothes Miss Eleanor has finished with would, of course, come your way for you to do with as you see fit. Many lady's maids make a tidy profit selling them on. Of course, they enjoy a higher status. Though, perhaps they have fewer friends among the staff."

"These all sound like good reasons to take the job," Lily murmured.

"Those are indeed the benefits, but you should also consider your long-term prospects, Lily. Once you go down that route, there is little opportunity for furthering your career. Lady's maids rarely become housekeepers." Mrs. Cadeby replaced her cup gently on its saucer.

Lily straightened. "Do you think I might be able to do that one day? Become a housekeeper?"

The other woman nodded. "Not only do I think you are able, but I think you should. You have shown initiative and ambition in a short time. I think you have the makings of a fine housekeeper."

Now it was Lily's turn to replace her cup. "With respect, Mrs. Cadeby, why are you telling me this?"

The housekeeper smiled. "Because, my dear, you rather remind me of myself at your age. I was only thirteen when I was sent as a tweenie to Mrs. Grove's grandfather's household. A huge mansion, it was. Well, he was an earl, of course. There were at least twenty maids and six footmen. His lordship and Lord James had a butler, under butler, and valets, while the countess and Lady Constance, Mrs. Grove's mother, had lady's maids. Outside, there was an army of gardeners as the countess was very keen on the garden. Lady Constance left to marry almost as soon as I started there. Her wedding was the biggest event in Yorkshire that year. When she left, she took her maid with her. As it happened, Lady Constance's maid took ill, so one of the chambermaids became her lady's maid, which meant there were opportunities for us maids to climb the ladder—one rung at a time.

"In those days, the hierarchy was very strict, and the work was hard. As a tweenie, I carried many buckets of coal upstairs and had to polish the coal scuttle. The earl wouldn't have a single speck of dust on it, which was ironic, really, seeing as how his fortune was largely from the mines he owned. Eventually, I became a housemaid, parlourmaid, and then chambermaid. When Lady Constance's daughter married and became Mrs. Grove, I came here as her housekeeper."

"Didn't you want to stay at the big house?" Lily couldn't help asking.

"I was glad to get out. The trouble with these huge places is you're never warm. The earl would never allow any modernisation, so buckets of coal and water still had to be taken upstairs by hand, not to mention the chamber pots. I don't believe Lord James, the new earl, has changed much." She looked around her sitting room. "No, this place suits me. Mr. Grove might not have the status of earl, but he is the future. Times are changing, Lily, and it is important to be part of that change. You will be part of that change."

"I would like to be independent one day," Lily said, thinking of when she had learned that half of her wages would be paid to her father.

"Then being a lady's maid is not for you. I pointed out the benefits, but the fact remains that this lifestyle is only enviable while the mistress favours you. I have known maids who have been tossed out because they fell out of favour, sometimes for something as trivial as overlooking a loose thread in a carpet or lacing a corset too tight." She leaned forward. "But if you aspire to be a housekeeper, I shall be only too pleased to train you."

"But what about Aggie?" Lily asked. "She's been here longer than me. Surely she should be next in line."

"Aggie is a good worker and a fine girl, but she doesn't have the ambition or the steel in her spine that you have."

"And what about Miss Eleanor?" Lily frowned. "I shouldn't like to get on the wrong side of her."

"You leave Miss Eleanor to me." Mrs. Cadeby smiled.

five

Lily didn't know how she'd done it, but Miss Eleanor was somehow pacified by knowing Lily couldn't be spared for the full-time lady's maid position. Although, she would be able to help with Miss Eleanor's hair when needed. So far she had only been called on twice when the young lady was going to a ball at the Cutler's Hall in Sheffield, where she had met a young man she had high hopes of marrying. She seemed to have completely forgotten the young man who had caused the unfortunate incident with the vase, which still sat on her dressing table surrounded by pots and bottles of perfume.

It was hard to believe Lily had been at the Groves' for almost four months. For the first time, she was going home on her afternoon off. Jimmy, the stableyard apprentice, had to go into Hope for supplies and had agreed to give her a lift on the cart, for which she was grateful. It would take a quarter of an hour to reach the gates at the end of the driveway were she to walk. She was looking forward to seeing her mother, brothers, and sisters. She was less inclined to see her father, but she was also determined to confront him about the cavalier way he had appropriated her wages.

"Does yer want me to drop yer at t' end of yer street?" Jimmy asked as they entered the town.

"No thanks, Jimmy, the High Street will do," she replied. "I want to buy a treat for my family."

"Right, no bother. I'm goin' down the 'igh Street to Charlesworth's farm in any case. That do yer?"

"Perfectly."

The High Street had not changed in the few months she had been away, and it was foolish to think it might have. There was a comfort, though, in familiar things. The newly built town hall was imposing, the new clock striking two as they passed. It was market day, and the old quarry, where the market had been for years, was busy with housewives buying tripe, fish, vegetables, and meat. Some couldn't afford the market's wares. She could see a woman buying a ball of wool from what they had put away, not being able to afford enough for whatever they were knitting at one go. Her mother did that.

As usual, there were men lined up outside the Prince of Wales public house while their wives did the shopping. No doubt they would carry the heavy bags home, or at least some of them would. Lily wanted to go to the toy stall and buy something for her brothers and sisters, but she knew food was more important for all of them.

"I'll be goin' back at seven," Jimmy said as he helped her down from the cart. "As well as this, I've to get the horse's shoe redone and do a couple more errands for Mr. Grove. If yer want a lift back, meet me outside t' market, then. Otherwise, it's a long walk 'ome."

"Thanks, Jimmy," she replied.

In the end, she bought herself a piece of ribbon to decorate her Sunday hat, a meat pie to feed the whole family, and—with the little bit of money she had left—a quarter of humbugs for her siblings.

As she passed the butcher's, Mr. Butterfield called out,

"Why, hello there, Lily. It's been a long time since I've seen you."

"I'm working now, Mr. Butterfield, for Mr. and Mrs. Grove at the big house," she replied with a smile.

Mr. Butterfield had always been kind to her when her mother had sent her to get some "bones for the dog." She had a feeling he knew as well as she did that they did not have a dog.

"This is my afternoon off," she added.

"And how are you enjoying life at the big house?" he asked.

"It's hard work, but it's better than the factory, or so my mum tells me."

"Mrs. Cadeby is the housekeeper, isn't that right?" He paused before adding, "She's a fine woman."

"Yes, she is," Lily agreed, wondering how Mr. Butterfield knew her.

"I met her when she first moved to the big house. I used to deliver the meat order for my father. You trust her, young Lily. She'll look after you. Here." He handed her a package. "A little piece of beef for your mum."

"Thank you, Mr. Butterfield," she replied. Her family would eat well for a few days at least.

It did not take Lily long to walk the few streets to Milsom Street. It was quiet now, but when the children emerged from school, it would be alive with games of football and hopscotch. Someone had slung a rope around the gas lamp. She had no doubt her brothers would be swinging from it like monkeys until the lamplighter came and told them off. Every doorstep was white, as were the net curtains at the windows. The housewives had little, but cleanliness was a matter of pride. It was not an easy task battling the smoke and coal dust daily, but woe betide the woman who didn't keep her area clean.

Lily approached the door but didn't knock. The door was

unlocked. No one locked their doors. None of them had anything to steal in any case. Her mother was sitting on the old Windsor chair in front of the range, the baby in her arms and her eyes closed. Not for the first time, Lily noticed the lines of strain around her eyes and mouth and the silver hairs among the faded gold. Her mother had once been a beauty. That was clear. But the harsh life she had led as the wife of Joey Russell had prematurely robbed her vitality. She thought of Mrs. Grove, who was of a similar age. Money certainly made a difference.

As quietly as she could, Lily placed the meat pie in the oven at the side of the fire, found an apron, and began to peel the potatoes and carrots she found in the pantry. It was almost the end of the week, so the portions were less than generous, but the meat pie would be appreciated. Hefting a pan of water onto the hob, she realised her mother was now awake.

"Hello, love. It's good to see you. I've missed you."

"I've missed you too, Mum," Lily replied.

Clara Russell surprised her daughter by gently putting the baby in the wooden box that served as a crib during the day and pulled Lily into a fierce hug. "It's been a lot harder without you, Lily. Vera and Betty try to help a bit, but Nora's too small, and the boys know more about making a mess than clearing it up."

"They're all just kids, Mum," Lily replied.

"I feel so tired all the time since this baby came," her mother admitted.

"Well, I'm here now," Lily said brightly. "I'll do what I can. See —" She indicated the pan heating on the hob. "—there's a pie in the oven, and the vegetables are ready to cook."

"You're a good girl, Lily. You always have been."

To Lily's horror, her mother, whom she had never seen cry, had tears in her eyes. Though she tried to hide it by quickly wiping them away with the corner of her apron.

"I should never have let you go out to work at the Groves," she added. "I should have stood firm against your father and sent you to the grammar school."

"We couldn't afford it, Mum, what with the uniform and getting there. You did well, between you and Miss Hodgeson, persuading Dad to let me stay on the extra time. Besides, we needed the money I could bring in now that Dad can't earn what he used to," Lily replied.

"We could have managed somehow, and if you'd have gone to the grammar school, you would have been able to eventually get a better job with more money."

"Well, I didn't, so there's no use crying about it now," Lily said firmly. "But I am going to be trained so that I can be a housekeeper one day. Mrs. Cadeby is going to train me."

For the first time since she'd arrived, her mother smiled. "I don't know how anyone could have doubted it, Lily. You were always going to make something of yourself."

six

Lily rolled up her sleeves to help her mother with the pile of ironing and washing the dishes that had no doubt been sitting in the sink since breakfast, something that would never have happened had her mother been feeling well. It was not long before the door was flung open and her brothers and sisters erupted into the room. As always, the boys were poking and pulling at each other, and the girls were complaining that the boys had made them run home from school. The boys were not keen on school and could not wait until they were old enough to go down the pit, which Lily knew her mother would do anything to save them from. Working for Mr. Grove would even be better than that. Once Lily had produced the humbugs, the noise subsided as each child savoured the minty sweetness. A calmness settled over the house for the next hour or so. The girls wanted to tell Lily about their day at school.

"I moved into Miss Hodgeson's class," Betty told her. "She hopes I'm as good a pupil as you."

"You work hard. Miss Hodgeson's a good teacher," Lily replied. A pang of sadness hit her as she thought of what she might have done had she gone to the grammar school.

"I can read any book from the shelf now," Vera told her

proudly. "I don't have to read from the reading books. I don't like the sums, though," she added with a frown.

"Sums are the best part," Tommy said, chipping into the conversation. "Come on, John. Let's take this outside and see how far it flies." The two boys rushed out of the door to test their paper aeroplane.

"You'd better be back when your dad gets home for his dinner," their mother shouted after them.

"We will," they chorused as the door slammed.

They would be back in time. All of Joey Russell's children knew that if they were late to the dinner table, they would get nothing or, depending on the mood he was in, a beating.

Betty and Vera helped Lily set the table as their mother finished preparing their meal. "It was good of you to bring the pie, Lily. Otherwise, tonight's dinner would have been a very sorry affair," her mother said as she stirred the gravy. "With that and Mr. Butterfield's meat, which I can eke out over two days, we shall eat like kings."

How different Lily's life was now. The food at the Grove's was plentiful and well-cooked. The continuous struggle for her parents, and many like them, to keep food on the table angered her. Wages never seemed to stretch far enough to satisfy all the mouths needing to be fed. She knew her mother often went without so that there was more for the others. She claimed not to be hungry, but Lily knew that was a lie she frequently told.

As the clock struck a quarter past six, the door opened and her father walked in, followed by her brothers. As usual, his face was covered with grime from his day on the building site. Without comment, he sat down to remove his boots and the old cap, jacket, and shirt he wore for work before moving to the sink and washing. Clara handed him a clean shirt. When he was dressed, he sat down at the head of the table.

"Something smells good," he commented.

Her mother smiled brightly. "Lily brought a pie," she said.

For the first time since entering the room, he acknowledged his oldest daughter. "So it's bringing food to the poor now, is it? Lady Bountiful from the big 'ouse?" he sneered.

"I'll remind you that I'm working for the Groves because you decided I should leave school and go out to work," Lily shot back at him, suddenly aware that he no longer intimidated her. "In any case, if you don't want it, you don't have to eat it."

There was a pause as the rest of the family seemed to hold their breath. No one spoke back to Joey Russell.

"I'll eat it," he replied. "Can't let food go to waste."

The meal passed in near silence. And as usual, not a scrap of food was left at the end of the meal. When everyone had finished and the dishes were cleared away, her father put on his jacket and cap and announced he was going to The Horseshoe. The boys had already escaped to play outside, having been told to be back when the lamplighter did his rounds. As she helped her mother put the younger ones to bed, Lily asked her mother if her father had increased the housekeeping money since she left. The puzzled look she received from her mother told her all she needed to know.

"I'll walk with you, Dad," Lily said, picking up her coat and hat. "I need to get to the market to get a lift back to the Groves' house in any case."

"As you like," her father replied.

They walked in silence for a few yards. "About the money from my wages, Dad," Lily began.

"What about it?" He was instantly defensive. "Don't yer think yer owe yer mam and I something? After all, we fed and clothed yer for sixteen years. Don't yer think it's time yer paid something back?"

"Oh, I do, Dad. I really do," she replied. "I'm only too happy to help put more food on the table."

"Well, there yer are, then."

"But it's not going to put food on the table, though. Is it, Dad?" she said.

"What do yer mean?"

"You've had a share of my wages for weeks now, and I don't believe Mum has seen a penny of it." Lily did not bother to keep the contempt out of her voice.

His eyes narrowed. "What's yer mam being tellin' yer?"

"Nothing," she replied. "She couldn't tell me anything because she has no idea about the extra money. You've been pouring it down your throat at The Horseshoe."

They turned the corner. The conversation ceased as a couple walked past.

Her father turned to her again. "I don't like yer tone, young lady. Don't think yer too old to feel the back of my hand."

Lily could feel the anger coursing through her. Her father, this man, who should have loved and protected his children, had brought them nothing but fear and humiliation at his hands. Well, no more. She stopped and stood still with her hands on her hips.

"I should have expected no less, should I?" she began. "Joey Russell could never win an argument unless it was with his fists. Well, you won't raise your hand to me ever again, and if I hear that you've done it to one of the others or to Mum, I'll have the law on you."

"A man has a right to chastise his wife and children..." he began.

"But he doesn't have the right to whip them within an inch of their lives. I saw what you did to Tommy. He'll forever bear those scars on his back. How many times has Mum had a black eye or two because she claimed she walked into a door? How many times have you come back angry and drunk and used her as a punch bag?"

"Keep yer voice down," he hissed.

"Why? So people can't hear what you do? They ought to know. The whole town ought to know what a despicable creature you are. You disgust me. You're nothing but a hypocrite and a bully. From this day forward, I never want to see you again." She began to stride away from him but stopped to face him one last time. "One more thing... You'll see the gaffer at Groves tomorrow and tell him my money is to be paid to me."

"So that's how it's to be, is it? My own daughter turning against me?"

Lily paused a moment before replying, "I will always be your daughter. But you forgot how to be a father."

Lily had not gone more than three steps when she felt a hand on her arm. Her father stood next to her. "Yer right, lass. I 'aven't been the father you should 'ave 'ad, and I will see to it that you get yer money. Yer right about the drink as well. It's no excuse, I know, but after the accident, it was a way of getting through the pain. Then it became a habit. I understand if yer don't want to see me again, but don't walk away from yer mother and yer brothers and sisters. It'd break yer mother's 'eart."

Lily looked at her father. She could see the lines of stress and pain around his eyes and the deep grooves around his nose. The broken veins told their own story of his fondness for a drink. He claimed his drinking started after the accident, but she knew it had gone on for longer than that. But at least, for the first time, he had acknowledged the problem. It was a start.

"All right," she replied. "You can keep the money. Just make sure you give it to Mum so she can put more food on the table for the kids."

He nodded. "I will. Yer 'ave me word."

"Very well. I'll trust you. But if I find out that you've lied to me..."

"Yer won't," he replied quickly. "I may be many things, but once I've given my word, I won't step back." With that, he turned and started walking back in the direction they'd come.

He was not going to prop up the bar at The Horseshoe. Not tonight, at least.

Lily walked on past the church and turned left onto the High Street. This was the first time she had stood up to her father and the first time she had ever seen him show some regret for his actions. She had no doubt he would struggle to change. He'd been used to having everything his own way for a long time, and he'd been drinking for so long it would not be easy, but he had, for tonight at least, shown he was willing to try to change. Perhaps the younger children would see their father sober for the first time. Perhaps her mother would see something of the man she had fallen in love with. Perhaps there would even be peace in the Russell household.

seven

The year passed by remarkably quickly, far quicker than Lily could remember from her time at school. The nights had drawn in, and the fires were lit a little earlier each evening. Some mornings, the lawn was covered in frost.

Since the confrontation with her father, Lily had visited home, but each time he had been out. Her mother did, however, tell her he had stopped drinking and there was a little more money coming in. The children looked a little less ragged and thin. The boys even had nearly new boots from the market.

War had been declared, but it all seemed so far away. Her birthday passed with little notice and no celebration, as it did every year. The routine at the Groves' continued throughout the early part of the autumn. She was increasingly called on to dress Miss Eleanor's hair as she attended more and more events with her new beau, the Honourable Bartholomew Cranston.

"I rather think Barty might propose soon," Eleanor said as Lily teased some tendrils from her loose chignon.

"Indeed, miss? He's the one, then, is he?" she asked, pinning the final curl in place.

"I rather think he is," Eleanor replied. "Of course, he's a younger son and unlikely to inherit anything, which is not what my parents want, but he's handsome, rich enough, kind, and makes me laugh."

"I imagine a married woman needs a sense of humour," Lily commented wryly, holding up a hand mirror so Eleanor could see the back of her hair.

"Well, I'm not sure Mama or her friends were overly endowed with that quality." The young woman laughed. "Still," she added, "I believe Barty has an aged uncle in need of an heir, so you never know. It would be quite a lark to be the Countess of Latham. Don't you think?"

"I imagine it would, miss," Lily replied, gathering the hairpins and dropping them into the small Wedgwood pot on the dressing table.

Miss Eleanor turned to face her. "By the by, did Mama tell you that Jonathon will be home shortly from Oxford? I imagine there will be much to do before the prodigal son returns."

"And is he, miss?"

"Is he what?"

"The prodigal son?"

Miss Eleanor laughed. "I shall have to leave you to decide. However, I imagine the fatted calf will be offered, knowing Mama."

The preparations for Christmas meant more work for everyone, especially the gardeners as the two young lads had gone off to join the army, much to everyone's surprise. The house was to be cleaned from top to bottom before it was decorated for Christmas.

"I wouldn't be surprised if Mrs. Grove doesn't go round with white gloves on to check for dust," Aggie puffed as they pulled out the oak sideboard to dust the skirting board behind it. "I wouldn't mind, but no one is going to see what's behind here, in any case."

"There might be a sovereign." Lily grinned.

"Nah, just a couple of old buttons and a sixpence." Aggie laughed. "I'll keep the sixpence, and you can have the buttons and any sovereigns we might find."

In fact, by the time they had cleaned every bedroom and reception room, their grand haul totalled ten shillings and eight pence, two pencils, and an assortment of buttons and collar studs.

"A Christmas bonus," Aggie said as she counted out Lily's share. "Enough to buy me a couple of lengths for a skirt, something to decorate my old hat, and a ticket to the pictures. What's yours going for?" she asked.

"Something to go in the kid's stockings," Lily replied.

Christmas had never been a particularly happy time in the Russell household. An apple and orange, a few nuts, and some chocolate were about all the children got. Gifts tended to be something that was needed, such as a new jumper or stockings knitted from wool carefully unravelled from a jumper and reworked by their mother during the long autumn evenings. This year, they would each have a toy or a book. Something they could call their own.

By the middle of December, Aggie and Lily had been into the attics and had pulled down boxes of Christmas ornaments for Mrs. Grove to inspect.

"The paper angels will have to be remade," she announced. "And we must have more fruits. You girls will now spend the next two afternoons working on the ornaments so they are ready for when the tree and greenery are brought in."

Neither Lily nor Aggie objected. Sitting in the dining room making decorations was infinitely better than sweeping, dusting, and polishing, even if it was only for an afternoon or two and the missed work had to be made up later.

"The house must be ready for Wednesday when Master Jonathon arrives," Mrs. Grove announced. For the first time, Lily saw life in the older woman's eyes.

It was a wonderful sight. Lily had never seen a Christmas tree in a real home before as her family had never had money for one. She and Aggie had spent much of the last few days cleaning each room before decorating it with holly, ivy, and mistletoe the gardener had brought in. It seemed almost that each surface was covered with greenery entwined with red ribbons, but it was the tree Lily's eyes feasted on each time she passed through the hallway. It stood near the base of the stairs and reached almost to the top. It was festooned with glass baubles and strings of tinsel that glittered in the light. At dusk, candles placed in small lantern holders among the branches were lit. The scent of pine was magical. She thought the whole thing was enchanting. The whole house was transformed into a place of light and beauty. Even its owners seemed to be lighter.

On the day appointed for Jonathon's arrival, a special meal was prepared and places were set in the formal dining room. But by ten o'clock, Mr. Grove had left, and it was obvious Master Jonathon would not be making an appearance.

"You may clear," Mrs. Grove ordered. "I shall not require coffee tonight." She swept from the room.

"Why don't you go on up?" Lily said to Aggie as they cleared the table. "There's only Mrs. Grove's things, as neither Mr. Grove nor Miss Eleanor are here tonight. Cook's already gone, and Mrs. Cadeby retired to her rooms when we served the main course."

Aggie smiled. "Thanks, Lily." She yawned. "I wouldn't mind. It'd be good to get some rest in before young Master Jonathon arrives. He'll break his mother's heart one day, that boy. Fancy not letting her know he wasn't coming."

"Perhaps he was delayed," Lily replied, replacing the unused crockery in the sideboard.

"He could have sent a telegram or used that new telephone Mr. Grove has had installed, which makes me jump every time it rings."

"He may not have been able to."

"I don't know why you're defending him. A right snob, he is. He's got his mother wrapped around his little finger. Make sure you don't fall for his charm because that's all it is, charm. There's nothing behind it." Aggie suddenly grinned. "Anyway, ta for the favour. I owe you one next time."

It did not take Lily long to clear the rest of the dinner things. Mrs. Grove had barely eaten anything. She left the dirty dishes in the scullery for Lottie to do in the morning and turned off the gas lamps. She was just putting out the last of the candles on the Christmas tree when there was an insistent banging on the front door. Although it was not really her place to answer the door, and certainly not late at night, she cautiously opened the door. Standing on the porch was a tall young man in an overcoat. He wore a dark fedora and was in the process of removing his leather gloves as she opened the door. Two suitcases stood at his feet.

"Hello," he said. "Devil of a journey. Had to change trains twice, and it took an age to get a taxi from Sheffield." He handed her his hat and strode past her into the hall.

"You must be Master Jonathon, sir," Lily said, desperately hoping she was right and that she hadn't just opened the door to some sort of burglar.

"I certainly am. Has Ma given up on me and gone to bed?"

"Mrs. Grove retired a little while ago, sir."

"And Pa?"

"Mr. Grove is away on business, sir, and Miss Eleanor is staying with an old school friend for a few days."

"Not much of a welcome, is it?"

"I believe you were expected earlier, sir," Lily explained. "It was assumed you would come tomorrow instead as you had not yet arrived."

The young man suddenly looked at Lily sharply. "I don't believe I've seen you before."

"No, sir. I've only been here a few months." She belatedly bobbed a curtsey.

"So what is your name?" he asked.

"Russell, sir," she replied.

He raised an eyebrow. "Russell? That's a boy's name. I can't believe your parents thought you were a boy."

Lily could not help but grin. "Of course not, sir. My name is Lily, sir. Lily Russell."

"Well, Lily Russell, do you think you could rustle me something up to eat? I'm starving."

eight

It was not long before Jonathon was sitting at the scrubbed table tucking in to the bread, cheese, meats, and pickles Lily had assembled and washing it down with a bottle of beer.

"This is the food of the gods. Thank you, Lily Russell," he said with a grin. He was good-looking. There was no denying it. A stray lock of his thick, dark hair fell over his eyes as he leaned forward. His eyes were blue, Lily noticed, but quite the bluest eyes she had ever seen. And any woman would have killed for his long, thick eyelashes. Any hint of femininity in his eyes was offset by his straight nose and firm jaw. He was the most handsome man Lily had ever seen. The lads in town generally had few teeth and battered faces, either from work or heavy-handed fathers.

"They must be pretty poor gods," she replied, "if they're reduced to a bit of bread and cheese. More the food of mice."

He laughed, showing white, even teeth. "Well, very well-fed mice. Now, Lily Russell, why don't you open another bottle of beer and join me for a drink?" he said, reaching for a second bottle.

"I don't think so, sir. It wouldn't be proper," she replied.

"I won't tell if you don't." He pushed the bottle towards

her. "Besides, it would be doing me a service, really. You shouldn't let a person drink alone."

"If Mrs. Grove, or even Mrs. Cadeby, found out, I would be out on my ear."

"I imagine Ma has taken one of her pills and is dead to the world by now. And don't worry about dear old Cadeby. She's actually quite a pussycat." He opened a third bottle.

"She might be a pussycat to you, sir. But trust me, to the staff, she's more of a tigress."

He laughed. "I can imagine. But don't worry. I can handle Mrs. Cadeby. Have a drink."

Lily picked it up. She shouldn't even entertain the idea. This was not what servants did at all, but she could not resist. Why shouldn't she be allowed to break the rules just once? How many times in her life was she going to be invited to have a drink with a rich, young man? Never, and in the morning, when she served him breakfast, she would be back to being Russell and he would have probably forgotten about tonight in any case. She took a sip and coughed.

"That is disgusting stuff." She wheezed, struggling to regain her breath. "Why does anyone drink it? How do they enjoy it?"

He laughed again, a rich, deep sound. "Practise, Lily Russell. Lots of practise." His eyes narrowed. "Don't tell me that's the first time you've drunk alcohol?"

Lily nodded.

He winked. "Well, now's a good time to start."

She took another sip. It wasn't quite the shock the first one had been. "Your parents will be very glad to see you've arrived home safely," she said, changing the subject.

"Ma will. Pa probably won't notice, and no doubt my dear sister is enjoying herself with her latest beau. In fact, I almost didn't come, as it happens, but if one doesn't come at Christmas, there's a chance of getting cut out of the will." He laughed.

"Mrs. Grove has certainly been looking forward to it," Lily replied.

"Oh, she does, what with the Christmas Ball to raise funds for the hospital and the lunch for the Widows and Orphans Fund as well as the Children's Christmas party. She wouldn't forgive me if I wasn't there to charm the old ladies into donating to her good causes." He grinned.

"Mrs. Grove certainly gives a lot of time to her charitable works," Lily replied.

"Yes," he said, thoughtfully. "Women of Ma's generation, especially ladies, weren't brought up to do much else. My grandfather apparently didn't approve of women being educated too much. I've often wondered what Ma might have done had she been born into a different family at a different time."

"Perhaps she might have been a housemaid," Lily said before clapping her hand over her mouth. "I apologise, sir. I should not have said that."

Jonathon threw his head back and laughed. "You're most refreshing, Lily Russell," he said. "So tell me, do you like working here?"

There was no point in saying otherwise, so Lily nodded. "Of course, the work is fine, and Mrs. Cadeby is training me so that I might be a housekeeper one day."

"And is that what you want? To be a housekeeper?" he asked.

Of course not. I wanted to go to the grammar school and then to university. I want the life you have, the life you take for granted, Lily thought to herself before replying, "It's what girls like me can aspire to," she replied.

"I'm not sure that's an answer to my question." He looked at her thoughtfully.

"I would have liked to have continued learning," she said, returning his gaze.

"Then why didn't you?"

She shrugged. Although they had grown up within a couple of miles of each other, they inhabited different worlds. He would never know how it felt to go to bed with a hungry belly or wear shoes with cardboard in the soles to fill the holes. She doubted he would even know what a hand-me-down was. His was a world of plenty.

"My parents couldn't afford for me to go to the grammar school," she replied honestly, adding, "They needed me to go to work. My wages help to put food on the table."

The easy smile left his face, and he looked at her with sympathy. "I apologise, Lily. You must think me an insensitive ass," he said softly.

It was not the response she had expected. "It's the luck of the draw, Master Jonathon. You were born where you were, and I was born where I was."

He drank the last of his beer. "Things won't stay the same forever, Lily. At Oxford, I rub shoulders with boys with titles, or the heirs to them. A few years ago, someone like me, whose father is from trade, wouldn't have been given the time of day, let alone a place."

Lily rose and began to clear the table. "Well, let's hope things do change," she replied. "Now, if you don't mind, Master Jonathon, if you've finished, I'll say good night. I have to be up early."

"Of course. Thoughtless of me to keep you from your bed. Good night, Lily Russell."

"Good night, sir."

Lily made her way to her room. As she climbed into bed, she thought about her strange evening. It had been nice to sit and talk with Master Jonathon almost as equals, but she would be wise to remember Aggie's warning: "He's a charmer." They were not, and never could be, equals, no matter what he said about things changing.

nine

With Jonathon Grove's arrival, it seemed as though the house had suddenly come alive. Mrs. Grove's listless lethargy was replaced by energy and an interest in life. Invitations to drinks, lunches, and dinners were swiftly dispatched. Soon, the house was filled with the local landowners and businessmen with their expensively clad wives. There was even a smattering of local gentry, on occasion, who seemed content to mix with people in trade as long as the food and drink were plentiful. As Lily circulated with endless trays of champagne and canapés, she couldn't help but notice that Jonathon was constantly called upon to accompany his mother as they circulated among their guests. Since their late-night meeting, he had, as she expected, barely acknowledged her presence.

"It's like this every time 'is nibs comes 'ome," Aggie grumbled as she lifted another tray of dirty glasses to return to the scullery. "She don't entertain unless 'e's 'ere. Then we're all rushed off our feet with little thanks and no more money. I tell you, I'm thinking of joining up." She produced a folded leaflet from her pocket. "Look."

"The Women's Auxiliary Army Corps," Lily read aloud. "I've never heard of it."

"Neither 'ad I," Aggie replied. "But I was in town the other day, and there were some women in the 'igh Street dressed in those uniforms." She pointed to the figure on the leaflet. "They gave me this. It's something to think about, innit? I mean, we're used to wearing a uniform and taking orders, and they're asking for domestic workers. It's right up our street. It could be an adventure. Don't you think, Lily?"

Lily thought for a moment before replying, "It could be, but we could end up doing more or less what we're doing here. Don't get me wrong. I'm happy to do my bit for the war effort, but I'd want to do something different, nursing or something."

"You'd have to do training for something like that, and I was never any good at school," Aggie replied.

"Well, let's wait and see after Christmas." Lily picked up her tray and headed towards the scullery.

"It might all be over by then," Aggie replied, following her.

On the day before Christmas Eve, the Groves hosted a dinner for several of the leading families of the area before they all went off to the town hall for Mrs. Grove's Christmas Ball in aid of the hospital. Several local girls were recruited for the evening, and Lily was put in charge of making sure they knew what their duties were.

"We're going to be feeding twenty-four," Mrs. Cadeby had said, "and there is no room for error. This is Mrs. Grove's principal fundraiser, and these are the people who will donate the most. Cook has prepared a lavish dinner, and it is our duty to ensure it is served correctly. If we do our jobs properly, the guests will not even notice we are there."

Lily knew exactly what Mrs. Cadeby had meant. By now, she had learned to stand behind each guest while they helped themselves to whatever food was in the dish she held. Most of them did not even look up as she silently moved from one guest to the next. Their glasses were filled and their empty plates removed without a break in the conversation. They were indeed invisible. She and Aggie did the waiting at the table while the local girls fetched and carried the dishes from the kitchen.

As Lily served, she could not help but overhear the many conversations across the table. Although there was talk about the ball later in the evening, and some talk about Christmas, much of the talk was about the war. There had been talk of it being over by Christmas, though it was clearly going to go on for longer.

"Of course," Mr. Grove stated, "the problem is that Germany has always been envious of The Empire. They believe that we and France are blocking their imperial ambition."

"That may be true, Pa," Jonathon agreed. "But the fact is that they came to this particular party too late. By the time the kaiser was ready to expand, we and the French had pretty much carved up the globe between us."

"Indeed," Sir Conroy put in, "and had it not been for the mishap with tea in Boston, we would have held on to America." He laughed.

"It should not take too long to defeat the kaiser, surely," Mr. Benson added. "After all, they are surrounded by the Russians, the French, and us."

"I agree," Mr. Grove replied, "and I hope to God it does not take too long. Far too many of my lads have signed up already. Can't run a building business with old men. That's for sure."

"Nor a coal mine," Sir Conroy added. "Still, it's good to see our young chaps doing their patriotic duty."

"It's true, sir," Jonathon chimed in. "Several of my chums from college are signing up. No one wants to miss out on the adventure."

"I hope you are not thinking of doing so," Mrs. Grove said. "War is not kind to young men."

There was a slight pause before Jonathon continued. "I would have thought you would have approved of my doing my bit for king and country, Ma. In any case, everyone says it's going to be a short war. One or two big battles and it will all be over."

"War is never an adventure, Jonathon. Remember that," Mrs. Grove persisted. She smiled brightly, looking around the table. "Now, everyone, let us talk of more pleasant matters."

———

As she finished clearing and setting the room to rights, Lily's thoughts turned to what she had heard. The thought of young men happily going off to fight a war in a foreign land made her thankful that, at fourteen and thirteen, her two brothers were too young to be involved. Life in Hope was hard enough without the men disappearing. It would mean even greater hardship for the families left behind. But Master Jonathon's words had rung true. Several of the boys she had been at school with had already left, thinking life in the army could be no worse than going down the pit, and Aggie was interested in joining up. She remembered Mrs. Cadeby's words: "Life was changing and changing fast."

She must have dropped off to sleep in Cook's Windsor chair by the fire. The fire had gone out, and the room was distinctly chilly when she awoke with a start.

"Don't mind me, Lily Russell." Jonathon's words made her jump. "I'm just helping myself to one or two of Cook's delicious mince pies." He sat on the scrubbed oak table in the centre of the room, idly swinging his legs. Although still in his evening suit, his tie hung loosely around his neck.

"What time is it?" she asked sleepily, rubbing her eyes.

He looked at his watch. "A little after three o'clock."

Lily shot out of the chair. "Three o'clock? Bloody hell. I have to be up in a couple of hours."

"I shan't tell Mother about your language, Lily Russell. After all, it's Christmas Eve." He grinned.

"It may be Christmas to you, sir, but it's a working day for me," she replied. The tiredness had loosened her tongue.

"Duly noted." He slid off the table and took her arm. "Allow me to escort you."

"I know the way, sir."

"A gentleman should always escort a lady."

Lily looked up at him. "Are you laughing at me, sir? We both know I am a maid. Under no circumstances that I can think of would your sort consider me to be a lady."

"Please, Lily Russell, I should like to play the part of a gentleman tonight."

They stopped at the foot of the staircase. "I think I can find my own way from here," Lily said.

Jonathon looked up. "Well, how fortuitous that we should stop here," he said, a gleam in his eye.

Lily did not need to see what he was looking at. She knew that above their heads was a large kissing bough because she and Aggie had hung it there.

"Now, Lily Russell, I simply refuse to pass up this opportunity," he murmured.

His arm slid around her back and pulled her closer as his lips found hers. It was a gentle kiss, until he ran his tongue along her lips, inviting them to open. When she did, one hand cupped the back of her head as his tongue plundered her mouth. Lily had never felt anything like it. Her whole body trembled as she returned his kiss, like for like.

"Lily Russell, what are you doing to me?" he whispered against her mouth, his hands roaming over her back.

Perhaps it was the use of her full name that brought some semblance of sense. She was, and always would be, Lily Russell, the maid. After all, he had barely acknowledged her since that first night. It was the ultimate cliché: the master's son and the maid.

She drew back. "Merry Christmas, Master Jonathon," she said, struggling to remain composed. "Pleasant though this interlude has been, there will not be a repeat of it. I will not be your plaything, sir." She stepped out of his arms and ran up the stairs without looking back.

Jonathon watched her until she disappeared.

ten

Christmas Day came and went. Once the family had returned from church, they ate their Christmas dinner. When Lily and Aggie had cleared the dining room and set out a cold buffet, the staff gathered downstairs to have their own meal. The crockery and silverware may not have been as fancy as what was used upstairs, but the food was just as good. The Groves had enjoyed a roast goose, but for the staff, Cook had prepared a fine, boned turkey with stuffing made from sausage, chestnuts and apples, roast potatoes, carrots, parsnips, and celery. The Christmas pudding was ceremoniously brought in and set alight. In truth, Lily had never had such a fine Christmas dinner, even though her mother saved all year to buy a turkey.

After dinner, all the servants, from both indoors and out, were allowed to play games together. The old gardener was surprisingly fast at Snapdragon, managing to snatch most of the brandy-soaked raisins before burning his fingers.

"A lifetime of gardening hardens the fingers." He laughed, popping the last one in his mouth.

There were charades and carol singing, and for the first time, Lily felt like they were all a community. No one had to dash off to lay or clear a table, dust the woodwork, scour the pans, or pick the beans. They were able to talk and enjoy each other's company.

Lily was given the afternoon off on Boxing Day. After breakfast, they had all lined up in the hall, and Mrs. Grove had given them all an envelope with their Christmas box. Each servant's Christmas box reflected both their standing in the household as well as their time of service. Lily's additional two sovereigns were a welcome relief and would go a long way to feeding her family through the worst of the winter when her father's building work was unpredictable.

As the family was to visit Mrs. Grove's family for a few days, the staff was given time off. and Lily was able to visit her family. Once again, she managed to get a lift in the cart as several of the servants' families lived in Hope.

"It's our Lily," Nora squealed as Lily walked through the door. "Look, Lily! I got a dolly! A real dolly from Father Christmas! She's called Patsy."

"And I got a paint box." Betty held it up from her seat at the table.

"I expect you saw the boys out playing with their football and hoop," her mother said before lapsing into a coughing fit. "Come in and close the door, Lily. The cold took my breath away."

"Yes, come in and put wood in t' hole," her father added, but his tone was not an unkind one.

Lily held out a small package. "I brought you these. Mrs. Grove's cook, Mrs. Thwaite, made them."

Her father reached into the packet. "Mince pies. Always been fond of a mince pie."

"Thanks, love," her mother replied. "They look lovely. I'll have one later with a cup of tea."

"So—" Lily looked round the room. "—Merry Christmas! How is everyone?"

"Fair, quite fair. Mustn't grumble," the older woman replied. "The baby and I have had a bit of a cough, but I think we're both on the mend. Fortunately, your father and the others seem to have avoided it."

Lily looked closely at her mother. She always seemed tired, but her complexion was quite grey, and she had clearly lost weight since Lily's last visit. "Are you all right, Mum?" she asked. "Do you think you should go and see Dr. Dickensen?"

"Of course not." Her mother laughed. "It's just a little cough and cold. I'll be as right as rain by the new year."

"I can pay," Lily urged. "I got a Christmas box from the Groves today."

"If yer mum says she's all right, then she's all right. We don't go botherin' t' doctor unless it's something serious," her father stated, speaking up.

"Well, if you're sure," she said, not convinced.

"I'm sure," her mother replied with a smile. "Now tell us all about Christmas at the big house."

The time passed all too quickly. In no time at all, she was pressing one of the sovereigns into her mother's hand and promising to visit again in the new year.

With Christmas over, the Grove household began to turn its thoughts towards the new year. Master Jonathon and Miss Eleanor had invited their friends for the celebration. There was to be a party for the young people.

"It's their bribe," Aggie surmised. "Master Jonathon and Miss Eleanor do the whole happy family thing at Christmas, and they get to have some fun at new year."

"Whatever it is, we've all the bedrooms to get ready," Lily replied, deftly tucking the sheet under the mattress. "It doesn't matter to us who comes so long as they don't cause extra work."

"They allus do," Aggie replied, picking up a pillow.

The weather almost scuppered the entire thing. It started

snowing two days after Boxing Day, and it looked as though no one would be able to come. Many of the lanes were blocked with deep snow drifts which froze overnight as more snow fell. However, somehow most of Jonathon and Eleanor's friends managed to make it through.

"Look at 'em," Aggie remarked as they were laying the table for lunch.

Through the dining room window, they could see the merry band making a snowman and hurling snowballs at each other. Even through the window, they could hear the shouts of laughter from the men and the shrieks and giggles of the women.

"It must be nice to be able to have fun like that. Not a care in the world, that lot," Aggie continued. "I bet they've never 'ad an empty belly or shoes with more 'oles than leather."

"I suppose not," Lily agreed. "Accident of birth made them what they are, just as it made us what we are. The thing is, Aggie," she went on, "we're survivors. Those women can't even get dressed without help. All they can expect from life is to marry some rich bloke who'll look after them. We know we can look after ourselves."

"I never thought of it like that," Aggie replied. "But don't you dream of a sweetheart coming along to sweep you off your feet and take you away from all this?" She raised her arm to indicate the room.

Lily thought for a moment. The two examples she had seen of marriage were not encouraging. Her parents seemed to have nothing in common, nor did Mr. and Mrs. Grove. Even Miss Eleanor, who had high hopes of a proposal from her beau, didn't seem to be head over heels in love.

"I don't know, Aggie," she admitted. "I'm not sure I want to depend on anyone other than myself." The one man who had shown any interest in her was so far beyond her that it was foolish to even think of him.

"You might be right at that," Aggie agreed. "Still," she went on with a wink, "we can 'ave a bit o' fun finding out."

———

On New Year's Eve, Mr. and Mrs. Grove went to spend the night with friends, so the young people had the run of the house. After dinner, the carpet in the large sitting room was rolled back, and one of the young men played the piano for dancing. As she cleared the dining room, Lily tapped her toes in time to the music. Later, they played party games. Several times, she had to avoid a couple as they careered out of the room to hide. Clearly a lot of Mr. Grove's fine wines had been drunk.

Eventually, the house went quiet, and she was on her way to bed when she heard a noise in the library. Cautiously, she opened the door to find the loudest of Jonathon's friends shuffling through the selection of Mr. Grove's decanters.

"Can I help you, sir?" she asked, coming further into the room. With the way the glass decanters were clinking, she could see the whole lot landing on the floor.

"Hope so," he slurred. "Thought I might find some of old man Grove's best port in here. The stuff they served after dinner was disgusting."

Lily instantly recognised him as one of Jonathon's titled friends, the Honourable Edgar Scott-Bishop, who, for some reason, everyone called Eggy.

"Well, come along, girl. Find it an' pour me one. Chop, chop." He leaned back against the bookshelves.

Lily found the appropriate decanter and poured a small amount into a glass. He took it and drank it down in one gulp before handing it back.

"Let's have another, and don't be stingy this time, girl."

As Lily poured the port, she could feel he had left his position at the bookshelf and was standing behind her. She turned, holding the glass out to him and pasting a bright smile on her face. "There you are, sir. I imagine you'll be wanting to turn in after this if you're planning on going out with the shooting party tomorrow."

Suddenly, the glass was dashed from her hand and smashed against the fireplace. "Don't tell me what to do," he snarled. Then his hands were all over her as she was dragged towards him. "Let's see what's under this uniform," he said, ripping at the buttons and yanking the bodice down so that her breasts were exposed to his greedy gaze and her arms were effectively imprisoned in her own sleeves. "Nice titties." He reached out and squeezed them.

"Stop. Stop now, sir, before you do something you'll regret." Lily raised her voice, trying to get him to listen. She raised her leg. If he wasn't listening, a knee to his groin should get his attention. He clearly wasn't as drunk as she thought, though, because he caught her leg before she could make contact.

"No you don't, you little bitch," he breathed. "I think you need to be taught your place."

He swept everything off the desk and pushed Lily face down against it, then held her in place with one arm across her back while lifting her skirt above her waist with the other. He tore at her knickers and began to undo his trousers. Lily closed her eyes. Her body was frozen. She concentrated all her efforts and let out a scream. He pulled her head back by her hair.

"Do that again and you'll regret it," he whispered in her ear. "Now spread your legs, you little whore. I've watched you serving meekly at the table, but I know what your sort want. You want it hard and fast, and that's what I'm going to do to you."

There was a crack as the door was flung open.

"What the hell is going on?" She heard Jonathon's voice.

"Get the hell out, Grove. I'm just about to fuck your maid.

If you want a go, you'll have to watch and wait until after I'm done. Then I'll watch you. Better still, fetch the others, and we can all have a bit of fun. You've probably already fucked her senseless a hundred times, haven't you?"

"The hell you are. Take your hands off her," Jonathon replied.

There was a whoosh of air as Jonathon grabbed the other man and flung him across the room.

"What the hell's the matter with you, Grove?" he protested. "She's only a bloody maid."

Jonathon looked quickly at Lily. "Are you all right?"

She nodded, clutching the open dress together in an effort to cover herself.

"Now—" He turned to Eggy, who Lily assumed was no longer a friend of Jonathon's. "—I suggest you get your belongings together and ensure you're out of this house by morning."

"Are you sure you want to do this, Grove? You know who I am, what I can do. Every door in society will be closed to you, and all for a maid? Look at her. She was asking for it."

There was a crack as Jonathon's fist connected with the other man's jaw. "Get the hell out, Eggy. I don't give a damn who you are or what you think you can do. If one word of this gets out, I shall ensure everyone knows what you were intent on doing."

The Honourable Edgar Scott-Bishop stood up. "I hope she's worth it," he said before leaving.

eleven

Lily could not bring herself to tell Aggie what had happened. The following morning, when Aggie looked at her, she said, "You're as white as a sheet, Lily. Are you sickening for something?"

"I don't feel too good," Lily admitted.

"Then best you stay there. T' guests are all leaving today along with Miss Eleanor, and the older Groves aren't coming back for a couple of days. I reckon we can manage without you."

"Are you sure?" Lily asked, thankful she wouldn't have to face either Jonathon or Eggy—if he were still there.

"Course I'm sure. You rest up, and you'll be as right as ninepence tomorrow."

Once Aggie had left, Lily buried her face in her pillow and allowed the tears to fall. If Master Jonathon hadn't come in when he had, she had no doubt his friend would have raped her. She not only wouldn't have been able to prevent it, but he would have gotten away with it. Who would believe or care about what a maid said against a man who would one day be an earl? The Groves wouldn't want to lose their hard-won society connections. The Honourable Edgar Scott-Bishop would go on with his life without a care in the world, but she would be dismissed and no doubt accused of making the whole thing up.

She sat up in bed and looked around the sparsely furnished room. There was very little in it apart from the two narrow beds, shared tallboy, and a few hooks to hang things on. She caught a glimpse of herself in the small mirror. She did not cry often, and she did not cry prettily, but she was damned if the Honourable Edgar Scott-Bishop was going to make a victim of her.

It took only a few minutes for her to wash, dress, and put her hair in order. As she entered the dining room, her attacker was leaving. His eyes narrowed. "I'm surprised you dare show your face here," he sneered. "I don't know what hold you have over Johnny, but however many times he fucks you, you'll never be more than a maid to him."

Lily stood up straight. "For your information, sir—" She didn't bother to conceal the contempt in her voice. "—Mr. Grove has never behaved in any way less than a gentleman towards me or any of the staff. I may be just a maid to you, but I am a human being, and if ever I think of you again, which I doubt, it will remind me that the term honourable before your name means absolutely nothing. Now if you'll excuse me, sir, I have work to do, and I have no wish to waste another second of my life talking to you." With that, she swept from the room. If she got sacked, it was worth it to see the look of astonishment on his face.

———

She was dusting the library when Jonathon entered, causing her to jump. Lily released the breath she had been unaware she was holding.

"I wanted to see you." He came into the room. "I wanted to know you are all right."

"I'm fine," she replied.

"When I think what that bastard was about to do to you..." he began.

"But he didn't," she said. "You came to the rescue."

"Only just in time. Thank God I heard your scream." He came towards her. "I don't know what you said to him today, but he's gone with his tail between his legs."

She shrugged. "I told him that although he might bear the term honourable, he was the least honourable man I've ever met and that I wouldn't waste another second of my life thinking about him."

Jonathon grinned. "Lily Russell, you are magnificent."

"And your friend is a miserable excuse for a man."

He shook his head. "I can assure you Eggy is no friend. I only brought him so Mother could have bragging rights that the heir to an earl was under her roof. He's an absolute snob, always boasting about his position. I can assure you he has very little to boast about. Heir to a title he may be, but there's no money, and believe me, any brains they had were bred out of them centuries ago. He'll have to marry a rich American heiress."

"I doubt anyone would want him," Lily replied. "I should think they would have more taste."

"That's the power of the title, I'm afraid." He grinned, then his smile left his face. "I can assure you he will never be a guest in this house again, title or no. In fact, I think you should report him to the police."

Lily laughed. "It doesn't work like that, sir. His father will no doubt know the chief constable, and the whole thing will be brushed under the carpet."

He shook his head. "That's not how it should be."

Lily nodded. "I agree. There are a lot of things that are not as they should be, sir. They might change one day. Who knows? But that's the way things are now."

He looked at his watch. "I have to go, Lily Russell, but

when I come back, I hope you and I can have a further chat. Talking with you has been one of the highlights of this Christmas." He bent and kissed her cheek, and then he was gone.

Once the guests had departed, Lily and Aggie set about clearing and cleaning the guest rooms. "Are you feeling up to this?" Aggie asked as she expertly stripped the bed.

"Of course," replied. "I feel a lot better. Whatever I had seems to have gone."

Aggie looked unconvinced. "If you're sure?"

"Absolutely," Lily replied. There was no doubt that once the front door had closed on the Honourable Edgar Scott-Bishop, her spirits had lifted.

They worked in companionable silence until all the guest rooms were ready for use again. Aggie stripped and remade the beds while Lily polished the furniture with beeswax.

"Well, that's that," Aggie commented as they closed the last door. "Let's 'ope there's to be no more entertaining for a while."

It was a vain wish, as Miss Eleanor returned late that afternoon sporting a sparkling engagement ring.

"Barty came up to scratch," she said as Lily styled her hair for the family celebratory dinner. "He wanted to make sure I would be here for him when he returns from the front."

Lily deftly teased one or two tendrils from the chignon. "Is he going off to war, then, miss?"

"He leaves within the week," Eleanor replied. "He's joining his family's regiment, The Green Howards. I must say he looks rather dashing in his uniform."

"Well, let's hope he comes back safe, miss."

Eleanor laughed. "Oh, Barty has the luck of the devil. I'm sure he'll be back with plenty of tales to tell. As a matter of fact, I thought I might join the VADs. What with all our young chaps disappearing off to war, life is going to be a little tedious. Don't you think? Might as well do something useful to pass the time."

"What is the VADs?" Lily asked.

"It's the Voluntary Aid Detachment. Rosie, Barty's sister, was telling me about it. Something like the Red Cross, I think, but nursing, at any rate. Mother will most likely be involved as well, given her association with the infirmary. We all have to do our bit, I suppose."

Lily nodded, putting the hairbrush down. "Aggie is thinking of joining up. They are advertising for women to work in Sheffield making munitions. Or there's always the land army."

Eleanor picked up her perfume bottle and applied it to her wrists and temples. "I don't think munitions or farming are quite my cup of tea, but I can see myself mopping brows and holding hands, so nursing is definitely for me. In any case, Lily, how will Mother manage without you and Aggie?"

———

At the end of the month, there was to be the formal engagement celebration. Barty had completed his training and was about to be sent to the front. Jonathon was also expected back from Oxford for the weekend. The war seemed a long way away. Life at the Groves' house continued as it had. Aggie had not yet left, though it was more difficult to get girls from Hope to come up to the big house, as many of them had gone to the munitions factories in Sheffield or Doncaster and were taken by omnibus. Lily was now helping Mrs. Cadeby with linen and ordering as well as organising the duty rotas. When Mrs. Cadeby had to visit her ailing brother, Lily stood in for her at her meeting with Mrs. Grove.

"You seem to have settled in well, Russell," Mrs. Grove said. "Mrs. Cadeby speaks highly of you, as does my daughter."

"Thank you, ma'am."

"Just ensure you continue to work well. We tolerate no slackers here."

"No, ma'am." It would not matter what she did. To Mrs. Grove, she was always going to be the servant that was foisted on her. Even worse, she suspected Mrs. Grove, even though she knew why Lily was given the job, half believed Lily had been employed because she was sleeping with her husband. It would serve the selfish woman right if she did leave and work in the factory. At least there the hours were shorter.

Lily had left her meeting with Mrs. Grove and was putting the finishing touches to the table when she heard a piercing shriek. Thinking someone was ill, she rushed into the hall to find Mrs. Grove weeping, and standing by was Jonathon, tall and handsome as ever dressed in the uniform of the Royal Flying Corps.

He put his arm around his mother's shoulders. "I told you I had a surprise for you, Mother."

"But this is so dangerous, Jonathon. Everyone says so. Fighting in the war is bad enough, but in those machines? I can't bear the thought," she wailed.

"Nonsense, Mildred." Mr. Grove appeared from his study. "A man has to do his bit. Jonathon has been in the cadets at university. It's obvious this is what he should be doing." He strode forward and shook his son's hand. "Well done, boy. Now that you're in the fighting, the war will no doubt be over within weeks." His tone was, as usual, loud and confident.

Jonathon certainly looked dashing, but Lily felt the fingers of fear clutch at her heart.

twelve

Lily could not help but notice that the celebrations for Miss Eleanor's engagement were somewhat subdued. Most of the young men were in uniform. Some who had been invited could not attend because they were already at the front. For all the laughter and congratulations, the air of gaiety seemed forced around the dinner table. Afterwards, when the ladies retired to the drawing room, there was much admiration of the ring. But there were also worries expressed about brothers and sweethearts. Once the gentlemen joined them, Lily returned to clear the dining room. She had just stacked the first tray when Jonathon poked his head around the door.

"Ah, Lily Russell, there you are."

"Did you want something, sir?" she asked.

"Yes, I do. When you're free later, would you meet me in the summer house for a chat?"

"You do realise it's winter, don't you? Begging your pardon, sir, but couldn't we chat somewhere warmer?" she replied.

"Of course." He laughed before adding, "How about the attic? The staircase is the one above your quarters."

"All right. I should be about another hour or so."

"Splendid. This should all be over by then. So many have to get back to barracks, thank God." He blew her a kiss and left.

Lily shook her head. This would do no good. No matter what her feelings were, his odious friend was right. Jonathon was so far above her. Nothing could ever come of it. Still, when she had finished setting everything to rights, she could not help herself from climbing the last set of stairs leading to the attics running along the whole of the house. He was there before her with a bottle of champagne open at his side and two glasses sitting on the step. He was always handsome, but the uniform gave him a dashing air.

"You came," he said, pouring a glass of champagne and handing it to her.

"Did you think I wouldn't?" she asked, taking a sip.

"Do you like it?" He watched as she took another sip.

"It's better than the beer," she replied.

He laughed. "I love talking with you, Lily."

"That's the first time," she said, taking another sip.

He raised his eyebrows. "The first time for what?"

"The first time you called me Lily."

He looked at her solemnly. "That's what friends do, isn't it?"

She took a breath. "Is that what we are? Friends?"

He smiled that lazy smile, his eyes glowing. "I like to think so. You're so unlike all the other girls I know."

She laughed. "That's because I am. All the other girls you know are like you—rich and carefree. My life experience has been somewhat different."

As they sat in the dark, they talked. Lily told him of her childhood and how she had passed the scholarship but there was no money to send her to the grammar school. She told him that while this happened to her, at least one of her brothers would go if they passed. He told her of his life at boarding school. As the son of a businessman, he was considered barely worth anything by the boys whose fathers bore the titles they would one day inherit.

"It just made me determined to beat them in every way I could, whether it was on the rugby pitch, in the classroom, or even in a fight," he confessed. "I wasn't going to let them win."

"I wanted to go on learning," Lily admitted. "In another life, I should have loved to have gone to the university. Not Oxford or anything like that. I know that's not the place for the likes of me. But somewhere I could have carried on learning. There's so much to learn, isn't there?"

He turned to her and took her hand. "I'm sorry, Lily, that you couldn't follow your dream. I rather took all that for granted."

She shrugged. "That's the way it is. At least working here I'm being trained to be a housekeeper one day."

"Is that what you want to be? A housekeeper?" he asked.

"It's a good opportunity for someone like me, if this war doesn't change things," she replied.

"That doesn't answer my question. But you're right. This war might very well change things." His tone was suddenly sombre. "I've heard things, Lily. I've heard it's not all going so well. I don't know if the rumours are true, but when all this started, a lot of lads went off saying it would all be over by Christmas."

"Then why are you going?" she asked. "Why are you going up in those aeroplanes? They don't seem safe. People were never meant to fly."

He laughed again. Lily liked to hear him laugh. It was a rich, deep sound. "Well, for one thing, most of my friends have already gone. For another, I have to do my duty to my country. And third, I didn't want to be given a white feather."

"You're no coward," she said firmly. "But why the Royal Flying Corps rather than the navy or the army?"

"Well, fond as I am of a tot of rum, I have to confess that I get seasick in a rowing boat on the park lake, and the army involves too much marching."

"Be serious," she admonished him. "I want to know."

He looked into the distance. "It's difficult to explain, really. I am in the Air Cadets at Oxford, and I was lucky enough to go up a few times. I have to say...I love it. I love to hear the wind rushing through the fuselage and the excitement of taking off and landing. There is a freedom one feels when one is up in the air."

She nodded. "It does sound exciting, but I would rather keep my feet on the ground." She thought for a second before adding, "What will it mean in terms of actual fighting?"

He smiled. "Well, for me, as well as being in the Air Cadets, I'm also in the Photographic Society, so I imagine most of my work will be taking photographs from the air." He put a finger on her lips. "But don't tell anyone I said that."

The air seemed to grow thicker as Jonathon looked down at her. He looked as though he was about to kiss her. She realised she wanted him to kiss her, kiss her until they both forgot about the danger he was about to put himself in.

He smiled and drew back. "May I ask you a question, Lily?"

She nodded.

"Will you write to me while I am away? I should like to have some letters from home to remind me it's still here."

"I imagine your mother and Miss Eleanor will write," she replied. "I doubt you'll be short of news from here."

"I imagine they will," he agreed. "But I would like to hear from you as well."

"I can't think why." She laughed. "I can't believe you'd be interested in hearing about me counting the linen or polishing the silverware."

"That's not what I want to read," he replied. "I want to know what books you're reading or what you've seen at The Empire, what you think about things generally. I want to know about you, Lily."

"But why? You'll be the one doing the big, dangerous things. I'll be living my small life."

He turned to her and put his hands on her shoulders. "Don't ever say that, Lily. It's as though you don't value yourself. Don't you see? That's what I'll want to know about when I'm away. The normal things."

She nodded. "All right, then," she agreed. "I'll write to you."

"At least once a week?"

She rolled her eyes. "How much time do you think I have to sit around writing letters? The beds don't make themselves, you know."

He threw back his head and laughed. "And that's the normality I want."

Later, in bed, Lily thought over the conversation she had with Jonathon. If only their stations in life were not so far apart. If it was a fairy tale, it was Cinderella all over again, and although she got the prince in the end, life was not a fairy tale. There would be no happily ever after for them. Mr. and Mrs. Grove would never countenance their only son with the likes of her. If Mrs. Grove knew about their clandestine meeting, Lily would be out on her ear. She could not deny it, though. She had feelings for Jonathon, but did he have feelings for her?

thirteen

The winter snow was slow to thaw, but most of it had gone by the end of February. Even so, Spring was late, cold, and wet. Farmers were worried about their crops, and Lily was fed up with picking her way along muddy lanes. Now that Jimmy had joined up, there were fewer lifts on the cart, which meant a long walk if she went to visit the family in Hope.

Her work at the Groves' house increased as Mrs. Cadeby was frequently called by Mrs. Grove to help with the setting up of the convalescent hospital in nearby Dentworth. Lady Dentworth had decamped to Canada with her daughters but had allowed Dentworth Hall to be used as a hospital. Mrs. Grove had been called upon to get it ready for the twenty or so officers who would be recovering there. Even though Aggie and Lily were employed in the afternoons and evenings to endlessly roll bandages, they were not called on to work in the hospital. As Mrs. Grove explained, the presence of young women might upset the men.

Aggie had disagreed. "You'd think they'd be glad of a sight of a young woman after fightin' and livin' like animals, and I'd certainly be glad of the sight of a young man. If Mrs. Grove thinks we'll faint at the sight of a little blood and a man's arse, she clearly didn't grow up with ten brothers." She'd laughed.

Lily was now in charge of keeping the linen supply, ordering food, supervising the household accounts, and ensuring things ran smoothly both in the kitchen as well as making sure standards did not slip in the house. It was fortunate for Lily there was little entertaining. There was no one to invite. Many of the young men were away. Even Miss Eleanor had gone to London to train as a nurse. Cook often complained it was hardly worth making anything. Mrs. Grove ate like a bird, and Mr. Grove was away even more than before. Houses were not being built. Fortunately, he had connections in the right places and had managed to get a contract to build military camps, but it took him all over Yorkshire. Lily doubted Mrs. Grove noticed or cared that he had gone.

Miss Eleanor returned from London to await her posting. She was pressed into service, driving her mother about in the new motor car Mr. Grove had bought her for an engagement present, even though he bought it for her so that she might drive to visit Barty if he was on leave. She loved the sense of freedom driving gave her and was often seen bowling along the lanes. Lily was less sure of Mrs. Grove's enjoyment, but as she remarked, "It gets one from A to B."

The weather continued to be cool. Many suggested they were paying for the lovely Indian summer of the previous year, in more ways than one. Life had changed. On the surface, things seemed almost normal, though there were certainly fewer young men seen about the place. Yet, the country was at war. People had also begun to dread the sight of the post-and-telegram boy. For most families, the news was never good. For Lily, however, it was a hand-delivered note that bore bad tidings.

As it happened, Miss Eleanor was driving into Hope to pick up some supplies that had been left at the railway station by mistake, so she was happy to drop Lily off in the High

Street. This visit would be a far cry from the happy one she had spent at Christmas. When she arrived at the house, the fire was out, the house was cold and dark, and there was no sound of any of her brothers and sisters. There was just her father sitting in his chair staring at the cold embers.

"Hello, Father," she said, taking off her hat and coat to hang them on the hook by the door.

He turned. "Yer came, then."

"What's happened, Dad? Your note said Mum was ill."

For the first time in her life, she could see tears in his eyes.

"She is, lass. Right badly. She's upstairs in bed. Mebbe yer can get her to eat summat. She's 'ad nothing for days, bar a few sips of water."

She headed towards the stairs, her heels clicking on the wooden floor. "I'll go and see her. Has the doctor been?"

Her father put his head in his hands. "She won't have the doctor. She says all she needs is a tonic, but I've never seen her like this. See if yer can get 'er to change 'er mind. I don't care what it costs. If she needs a doctor, we'll manage."

Lily nodded. For once, her father seemed at a loss. For all his bluster and rage, he was scared. He was scared his wife wasn't going to come through this.

The curtains had been pulled and the room was quite dark, but Lily was able to make out the shape of her mother in the bed she had shared with her husband for many years. As Lily approached, she turned to face her.

"Is that you, Lily?" she asked. Her voice was recognisable, but it was also certainly weaker than Lily had ever heard it.

"Yes, Mum. It's me," she replied. "Shall I open the curtains and let a bit of light in? It's not raining today. A bit of sunlight will do you good."

"Just a bit, then. Too much light hurts my eyes, though."

Lily drew back the faded curtains. A narrow shaft of light fell on the bed, and she was shocked to see how thin and gaunt her mother had become in the few weeks since she had seen her at Christmas.

"If you'd let me know you weren't well, I would have come sooner," Lily said, sitting on the bed and taking her mother's hand.

"I didn't want to make a fuss," her mother replied. "Besides, I know how this is going to go. You remember Mrs. Cameron? I helped to nurse her to the end and what happened to her is now happening to me."

"But Mrs. Cameron was a lot older than you, Mum, and it was a few years ago. Perhaps the doctors can—"

"No, Lily," her mother interrupted. "Mrs. Cameron had some treatment, but she always said it was almost worse than the disease. I knew when the baby was born there was something different, but it doesn't matter now."

"But Mum—"

"Listen, Lily. There are things I need to say to you, and I don't have a lot of time or energy, so please don't interrupt me. I've sent the children to my sister in Shropshire. Polly doesn't have children of her own, and they'll be well looked after. Polly and her husband have plenty of money, so they will want for nothing. Your father isn't happy about it, but he would never be able to look after them." She paused for a moment. "Polly is my younger sister. She married well. I was rather the black sheep of the family."

"So I have relatives in Shropshire I never knew about?" Lily was only partly surprised. She knew her mother had not been born and bred in Hope.

Her mother nodded. "In the top drawer are some papers with the details and Polly's address for you to contact your brothers and sisters. Don't forget them, Lily, and don't let them forget you."

"I won't."

"When I'm gone—" her mother started.

"No, Mum." She could not keep the anguish from her voice, nor the tears from her eyes.

"When I'm gone," she went on, "you are not to come home and look after your father, no matter what he says. He'll be lost, even though he doesn't know it, but he can either learn to look after himself or he can get one of his sisters to come and look after him. Alice or Dorothy would do it. Neither of them are married, and I imagine either of them would welcome the chance to escape from Aunt Mary. She rules them with a rod of iron."

She paused for a moment, the long speech leaving her short of breath. "I want you to carry on with your work, Lily. Make something of yourself. Take all the opportunities that come your way. I had every advantage growing up, and I threw them away. I'm not complaining, and for all his faults, I love your father. In his own way, he loves me. But you could do so much more, Lily, be so much more. Don't get drawn into looking after him and get stuck here in Hope. Go out into the world and make your mark, Lily."

She gripped Lily's hand tightly. "Now, it's time for you to go, and I don't want you to come again. I want you to remember me as I was when I was fit and strong. I don't want your last memories of me to be a frail, sickly woman. Your father will let you know when it's all over."

"Mum..." Lily could barely speak for the tears that choked her.

"Come and lie beside me for a little while, love, and then no more tears."

Lily lay down beside her mother and covered them both with the faded, rose, satin eiderdown. Her mother put her arm around her as she had done so often when Lily had needed comfort as a child, but this time it was difficult to know who was comforting whom.

As the light began to fade, Lily kissed her mother on the cheek. "I have to go now, Mum."

"I know, my love." Her mother kissed her and hugged her with all the strength she could muster. "Goodbye, my darling daughter."

"Goodbye, Mum."

Lily quietly got off the bed and walked to the door, taking one last look as she closed the door behind her.

fourteen

Within the month, the note she had been dreading arrived. Her mother was dead, and she was to come home. Mrs. Grove reluctantly agreed to give her a week off. Mrs. Cadeby was more sympathetic.

"Don't worry, Lily. With everyone away or busy, there's less work. Aggie and I can easily manage until you get back," she'd told Lily.

As her mother had suspected, her father had gone completely to pieces. He didn't even know how many spoonfuls of sugar he had in his tea. It fell to Lily to make arrangements for the funeral. Though, he was adamant the children should not be called back from Shropshire.

"They 'ave a new life now, lass. Best they forget us. In any case, a funeral's no place for little uns."

"They do have a new life, Dad, but they should never forget their mother," Lily replied. "I think it's only right to let Aunt Polly know. Mum was her sister, after all."

"Do what yer thinks best," he said. "That Polly was the only one who stood by yer mother, but I didn't know yer mum had kept in touch with her all these years."

"I think Mum kept a lot of things to herself," Lily replied. They sipped their tea in silence for a while.

Eventually, the silence was broken by her father. "Of course, yer'll 'ave to give up working at the big 'ouse and come back 'ere now yer mother's gone."

Lily took a deep breath, remembering the last conversation she'd had with her mother. "No, Dad. I won't be doing that."

His look of surprise was quickly followed by one of anger. "What? Yer refusing to look after yer own father? Where's yer sense of duty?"

"You'll have to learn to look after yourself," she replied.

He tried a different tack. "Yer mother would be very disappointed in yer, Lily, to know you were refusing to look after yer own father. It's what she'd want."

"Actually," she began, "the last time I was here, when Mum was dying, she was very clear I was not to give up my job and come back here."

His eyebrows shot up. "I don't believe yer. Yer mother loved me. She'd never say that."

"Oh, she loved you all right," she replied. "She told me that, but she also told me you would have to learn to look after yourself or get someone to do it for you."

"I'm not paying some woman to do what my own daughter should be willing to do," he protested.

"In that case, Mum also suggested you ask one of your sisters to come and be your housekeeper," she replied.

"Aye, I might just do that. I'll ask our Alice. She'd be 'appy to come and live here."

"Then that's settled," Lily said smoothly. "I don't want to fall out with you over this, Dad, but Mum thought it would be for the best, and so do I." The conversation was over.

At least there was money for the funeral. Lily found that her mother had taken out a penny policy when the Prudential insurance man came to collect the money. Fortunately, he was able to start the claim, and the undertakers were willing to wait, knowing that the money would come within the month. The day of the funeral dawned cool and dull. The air was damp, but it did not rain.

The right weather for a funeral, Lily thought as she put on the black hat Miss Eleanor had lent her.

Not having a special mourning dress, her black working dress would have to do. The night before the funeral, she had sat with her mother in the front room. Though, it was not until the undertaker arrived with the hearse that the finality of death began to sink in that she would not see her mother again. They did not have the money for the horse-drawn hearse, but their house was not far from the cemetery, and walking behind the hand-pulled hearse did not take long. Her mother, though not born and bred in Hope, had been well-liked in the town. There were many who stood with heads bowed as she made her final journey. Some made the sign of the cross, and the men removed their hats as they paid their respects.

The service took place in the Methodist chapel. Neither of her parents had been regular attendees, but they had sent the children to Sunday school. As the tall spire came into view, Lily wiped away a tear, trying desperately not to weep. She was afraid that once she started she would not be able to stop. It was with a grateful smile she accepted the snowy-white handkerchief her father held out. With surprise, she also accepted his arm as they walked behind the coffin. The hymns they had chosen were her mother's favourites, but she could not sing a note. During the eulogy, she tried to concentrate on what the minister was saying, but he didn't really know her mother. Did any of them?

Another short walk took them to the cemetery, which had

a few winter-flowering plants struggling to bring a dash of colour to the greyness surrounding them. In no time at all, she was throwing a handful of dirt into the grave along with a white rose. The flowers had been an extravagance, but she knew how much her mother loved flowers, roses most of all. She stepped back from the graveside. At least it was in the shade of a yew tree, for which she was illogically grateful. It would offer shade on hot days and shelter on cold days. Her mother had never liked being cold.

As they thanked their friends and neighbours for coming, Lily became aware of a well-dressed woman standing further back. When she reached her, the woman said, "I don't think you know who I am."

"I think you must be Mum's sister, my Aunt Polly," she replied.

The older woman nodded. "I haven't seen Clara since she left as a young woman. It was several years after she left that she made any contact, but it was only when she asked me to take the children that I actually knew where she was. I would have come sooner..." She left the sentence unfinished.

"How are the children?" Lily asked. "Do they know?"

The older woman smiled. "They're doing well. They're all at the local school, though the boys are quite a handful. They've settled in and have put on some weight. Those boys are forever hungry. And they do know. I told them yesterday. Of course, they are very sad, but I didn't think it would be a good idea to bring them today, not now that they've settled into a new life. I hope you don't think that's harsh."

"You have been kind enough to take them in, Aunt Polly. You must do what you think is best for them," Lily replied.

"I have waited a long time to hear you call me aunt, and you may rest assured those children will have the best life I can give them."

Lily reached forward and hugged her aunt. "Thank you. Just don't let them forget Mum, please."

Her aunt hugged her back. "I promise I'll always talk to them about her. We'll keep her alive in their hearts and memories."

"Will you come back to the house?" Lily asked.

The older woman looked at her watch. "I'm afraid not. I have a train to catch to Leeds to make my connection to Ludlow. I'm also not entirely sure your father would welcome me. My family was not kind to him. But," she added, pressing a piece of paper into Lily's hand, "here is my address. Please keep in touch with me. The children would love to hear from you, I know. Perhaps when you have some time, you might like to come and visit."

"I'd like that," Lily replied. "I'd also like to learn about what led my mother to leave the family. She referred to herself as the black sheep."

Aunt Polly laughed. "That she was. Grandmother referred to her as something of a hoyden. I don't agree with that, but she was certainly high-spirited. She stood up for herself, and Father didn't like it, but the story is too long to go into now. When you come for a visit, I'll tell you all I know."

By the time Lily got back to the house, her mother's friends were already serving tea and sandwiches. There was also whisky for the men and sherry for the women. The chatter was louder than she was expecting as there was much reminiscing about Clara. It was, she realised, a way for people to release tension after the emotion of the funeral, but she found it hard. She was not ready to hear laughter just yet.

fifteen

Within the hour, everyone, except for her father's two sisters who stayed behind to help clear up, had gone. They had used her mother's best china, so the three women were in the scullery washing up.

"Yer father tells me yer not wanting to stay home and look after 'im and the 'ouse," Alice, the elder sister, said as she rinsed the large brown teapot and set it on the wooden draining board.

"Mum wanted me to carry on working," Lily replied, hanging up the tea towel and turning to face her aunts. It was not a conversation she was looking forward to. "She suggested that perhaps one of you might like to move in and act as his housekeeper."

"A daughter should know her duty," Dorothy said. "Me and Alice 'ave looked after our Aunt Mary without complaint."

Lily nodded. They had indeed taken care of their elderly aunt, but did they do so without complaint?

"Yer only skivvying for someone else at the end of the day," Alice went on. "Yer might as well look after yer own flesh and blood."

"Yer should want to," Dorothy added.

"Mum wanted me to make something of myself," Lily replied. "I know you think it's only skivvying, but one day I shall be a housekeeper. It's a respected position in a big house." A thought occurred to her. "Did Dad ask you to try to persuade me?"

The two sisters exchanged a look. " 'E wants yer 'ome," Dorothy said. " 'E wants yer where 'e can keep an eye on yer."

Lily's eyebrows rose. "He wants me here so he can control me."

"Now, then," Alice replied more kindly this time, " 'e's not a bad man, lass. 'E doesn't know 'ow 'e's going to carry on now Clara's gone."

"No," Lily agreed. "I don't think he realised until she'd gone how much he would miss her."

"Nobody does," Dorothy stated, a distant look in her eyes. Lily knew there had been a fiancé a long time ago who had gone out to India and never returned. "Well, if you're sure, Alice and I will make sure Joey's all right."

"Yer mum was different to us," Alice put in. "She calmed our Joey down, and she was a good wife to 'im, but she was never really one of us. Was she?"

The two women removed their aprons and donned their winter coats and hats. As they left, Alice turned to Lily and said quietly, "Perhaps yer mum was right. Perhaps yer should aim 'igher than we've been used to. So if yer determined to keep working, make 'er proud. Don't worry about yer dad, we'll see 'im right."

"As for controlling yer," Dorothy added, "I doubt very much that any man's going to be able to do that. Yer too much like yer mother." Both sisters laughed and set off to catch the tram to Barnton.

Lily went upstairs. Her mother's clothes were already neatly folded and ready to be distributed among the poorer women in the neighbourhood. No one had much in the way of possessions, and no one would be too proud to accept second-hand clothes.

Lily sighed and shook her head. Some of the clothes had hardly been worn. Like many of the women, she had saved them "for best," but the occasions to use them had been few and far between. Still, they would not go to waste. Even petticoats would be cut down to make underwear and eventually be made into dusters.

The only thing left was a thick envelope along with a small muslin bag of lavender seeds in the drawer. Lily picked it up and put it in her bag. She would read it another day when she didn't feel quite so raw.

When she returned to work, she threw herself into whatever she could. She found that working took her mind off her grief. Linens were checked and rechecked, crockery was catalogued, and silverware polished. Cupboards were emptied and cleaned and Cook commented that the larder had never been so well-organised. Rugs were taken out and beaten within an inch of their lives. Lily and Aggie turned all the mattresses and washed paintwork and windows in all the bedrooms. Before she knew it, spring had turned into summer, and the leaves had turned into their autumn glory and were falling fast. Another birthday and Christmas had passed unnoticed and uncelebrated.

Lily had just started to take down the books in the library to dust them when she heard the door open. Since her experience at the new year, she had been reluctant to be there on her own, but she refused to let that man get the better of her. She turned and was both surprised and delighted to see Jonathon enter the room.

"There you are, Lily. Mrs. Cadeby said I might find you here. Now come down from that ladder so that I may have a look at you properly." As ever, his grin was infectious.

"It's lovely to see you, sir," she replied, descending slowly. She squeaked with surprise when a pair of strong hands grasped her around the waist and lifted her down the last three rungs, setting her gently on the ground.

Jonathon wore his uniform with his hat at a jaunty angle. His face bore a wide grin, but there was no mistaking the lines of tension around his eyes and mouth. More than anything, he looked exhausted.

"You're looking a bit tired, sir. Shall I get some tea?" she asked.

"Well, it was a devil of a journey, and I'm only in Blighty for a day, but I wanted to come home before going back," he admitted. "Tea would be lovely, though. You have no idea what they serve up as tea out there. Looks like mud and tastes like it too."

"I'll just run down and order some for you." Lily was out of the door before he could respond. When Cook knew who it was for, she quickly cut sandwiches and hot scones as well as a generous slice of cake and placed them on a tray. "He'll be hungry. Master Jonathon's always hungry," she said as she handed the tray to Lily.

When she returned, Jonathon was lying on the chesterfield, he had taken his cap and boots off and had his eyes closed. Lily hesitated, unsure of whether to leave him to rest or serve the tea. "The tea please, Lily," he said without opening his eyes, "and please come and sit beside me. I want to know all the news, though I know yours is not good. Please accept my condolences, Lily. You must miss your mother very much."

Lily poured the tea and handed him the cup. "Thank you, sir," she replied, unwilling to say more. "But what about you? Your news must be far more exciting."

He looked into the distance. "I don't know that exciting is quite the right word. War is a terrible business, Lily. Something I knew but did not understand until I saw it with my own eyes. They talk about the glory of war, of heroism, but let me tell you, there is no such thing as dying a hero's death. Death is death, and that is the end of it."

Lily said nothing, waiting for him to continue. She sensed he had more to say, more he *needed* to say.

"Eggy is dead," he said without emotion. "The victim of friendly fire, though it would not at all surprise me if his own men knew exactly what they were doing when they shot him. He was not a popular officer."

Lily's hand stilled as she poured more tea. "His parents will miss him" was all she could say. Words of condolence and sympathy would not come.

"They will," he agreed. "Eggy was their only son. Now that he's gone, the title will die out unless they can find some cousin or something to inherit. Rather ironic, really. His whole life was based on the title he was going to inherit one day."

"A title doesn't make a man," she replied.

"You're right. Eggy was a bully and a coward. He led from behind, exhorting his men to go over the top, and hung back until the last minute. If he hadn't died in battle, he'd have been killed sometime by a jealous husband. At least his parents have the story that he died with honour, however much it's a lie."

"Well, they can take comfort from that." She couldn't feel anything but contempt for the man, but she understood his parents needed the fable of the brave soldier's death to help them grieve.

"Your parents aren't here, sir. Mr. Grove is near Richmond overseeing the building of something for the army, and Mrs. Grove is staying overnight in Leeds with Miss Eleanor doing some kind of nursing training."

"So it's just you and me, is it, Lily?" He wiggled his eyebrows and grinned. He sat up, suddenly energised. "I've just had a marvellous idea, Lily. Let's go out tonight. We can have dinner and go dancing."

Lily laughed and shook her head. "I don't think so, sir. What would people think?"

"Damn what people think."

"That's easy for you to say. My job here depends on what people think," she replied.

He took both her hands in his and looked into her eyes. "Lily, I just want a normal evening where I can go out and have dinner with a beautiful, young woman and feel for the first time in months that life is normal. For one evening, I want to put the thought of war and death out of my mind. Surely you can't deny me that?"

Lily returned his look. What could she say to that? She had no idea what life was like for him. The newspapers were full of the talk of victory, but the long lists of casualties would suggest that the war was not going as successfully as the government would wish. There had also been some of the lads from Hope lost.

"All right." She nodded. "I'll go with you."

"Hardly the most enthusiastic response." He smiled and raised her hands to his lips. "However, I promise you won't regret it. I'll book a table at The Queen's."

"What about Mrs. Cadeby?" she began. "And I don't have the right kind of thing to wear to go to The Queen's," she squeaked, having walked past it many times and wondering what it would be like to go inside.

"Leave everything to me, Lily. I promise I won't let you down. Ever. Tonight is going to be special."

sixteen

How he had achieved it, Lily did not know. But later that evening, she sat opposite him at The Queen's for dinner. Electric chandeliers hung over tables set with snowy, white cloths, shining silverware, and glittering crystal glasses. Each table had a small vase with bud roses. Plush, red drapes hung at the large windows, and the same material covered the chairs. Her feet sunk into the red-and-gold carpet as she followed the manager to the table. Clearly, Jonathon was well-known here. The manager had not needed to ask his name.

She waited until the manager pulled out a chair for her and left before whispering, "I've always wondered what it looked like in here."

Lily wore a pale green taffeta with a lace overlay, capped sleeves, and a V-neckline. It was one of Miss Eleanor's cast-offs Lily had altered. It was her best dress, but she still felt a fraud, as though any moment someone was going to tap her on the shoulder and tell her to leave.

Jonathon looked around him, perhaps noticing his surroundings for the first time. "It is rather grand for a provincial railway hotel, I suppose. Father always says it reminds him of a Paris bordello."

"Well, I wouldn't know what a Yorkshire bordello looks like, let alone a French one." She laughed.

He reached across the table and took her hand. "That's what I like about you, Lily. I admire your sense of humour and never being afraid of saying what you think."

She looked down at their hands, his large one and her smaller, work-roughened one. If anything summed up the difference between them, there it was. She gave his hand a slight squeeze before removing her own, firmly ignoring the thrill that had shot through her as he'd touched her. He was a nice man who had taken her out for a nice dinner. That was all. She could not let herself believe anything else.

"So tell me how you managed to persuade Mrs. Cadeby to let me out for the evening?" she asked, putting the conversation on safer ground.

"I must confess to telling a little porky." He grinned. "I told Mrs. Cadeby that a friend of mine desperately needed a maid tonight as my chum was going to propose and her maid had joined up, so she couldn't manage on her own and needed to look her best."

"And Mrs. Cadeby believed that nonsense?" She was incredulous.

"I doubt it, but who cares? She let you out, and that's the main thing. Now let's enjoy ourselves."

"But what if she asks about it?"

"You'll think of something. Besides, there's less for you to do now, what with Mother, Father, and Eleanor out of the house most of the time. You'd just have spent the evening sitting in your room darning socks or knitting a scarf or something." As ever, his grin was contagious.

"That's beside the point, and I might point out that you were the recipient of the scarf I knitted," she said firmly. Lily could not help grinning back.

"And jolly welcome it was too, but let's not talk of reality. I'm out on the town with a pretty girl about to have a nice dinner. I don't want to think of anything to do with war. Tell me about life in Hope while I've been away. But first, let's order. I'm starving."

Lily let him order for her. Although she had served many fine dinners, she had never eaten them. The food served below stairs was plainer fare. She enjoyed the consomme and the fish and was amused by the sherbert. By the time they had eaten the roast beef, she complained that she'd never be able to eat again, but the thought of the chocolate pudding was a temptation she could not resist.

As they sipped their coffee, Jonathon said, "I was sorry about your mother, Lily. You must miss her very much."

Her eyes misted over. "I do. Mum was the glue that held our family together. Father is not a kind man. His life has been hard, and that has left its mark on his personality."

"What about your brothers and sisters?" he asked.

"They've gone to live with my Aunt Polly in Shropshire." She smiled. "It's funny. Until Mum died, I didn't even know I had an aunt."

Jonathon raised his eyebrows. "Your mother was from Shropshire? I had assumed she came from Hope."

Lily shook her head. "Mum never spoke about her life before she met Dad, but she didn't speak like others in Hope. She was always well-respected in Hope, but I don't think she had many friends because she didn't grow up there."

"Then how did she end up in Hope?" he asked, taking a sip of brandy.

"I don't know. I think her family has money, from what Aunt Polly said. She also told me Mum was considered to be the black sheep." She paused. "Mum left me a letter and some papers, but I haven't had the heart to read them yet."

"You will one day," he assured her. "Your mother clearly wants you to know her story," he added. "Now, I think we have been serious for long enough. I can hear the band from here. I think it's time to find the dance floor."

"Ah," Jonathon murmured in her ear as he took her in his arms. "This is the foxtrot, my favourite new dance. Do you know why?"

"No," she replied.

"It's because I get to hold you in my arms the whole time. Heaven. You really are beautiful. I am the envy of every man in this room," he breathed into her ear, causing shivers to dance down her spine.

"You really shouldn't say such things," she whispered.

"Why not if it's what I feel? I mean it, Lily. I have thought of you all the time I've been away. I've read and reread your letters. It's the thought of coming back to you that keeps me going."

As the music changed to a waltz, he pulled her closer.

"You have no idea what you do to me, Lily. I want you. I can't bear the thought of dying without making love to you. Tell me you feel something for me."

"I do, Jonathon. I know I shouldn't, but I do, even though I know nothing can ever come of it," she admitted. "You're so far above my station," she added sadly.

"The war is changing things, Lily. There's no reason why we can't be together. At least tonight," he said softly. "I have to go back to base, and in a day or so, I'll be flying. God knows when, or if, I'll get back. But tonight... Tonight is for us."

Her step paused for a second. "I'm not sure I can do what you're asking, Jonathon. Where I come from, girls are judged harshly, if you know what I mean."

"I will happily put a ring on your finger, if that's what you want. When this is all over, we'll be married, Lily. Not because I have to, but because I want to."

As she looked into his eyes, Lily could see he was in earnest, but there was a naivety as well. "I'm not sure that counts as much of a proposal," she teased, trying to lighten the mood.

"I am more than willing to go down on bended knee if only you will promise to say yes."

"Oh, Jonathon, I would be the happiest woman alive to be your wife, but I doubt your parents would ever permit it." Someone had to be realistic.

"Then they can go to the devil," he replied stoutly. "But once they get used to the idea, they'll accept you."

"And what if they don't? What if you are disinherited like my mother was? Cut off from the family, never to see them again? I don't know that I could live with myself if I was the cause of that," she replied.

He smiled down at her. "I'm their only son. There's no spare. They'll welcome any bride I choose."

"If you marry a rich woman, preferably with a title," she replied. "I doubt if even in their darkest nightmares they imagine their son marrying their maid."

The final waltz ended. Lily collected her coat as Jonathon hailed a taxi. It had been a magical evening, one she would remember for the rest of her life. Jonathon was sincere in his proposal, but he could only see the bright side. Perhaps he needed an escape from the horrors of war.

In the taxi, he held her hand. The taxi ran over a bump in the road, pitching her into his arms. Then he kissed her. Softly at first, until she sighed, and then he deepened the kiss. His tongue ran over her lips and plunged into her mouth as she opened for him. For all her common sense, Lily knew she was lost.

seventeen

The house was dark and silent when they returned.

"Would you like a drink?" Jonathon asked.

"No, I think I'll just go to bed," Lily replied, but she didn't move.

He held out his hand. "Then come with me."

She paused before putting her hand in his, knowing that nothing would be the same from that point on.

"I promise you, Lily, that I won't do anything you don't want," he said softly. At the door to his bedroom, he stopped. "If you want me to stop at any time, just say the word. I mean it."

"I know," she replied.

His room was familiar. She had dusted, swept, and made the bed many times, but it felt strange to be inside it without some chore to do. As she looked at the large bed, she shivered, partly in unease and partly in anticipation. For all his fine words about marriage, she had no real expectations. She knew she felt something for Jonathon and he felt something for her, but whatever happened between them tonight, she told herself she would expect no more.

"Are you cold?" he asked, helping her out of her coat and tossing it onto the chair.

"No, it's just a little..."

"Overwhelming?" he suggested.

"Unexpected," she replied.

"Why don't we sit down and talk awhile?" he suggested.

"All right," she agreed. There was no other place to sit than on the bed.

As he sat, Jonathon gently took her hand and stroked her fingers. "I want you to know that, although this might seem sudden to you, Lily, I have had feelings for you almost since the first time I met you. Feelings, which to be honest, I fought for a time. But this war, it changes everything. I don't know where I'll be when I leave here, but the Royal Flying Corps is flying more and more sorties. Mother thinks all I'm doing is flying over and taking photographs, but the reality is that guns are now attached to planes. I have to be honest with you. I'm no longer an observer."

"Are you supposed to be telling me this?" she asked.

"I want to be honest with you. I'm saying the chances are high that I might not come back from this alive, but I will take care of you. I promise. I just don't want to die without..." His words trailed off.

"Without?" she prompted.

He took a breath. "Without making love to you, Lily. Without making love to anyone," he finished quietly. "I've never..."

"Neither have I," Lily replied. "Why don't we learn together?" She looked down at their hands. Even just the touch of his fingers on hers was causing a riot of sensations in her body.

"Oh, Lily, are you sure?" he murmured.

She nodded as one hand cupped the back of her head and drew her towards him. Her lips opened, and he deepened the kiss as they sank onto the bed. His hands roamed over her arms and back as hers went around his neck.

"I want to touch your breasts now, Lily. May I?" he whispered.

"Please," she replied, realising she wanted him to touch her. Even through the material of her dress, he could feel her nipples bud as his fingers sought them.

"Please tell me when you want me to stop," he said.

"Don't." She gasped as he increased the tension.

"Don't what?" he asked.

"Don't stop," she replied with a smile.

"I want to see you."

"I think the next part is accomplished without clothes," she replied, her fingers reaching for the buttons on his shirt.

He remained still while she removed it. His time in the military had changed his body from that of a youth to a man. His shoulders were broader than she had remembered. His chest was scattered with a dusting of dark hair that narrowed down the flat plane of his stomach, eventually disappearing. She could not resist running her fingers over his flat, male nipples. At his sharp hiss, she drew back her hand.

"Sorry," she murmured.

"Don't stop," he replied. "For God's sake, don't stop."

Lily began a leisurely tour of his body, gently stroking his muscles and noticing, with some satisfaction, the result of her teasing.

He caught her hands in his. "My turn," he breathed. "Turn around."

When she did, his fingers went to the row of tiny buttons down the back of her dress. As he released each one and revealed her creamy flesh, he planted a soft kiss. "Why are women's clothes so damned complicated?" He finished the last button.

"It's an old one of your sister's," she explained. "That's why ladies need maids."

"Then I'll be your maid." He chuckled.

Within moments, her dress was in a pool on the floor. It

was quickly followed by her silk underwear, another gift from Miss Eleanor.

"You are so beautiful, Lily." His breath caught as he greedily took in every inch of her gloriously naked body.

"This hardly seems fair," she protested. "Here I am, and yet you're still clothed."

His hand went to the buttons on his trousers, but he stilled. "Are you sure, Lily? Once these are gone, there will be little chance of going back."

"I'm sure."

His trousers and underwear joined the pile of clothing on the floor as he had enjoyed looking at her. Lily felt her mouth go dry as she took in his narrow hips and the sight of his erection standing proud. She had brothers, so she was no stranger to the male body, but she had never seen one in an aroused state before.

"You're like one of those statues at the museum," she said.

"I hope not." He laughed. "I always thought those chaps were less than well-endowed."

She giggled, and the tension was broken. The only sounds in the room were the ticking of the clock and the gasps and moans of pleasure as they explored each other.

Finally, Jonathon said, "If you want me to stop, tell me now, Lily."

"I don't want you to stop. I want all of you. I don't want you to hold back." She raised her glazed eyes to his.

"There might be some pain, but I'll try not to hurt you. I would never knowingly hurt you."

"I know."

She winced as he pushed into her, but within seconds, she began to move with him until the sensations roared through every cell in her body.

"Jonathon," she cried as wave after wave hit her.

A second or two later, he found his own release. When he

rolled onto his back, he tucked her to his side, her head against his chest.

"That was wonderful," he said. "I had no idea."

She turned her head to look up at him and smiled. "I imagine it's why people are keen to do it."

"But only with you, Lily. Only with you," he replied, kissing the top of her head. "Did I hurt you?"

She shook her head. "A little, but it was soon gone," she replied. "Though I think I had better make sure it's me who changes this bed."

"Let's not think about that now," he said, reaching for her again.

They made love twice more during the night. One time, Jonathon took it so slowly that Lily was almost crying for release. The last time, he thrust into her again and again with a kind of desperation. It was almost as though he wanted to imprint his body onto hers so that neither he nor she would forget.

As she awoke languidly and stretched, she realised the bed was empty. The side where he had laid was cold. He had been gone some time. She glanced towards the tallboy to find a note leaning against the clock.

Whatever happens, I won't forget last night. Thanks, Jonathon.

eighteen

Jonathon had not, she concluded, ever had any intention of marrying her. The note was proof of that. He had used her innocence and naivety. Like a fool, she had fallen for it—hook, line, and sinker. It was a wonder he hadn't left her money as a tip for services rendered. She was angry with him, but she was furious with herself for being so stupid as to think he was different. At least with the late, unlamented Eggy, he wore his contempt for the lower class openly. Jonathon had seemed different, but it was all smoke and mirrors.

As she always did, Lily threw herself into her work. There was more now that Aggie had gone to join the Women's Auxiliary Army Corps.

"Better pay and better hours," she had said, "and I rather fancy myself in that uniform." She had laughed as she kissed Lily goodbye. "Yer take care of yerself, Lily. Don't let them put on yer."

For all she had the bedroom to herself and appreciated the additional space, she missed Aggie's acerbic wit and ready laughter. In addition to her housekeeping duties, she was often given bandages to roll and boxes to pack for the men on the front. Mrs. Grove had read about comfort boxes being sent out to the troops and had begun to organise some to go to the men who had left Hope to fight. So Lily packed socks, sweets, chocolate, cigarettes, writing paper, and pencils, among other things in the afternoons. She didn't mind the extra work. It filled the time and took her mind away from thoughts of Jonathon.

Christmas came and went with little celebration. With the death and destruction going on, it didn't seem right to celebrate lavishly. Each day, the women looked for the arrival of the postman with feelings of both anticipation and dread. Eleanor looked for a letter from her fiancé. Both Mrs. Grove and Lily looked for something from Jonathon, though it was some weeks since he had written.

There was, however, a letter for Lily from Shropshire. As she had promised, her Aunt Polly had written several times since her mother's death. The children had settled splendidly in school, Nora was quite the promising academic, Betty was learning the piano, and Vera had won a prize for art. The boys were enjoying sport and had begun to settle, and the youngest, Emily, was doing well. They had celebrated Tommy's sixteenth birthday with cake and a visit to the music hall in Shrewsbury.

As she opened this letter, for some reason, Lily had a sense of foreboding. Her aunt wrote,

I am sorry to have to tell you that Tommy and John have gone. The army came through town on a recruitment drive, and they were very taken. They have been collecting every scrap of information about the war since it began. Their bedroom is full of items they have cut out of the newspaper. As you know, they are fine, strapping boys and have grown a lot since living here. The upshot is that, unknown to us, they took the omnibus into Shrewsbury and went to the recruitment office. They lied about their age and signed up. The girls and I are beside ourselves, but there is nothing we can do, apparently. We didn't have birth certificates for them to prove they were underage, and the recruiting sergeant was not going to give up his two shillings and sixpence for each boy. I can only hope that they write to let us know they are well. I am so sorry, Lily. I feel I have let you down.

I have written to tell your father.

Yours with love,

Aunt Polly.

On the next Sunday afternoon, Lily walked into Hope, thinking Tommy had written to Dad to let him know where he was. As she arrived, Alice was just laying the table for tea.

"This is a turn up," she said, looking up. "Yer dad thought you'd forgotten where 'e lived."

Alice and Dorothy had clearly made an impression. The living room had been given a fresh coat of paint, and a new colourful rag rug was laid in front of the fire. The table was scrubbed, and copper and brass ornaments Lily had never seen before gleamed in the firelight.

"Yer dad's just popped down to get a jug of cream from Low Laithes farm," Alice said, lifting down the well-used breadboard and beginning to cut slices of bread. " 'E'll be pleased to see yer," she added. "Take off yer coat. You'll be stayin' fer tea."

Lily removed her coat and hung it on the hook on the back of the door. "How's he been?" she asked.

Alice paused, bread knife midair. "Fair. Misses yer mam more than 'e thought and definitely more than 'e admits to. We've kept 'im busy to try and stop 'im gettin' morbid." She waved the knife, indicating the improvements. "It's just a pity 'e never did this fer yer mam," she added.

"He hasn't started drinking again, has he?" Lily asked.

Alice shook her head. "Funnily enough, no. We thought 'e might, but 'e's adamant 'e's not goin' to take a drop. 'E's even started goin' to t' Methodists, and they don't 'old wi' drinkin' at all."

Lily raised her eyebrows. That was a surprise. "Does he know about Tommy and John?" she asked.

" 'E does, an' 'e's not best pleased."

"With Aunt Polly?"

"With the lads. Yer dad don't 'old with this war. Says it's a waste of men and money," Alice replied.

"And it is." None of them had heard Joey come into the room. He put the cream jug on the table and removed his coat and cap and sat down to remove his boots. "Now then, our Lily, 'ow are yer?"

"I'm fine, Dad. Just worried about our Tommy and John," she replied.

He frowned. "Silly buggers. Cannon fodder, that's all they are. They should've known better."

"I think they all seem to see it as an adventure," she replied, thinking about Jonathon and his friends.

"Adventure? War's not adventure. It's a bloody waste of life and money. We shan't be seein' either of 'em again. You mark my words. They'll be put in t' front line like all the other silly young buggers who signed up thinking there's some glory in it. Well, there isn't, and there never was."

"I had no idea you felt like that, Dad." Lily was surprised by the passion in his voice.

"We," he indicated his sisters, " 'ad two brothers. Twins, they were. Tom an' Arthur. They joined up rather than go down t' pit. They ended up in Africa, and neither of them came back. Tom died from wounds, and Arthur caught a fever. That's why I have no great love for the army."

"I didn't know," Lily replied.

"No reason why you should," Dorothy chimed in. "They were dead an' gone almost before we knew them."

"Aunt Mary couldn't bear to 'ear their names, so we just stopped talking about them," Alice said, continuing the story. "What grieved 'er most was not 'avin' a grave to visit."

"We don't even know if they 'ad a proper burial," her father went on. "Or if there's a grave to visit, even if we could've afforded to go, which we never could."

"Has our Tommy written to tell you where he is?" she asked.

"Not yet," her father replied. "I expect 'e will when 'e can. At the very least, they'll let us know when anything 'appens to 'im. They all 'ave to write a letter 'ome before they go into action, so I 'eard."

"Well, enough of that talk now," Alice said briskly. "Tea's ready."

There was boiled ham, potted-meat sandwiches, jam and lemon-curd tarts, and an apple pie, for which Joey had been sent for the cream. Lily barely ate a thing. Her stomach churned as she thought not only of Tommy fighting in the war but also of Jonathon. No matter that Jonathon had broken her heart. She couldn't stop thinking about him facing danger.

"Are yer all right, our Lily?" Dorothy asked, refilling her teacup with the strong brown liquid. "Yer lookin' a little peaky, truth be told."

Lily smiled back. "I'm fine," she replied. "Just had a stomach upset a couple of days ago. Something I ate, I expect. Nothing that a good cup of tea won't cure."

"Yer want to make sure yer don't overdo it," her father added. "I know what them rich folks is like. Want their pound of flesh out o' the working class, they do."

"You got me the job, Dad." Lily laughed. "Besides, I like working there. Mrs. Cadeby is a good boss. And now that Mrs. Grove's doing war work, I barely see her, and Mr. Grove was never there much anyway."

"They don't do nothin' but that it benefits them," he said.

"You'll be joining the Labour Party next," she replied with a smile.

"I just might," he said. "But mark my words. Never think they'll be your friend, Lily. They'll chew you up and spit you out when it suits. That's all I'm sayin'."

nineteen

Lily had begun to enjoy spending some of her evenings with Mrs. Cadeby in her sitting room. The two women had always gotten on well. They were enjoying a cup of tea together as they sat knitting socks and scarves for the troops.

"You've been looking a little pale, Lily," the older woman said as she poured more tea. "You're not sickening for something, I hope."

"Of course not," Lily replied firmly. "My stomach is just a little tender," she continued. "At first I thought it was something I ate, but it just won't go away. Every morning it's the same."

Mrs. Cadeby put down the teapot. "Oh, Lily," she said.

Lily looked up. "What?"

Mrs. Cadeby shook her head and, for once, allowed a Yorkshire idiom. "You should know the signs by now, lass. Your mother was there often enough."

Lily's face went pale as she took in the significance of Mrs. Cadeby's words. "Oh my God. How could I have been so stupid?" Her fingers trembled as she carefully placed the cup and saucer on the table. "It was one night," she added, her face stricken.

"It only takes the once sometimes," Mrs. Cadeby replied. "I take it that it was with Master Jonathon?"

Lily nodded. "Just the one night with the one man," she replied.

"I'm not judging you, Lily," Mrs. Cadeby said, her voice kind. "The question is, what are you going to do about it?"

Lily shook her head. "I really don't know."

Mrs. Cadeby took a deep breath. "Of course, you're going to have to tell Mrs. Grove."

"I can't imagine she'll be thrilled at the thought of me and Jonathon." Lily sighed.

"No, she won't," the older woman agreed. "But you're going to have to tell her before it becomes too obvious."

Lily looked up. "Jonathon said he wants to marry me."

Mrs. Cadeby patted her arm. "Lily, men say all sorts of things when they want to get you between the sheets. Did you really believe him?"

"I did at the time," Lily replied. "He was so charming and sincere."

"Oh, he can be charming. Of course, he can. Especially when he wants something. He learned that as a small boy. That's how he has his mother wrapped around his little finger."

Lily's shoulders slumped. "I suppose you think I'm a fool."

Mrs. Cadeby smiled. "Of course not. Naive, perhaps, but you haven't been brought up to deal with the likes of Master Jonathon." She paused. "Perhaps I should have warned you."

Lily smiled. "Do you think I would have listened? My dad would tell you how stubborn I can be."

"Will your dad take you in?" Mrs. Cadeby asked.

Lily thought for a moment. "I don't think so, and I don't think I want to listen to his endless socialist lectures on how I should have known better than to trust a toff, let alone the moral diatribes now that he's gone religious. Besides, I didn't go and take care of him when Mum died, so why should he take care of me now?"

"He is your father."

"He would be my jailer."

"Then we must think of something else. But first, you must speak with Mrs. Grove."

As it happened, both Mr. and Mrs. Grove were in the library when Lily asked to speak with them. Mr. Grove sat at his desk reading papers, and Mrs. Grove was seated on the leather chesterfield reading the newspaper when Lily entered the room.

Mrs. Grove looked up. "You wished to see me?" Her tone, as ever, was discouraging.

"Yes, ma'am," Lily replied.

"Then get on with it, girl. I haven't got all day." The newspaper rustled.

"It's rather a delicate matter, ma'am," Lily replied, casting a glance at Mr. Grove, who didn't seem to notice she was there.

"Delicate or not, spit it out."

"The fact is... The fact is," Lily began. "I have to tell you that I find myself in a difficult position."

Mrs. Grove's eyes narrowed. She put the newspaper down next to her. "What sort of difficult position?" she asked.

"I'm going to have a baby." The words tumbled out before Lily could stop them.

"I see." The tone of her voice and the look in her eyes were like shards of ice. "What has this to do with us?"

"I thought you should know," Lily replied.

There was a pause before Mrs. Grove replied, "Is the father prepared to do the right thing?"

"He said he was," Lily replied, adding, "but he doesn't know about the baby yet."

"What if he does not do the right thing? What if he denies the child is his?" Mrs. Grove asked.

"I was hoping you would help," Lily replied.

Mrs. Grove's eyebrows raised. "I? Why should I help? Your predicament has nothing to do with Mr. Grove or myself. You are entirely to blame for the condition you find yourself in. If you are prepared to sleep with any Tom, Dick, or Harry, what do you expect?"

"I slept with one man," Lily shot back. "Your son."

The silence was broken by the ticking of the clock on the marble mantelpiece.

"What did you say?" Mrs. Grove asked.

Mr. Grove's pen stilled over the document he was writing.

"The baby I'm carrying is Jonathon's," Lily replied.

Mrs. Grove stood up and walked quickly to where Lily stood. "How dare you say that you wicked, wicked girl!"

"It's true," Lily shot back. "It happened when you were both away and Jonathon came back for one night before going back to war. He told me he loved me and that he would marry me."

"I don't believe for a moment that Jonathon would sleep with you, a servant, let alone talk of love and marriage. He will marry one of his own kind, a lady with breeding and money. Do not forget I am the granddaughter of an earl." Mrs. Grove was incandescent with rage.

"Is it money you're after?" Mr. Grove questioned, putting his pen down and staring at Lily. "Because it wouldn't be the first time a Russell had demanded money from me."

Lily turned to look at him, knowing she was alone. Neither Jonathon nor his family would want anything to do with her or the child. What they wanted to do was wipe them from their memory.

"I had hoped you might be interested in your grandchild," she replied. "But that is clearly not to be, so I want nothing from you."

"We don't even know that Jonathon is the father of this

baby. He wouldn't be the first man to be burdened with bringing up another man's child," Mr. Grove commented.

"If you believe that, then there is nothing I can say or do that will change your minds," Lily replied as she turned to go.

"One moment, young woman," Mrs. Grove's voice stopped her. "Clearly, your employment here is at an end."

"I know." Lily didn't bother to turn around.

"I shall give you a week to get your things and leave this house. If I ever hear tell that you have spread this vile rumour about my son being the father of your child, I shall see to it that you are never employed again. Do I make myself clear?"

Mr. Grove cleared his throat. "I shall pay you one month's wages in lieu of notice, which is, I think, more than reasonable given the circumstances."

"One more thing," Mrs. Grove added. "You are not to attempt to contact Jonathon. He is never to know this conversation has taken place or that you have tried to pass off your bastard as his child in the most shameful manner."

Lily turned to address them one last time before leaving. "I understand perfectly," she said. "But one day, the truth will come out, and I hope it's not too late, for Jonathon or his child."

twenty

The visit with her father did not go well.

"I warned yer about them," he replied when she told him of her situation. "I told yer to be careful."

"You were the one who sent me there, Dad," she replied. "You were only too happy so long as the money was coming in."

"Well, yer won't be stayin' 'ere. Yer made yer bed an' now yer'll 'ave to lie on it," he replied. "Yer didn't want to come back after yer mum died, and there's no room for yer and the bairn now that Alice lives 'ere. Apart from that, Alice won't 'old with yer 'avin' a baby with no weddin' ring in sight."

"You are such a hypocrite," she shot back. "Did you think I didn't know that the reason Mum was thrown out of her family was that she was pregnant with me?"

"At least I 'ad the conscience to marry yer mum," he replied. "Where's the fella that's fathered your child, eh? You think 'e'll marry yer? Course 'e won't. Because 'im and 'is kind think they're better than the likes of us. Yer'll be lucky if yer ever 'ear of 'im again."

He strode over to the mantelpiece and took down the Queen Victoria tea caddy.

"'Ere," he said, holding out a five-pound note. " 'Ave this. It's not much to yer fancy fella, but it's what I was savin'. It should see yer through until yer get settled."

Lily looked at the crumpled note in his outstretched hand, wanting to refuse it. But knowing she would need all she could find, she took it.

"Thanks. If you want to get in touch with me, Mrs. Cadeby will know where I am."

Taking one last look around her childhood home, she left. When she returned to Grove House, Mrs. Cadeby was waiting for her with tea.

"I take it your father was unhelpful?"

"He wants nothing to do with me or his grandchild," Lily replied, sinking into the chair, exhausted after her seeing her father. "He was never much of a father, so I shouldn't be surprised. He's become religious and respectable, so a pregnant, unmarried daughter doesn't fit with his new life."

"Well, you had to try and give the man a chance," Mrs. Cadeby replied, pouring a cup of tea and handing it to Lily. "You're not the first girl to get into this situation, and you won't be the last."

There were a few moments of silence as the two women sipped their tea.

"I do have a suggestion," Mrs. Cadeby said, breaking the silence. "I have an aunt up in the North Riding, not far from Hawes. She's getting on a bit now and would appreciate a bit of help. You could stay with her and help with the housework, shopping, and such."

"What about when the baby comes?"

"Annis has helped women to birth babies in the area for years. She's no stranger to childbirth," Mrs. Cadeby replied.

"But what about this baby with no father?" Lily asked.

"Annis can be a bit of a tartar, make no mistake, but she won't judge you for that. It takes two to make a baby, but it's always the girl who takes both the responsibility and the blame."

"Well, if you think your aunt will take me, I don't seem to have much of a choice," Lily replied.

"That's settled, then. I'll write to her this afternoon."

As she was packing her small suitcase, Lily was surprised to see Eleanor standing in the doorway to her room.

"May I come in?" the young woman asked. "I don't think I've ever been up here before," she commented, looking around at the bare, whitewashed walls, tallboy, and wardrobe, which had seen better days.

"I don't imagine there's any reason you should," Lily replied, folding a blouse and placing it neatly on the top of the case. "How did you find out?" she asked. "Your parents made it very clear no one was to know."

"My parents rarely talk to each other, but on this topic, they have been unable to stop. I overheard them at breakfast. I've brought you these." Eleanor held out her hands. There were some stockings and a jumper. "Mrs. Cadeby said you were going up north. I thought you might need the extra layers," she explained.

"Thank you," Lily replied.

"For what it's worth, I think my parents are treating you extremely shabbily." She sat down on the bed. "If only Jonathon knew."

"Well, he doesn't, and Mrs. Grove has made it very clear that I am not to contact him at all, not that it would have made any difference. I haven't had a letter from him since he went back."

Eleanor's eyes widened. "My God, you don't know, do you? Nobody's told you, have they?"

"What?" Lily could feel fingers of dread grasping her throat.

"The telegram must have come when you visited your family, or I assure you, you would have heard mother's screams. That's why she's been confined to bed for the last few days. Jonathon is missing."

"Missing?"

"Missing, as in, his aeroplane came down behind enemy lines and nothing has been heard of or from him since," Eleanor confirmed.

"But does that mean..." Lily couldn't bring herself to finish the sentence.

"It just means he's missing," Eleanor said firmly. "That is all the telegram said. It did not say 'Missing, believed killed,' which is what Bertie Wright-Mellor's parents received, and I hope to God that Barty is keeping himself out of trouble."

Lily sat down before her legs gave way. "I had no idea," she whispered. "Here I have been going on about Jonathon not bothering to write, and all the time..."

Eleanor patted her arm. "Try not to worry, sweetie. Knowing Jonathon, he's probably got his feet up somewhere in a bierkeller, enjoying large quantities of fine German beer. He's like a cat, that one. Always lands on his feet. Now," she said as she rose, "I must go. I promised to visit Barty's parents."

"Please, Miss Eleanor, would you let me know if there's further news about Jonathon? I should like to know, one way or the other, so that I can tell his child one day," Lily said, her hands protectively on her stomach.

"Of course." Eleanor smiled. At the door, she paused. "Good luck, Lily. If there's anything I can do to help you, write and let me know. I'll do what I can."

"Thank you, miss. I appreciate that, but me and this baby will be fine," Lily replied with a lot more conviction than she felt.

The journey would take all day. The station in Hope was only two tracks, one towards Sheffield and the other towards Leeds. Lily was grateful for the roaring fire in the waiting room. Her ticket to Leeds was in her hand as she waited for the train. It was one of those "damp, dark days before Christmas," as her mother would have said, regardless of the time of year. The clouds were low, and fog hung around the lamps, giving them a mysterious glow in the early morning half-light.

It was the first train of the day, and among her fellow travellers were shopworkers in nearby Barnwell, women who worked in the nearby clothing factories, and men in their working clothes going to their shifts at the foundries and glassworks. There were also a few young lads in uniform, laughing and pushing at each other in camaraderie with a bravado she thought they probably didn't feel.

The whistle announced the arrival of the train. The waiting room quickly emptied as people stood at the edge of the platform waiting to board and get a seat. The train was halfway along its journey from Sheffield to Leeds, and sometimes seats were scarce. On this occasion, though, Lily was lucky and managed to find a seat near the window.

The station was at the end of Hope, so the rows of terraced houses were quickly left behind. The fog hung to the trees as the train passed the edge of the wood where she had picked the bluebells on her last day of school, which seemed like half a lifetime ago. There were some bedraggled-looking allotments with little growing at this time of year. Soon, there were open fields with sheep and cows dotted about. As the train chugged into Barnwell, they passed the brewery, glass, and chemical works the town was known for.

At the station, the workers got off ready to go about their daily business, probably following a routine they did every day. That was something Lily was putting behind her. This journey would be the beginning of a new life for her. Who knew what it would hold? As the train drew away from the station, Lily noticed the manual workers had been replaced by others.

People who worked in the textiles factories and offices of Leeds, she thought.

It was funny that although it was only twenty miles or so, it might as well have been two hundred. Yet here she was, travelling further to a place she had never even heard of before Mrs. Cadeby had suggested it.

twenty-one

Lily sat on the wooden bench, waiting for the Carlisle train, grateful for the packet of sandwiches Mrs. Cadeby had insisted she take when she left. She had bought a cup of tea from a boy as he passed with his trolley and enjoyed the warmth as she sipped it. Leeds New Station was the biggest building she had ever seen. The glass-and-metal arches reminded her of the pictures she had seen of Westminster Abbey in the Encyclopedia Britannica in the library at Grove House.

What she hadn't been prepared for was the constant noise of engines hissing as they stood ready to depart and the shouting of guards, drivers, and porters as they readied the train and passengers for departure. The constant banging of doors as passengers boarded and disembarked the trains also contributed to the noise.

On the opposite platform were what looked like hundreds of young soldiers ready to depart, looking smart in their new uniforms. Some wore their caps at a rakish angle. There was a lot of laughter and joking.

Probably, Lily thought, *to cover up the fear and apprehension they were feeling*.

The war had been going on for over two years now, and they no doubt knew of other young men who had gone before them who would not be coming back. In Hope, she knew of at least four families whose sons were dead. Two of them were brothers. She sent a silent prayer that her own brother, Tommy, was safe.

There was a lot of shouting as the men began to board the train. In a surprisingly short time, the platform was empty, the whistle sounded, and the train slowly drew out of the station. At every window, faces peered out. For some, it would be the last time they would see their home.

Almost immediately, another train steamed slowly into the station, and Lily noticed the red crosses painted onto the side. The timing was impeccable. It would not have boded well for the new recruits to see what awaited them across the channel. Once the doors were opened, its sad cargo began to be unloaded, some walking slowly unaided while more walked with the aid of others. Many were laid out on the platform on stretchers waiting patiently for people to come and take them on to the next stage of their journey. Some were moaning softly. For the most part, they bore their pain with silent fortitude. Her thoughts turned to Jonathon. She sent a silent prayer on his behalf, praying he wasn't among their number on a hospital train or ship or lying injured behind enemy lines. She could not bear to think of the alternative.

As she boarded her train and found a seat, her thoughts turned to the new life she was having to forge. She must put her old life behind her and think of the child. Whatever happened, she would give her child the best life she could. It may never know its father, or even its grandparents, but she would make up for all of them. She watched as the small, terraced houses gave way to larger ones with gardens. Eventually, the houses became fewer and fewer, giving way to green fields with sheep dotted about. As they rattled over viaducts, she could see for miles where fields were now surrounded by small, drystone walls as they wound their way across moors and dales. How different this part of Yorkshire was to Hope.

The train slowed to a stop, and the guard announced their arrival at Garsdale, where, once again, she would wait for the local train to take her to Hawes. Lily welcomed the chance to stretch her legs, but the sun was setting, and the temperature had dropped quickly. She was grateful for the warmth of the fire in the small waiting room.

The train arrived promptly for the six-mile journey, wending its way through small areas of woodland and sometimes running alongside a small stream. They passed areas where sheep ignored the train and continued to graze on the rich grass. At Hawes station, she was the only passenger to get off. The station was deserted, and it was getting both cold and dark. She could not help but feel some unease as she watched the lights of the train recede into the distance. Lily took the piece of paper on which Mrs. Cadeby had written a name and address out of her pocket, but it was of little use when she didn't have a clue in which direction to start walking. It was a relief when she heard the clopping of a horse and saw the lantern on a small cart.

"Are yer t' lass who's to be staying wi' Annis Clayton?" he asked.

"Yes," she replied, though in all honesty there was no one else in sight.

"Jump up, then," he said, indicating the seat next to him. "Chuck yer luggage in t' back an' we'll be off."

"Thank you, Mr....?"

"Dinsdale. Jack Dinsdale," he replied. "Yer'll 'ear that name a lot round 'ere." He clicked his tongue, and the horse set off out of the station yard and over the bridge the train had passed under. Shortly after, they went over another bridge, which was clearly over a river as Lily could hear the rushing water. Then the road rose sharply.

"I 'ope yer used to a few 'ills," her driver commented as he steered the cart round a bend to the right. "It's all 'ills and dales 'ere, and Annis lives at t' op of one of steepest."

"We had a few hills in the West Riding as well," she replied.

He grunted a response as the road rose again. She could see the town of Hawes, where they had come from, down in the valley below. Its lights were a welcome sight against the darkness enveloping them. He pulled on the reins, and the horse slowed as they took a tight turn to the left.

"Yer might want to 'old on a bit," he commented as the cart tilted back up the steepest hill Lily had seen.

"You were right about the hills," she replied, holding onto the side of the cart.

The horse slowed a little but carried on steadily. The road wound round, and Lily made out a farmhouse with a couple of barns and a terrace of cottages on either side of the road with lights shining from the windows. There was a second row behind the first row. Beyond the lights of the small community, there was complete darkness. The silence was broken only by the occasional bleating of a sheep. The cart stopped, and Jack jumped down.

"The lane's too narrow for t' cart. It's only a short step from 'ere," he said, picking up her suitcase and bag. "Follow me." He strode down a narrow path and through a gate. He rapped on the door and opened it. "Annis, yer lass is 'ere," he shouted, putting her luggage inside the doorway.

"Well, don't just stand there letting the cold in," replied a voice from within. "The kettle's about to boil."

"I can't stop. I've a ram to deliver to Askrigg, and our lass'll 'ave me guts for garters if I'm late for supper again. I'll pop round tomorrow an' 'ave a look at the water pump. In yer go, lass," he said as he turned to Lily. " 'Er barks worse than 'er bite," he added softly.

A blast of warmth hit her as Lily stepped into the room. There was no hallway. The front door opened straight into the living room. A cheerful fire burned in the grate, giving both light and warmth. The walls were white with a variety of pictures hanging and red curtains framing the window. A faded sofa stood along one wall, and a worn armchair stood near the fireplace. Oil lamps cast a gentle glow over small tables and shelves. Both of the alcoves beside the chimney contained full bookcases, but there were few other ornaments, something Lily's experience as a maid had taught her to look for.

Less to dust, she thought.

At the other side of the room, there was a door she assumed led to the kitchen. As she stood, wondering what to do, a woman appeared in the doorway, wiping her hands on her apron.

"Come through to the kitchen. I've a fresh pot of tea, fresh-baked bread, and a stew ready. You must be hungry. It's a fair step from Hope." She indicated the hook by the door. "Hang your coat and hat on there and come through."

Lily did as she was told. She would have known Annis Clayton was Mrs. Cadeby's aunt anywhere. Like the house-keeper, she was tall and slim with the same intelligent blue eyes and straight nose. Her hair, though, was white and drawn into a tight bun. Although she seemed to be in her seventies, her skin was clear and remarkably unlined. As she entered the kitchen, the older woman was bent over the range, stirring the pot from which a delicious aroma was coming.

"Sit yourself, love, and pour the tea while I dish this up. You look tired and half-frozen. Once you've had something to eat, it's bed for you. We can talk in the morning."

For the first time since being homeless, jobless, and pregnant, Lily cried.

twenty-two

"Now then, lass."

Lily felt a friendly hand on her shoulder.

"No need to take on. You'll get through this and come out stronger on the other side." The older woman spoke kindly.

"Thank you, Mrs. Clayton," Lily replied, wiping her eyes. "I don't know what came over me. I'm really not one to cry."

"Good. I can't be doing with women who turn on the tears. You'll call me Annis. Everyone does. Now eat. I don't want to see anything left on that plate."

When she had finished, Annis said, "Come on. I'll show you to your room. It's nothing fancy, mind." She lit a candle and started up the stairs.

The room was large enough to accommodate a double bed with a beautiful patchwork quilt over it. Heavy, deep red drapes hung at the window. There was a wardrobe and tallboy in dark wood and a washing stand with a marble top. On it stood a white porcelain washbowl and jug decorated with pink roses. Annis lit candles by the side of the bed.

"I think you'll be comfortable enough, and there's room enough for a crib when it's needed. Now get some rest. I'll see you in the morning."

"Thank you, Annis," Lily replied.

The older woman nodded and left.

Lily suddenly felt exhausted. She quickly undressed and climbed into bed, blew out the candles, and fell into a deep dreamless sleep for the first time in several nights.

It was impossible to tell what time it was when she woke up. Through a slit in the curtains, she could tell it was daylight. She got out of bed and padded to the window. The view took her breath away. In front of the house was a small garden. A narrow lane gave way to a grassy bank below where she could see the track she assumed she had come up the night before. On either side of the track, there were fields with sheep dotted about. She could hear their faint bleating through the window.

To her right, she could make out the town of Hawes, with the church tower standing above everything else. Beyond Hawes, another hill rose with even more fields dotted with sheep and crisscrossed with drystone walls and small barns. She could barely make out another small village to her left on the other side of the dale. At the top of the hill, the land became more rugged. She had never seen so many different shades of green.

She washed and dressed quickly. The water in the jug was tepid, which suggested Annis had been in earlier while Lily slept. As she went downstairs, the aroma of coffee hit her, and her stomach rumbled.

"Good morning." Annis smiled as Lily entered the kitchen. "I left you sleeping this morning, but you'll have to be up earlier in the future."

"Of course," Lily replied.

"Here." Annis handed her a mug of steaming coffee. "Most of the folks around here drink nothing but tea, but you can't beat a cup of coffee in the mornings. Only the one, mind, or that baby will be dancing a jig in there." She smiled again. "Now, I've boiled you a couple of eggs, and there's toast on the table. Mary was most insistent that I made sure you eat something, and she was right. There's nothing of you."

Lily began to eat. Annis was not a woman to argue with. As she ate, she looked around at her surroundings. The walls were freshly whitewashed, and blue gingham curtains hung at the window. The range was black leaded, and the table was scrubbed. There was a Windsor chair to the right of the range and a tab rug on the flagstone floor. Above the range was a rack with a wide selection of what she assumed were herbs hanging to dry. Further back, there was a small scullery with a sink and dolly tub for washing clothes as well as another wooden table and shelves with gleaming copper pans. There were also shelves containing jars of all sizes.

"It's very kind of you to take me in, Annis," Lily began, trying the older woman's first name for the first time.

Annis shrugged. "Mary said you were a good girl. You've made a mistake. That's all," she replied gruffly. "Many a lass has believed a young man when he promised a ring."

"No one seems to want anything to do with me," Lily admitted. "My father has gone all religious and sees me as a sinner, and Mr. and Mrs. Grove don't even believe I'm having their grandchild." To her horror, Lily could feel her eyes filling with tears again. "I'm sorry," she said. "I don't usually cry like this."

"Better out than in," Annis replied. "A lot of women cry easily when they're expecting." She took a sip of coffee. "Now, we must sort out what it is you're going to do while you're here. No use sitting about moping. Best to keep busy."

"I'll be happy to do whatever you need me to do," Lily replied. "As you know, I was a housemaid, so cleaning is something I'm used to."

"Well, that would be a help," the older woman said, leaning against the table. "I'm not as young as I was, and although I can still do it all, I can't do it as quickly as I used to. Do you know anything about gardening?"

"Not really. We didn't have a garden at home, and there were gardeners at the Groves' house."

"Well, you'll soon learn. I keep a kitchen and herb garden. You'll have seen the kitchen garden under your window. These —" She indicated the rack above her head. "—are grown at the back. You'll soon get the hang of it, and my knees will appreciate the help." She laughed a throaty laugh. "I shall need you to go into Hawes for me. Mostly to the post office. It's a tidy walk, and I don't keep a cart, but the exercise will be good for you and the babe. The rich women who sit around all day throughout their pregnancies are the ones, in my experience, who have the toughest time during the birth."

"I don't have anything yet for the baby," Lily said suddenly, her eyes wide.

"We'll have plenty of time to get ready," Annis assured her.

"But I don't sew very well," she admitted. "My mum was good at all that sort of thing."

The other woman's eyes softened. "Well, you're fortunate I do. I'll teach you sewing, knitting, and crochet if you like. There's not much else to do around here in the evenings."

After breakfast, Lily finished unpacking, placing her two books on top of the tallboy. At least now she wouldn't have to hide them from anyone. She cleared the washing bowl and jug in the sink in the scullery. Annis was already in the herb garden. It was a fine day, so she went outside to join the older woman, who was hoeing between two rows of plants. It was good to feel the warmth of the sun. The garden was larger than she had thought. It was surely too big for one woman to manage, let alone eat all it produced.

Annis looked up and beckoned her over. "This is parsley, that one is chervil, and the next row across is dill," she said, pointing to three rows of plants.

"They all look the same. How can you tell the difference?" Lily replied.

"Look again," Annis replied.

"I suppose the leaves get more feathery," Lily said.

"Quite," Annis agreed. "Parsley has the broadest leaf. Dill is the most feathery, as you put it. Chervil is in the middle. I'll make a gardener of you before long." She picked up a pile of plants and walked swiftly towards the house. Though Lily could not help but notice her surreptitiously rub the small of her back. "Now, I need you to go into Hawes and pick up one or two bits for me. There's a list on the table. Here." She held out a brass curtain ring. "I'm not one to judge, but there are others who might. Best wear this and say you're a widow. Nobody'll be any the wiser, and it'll be easier to explain when the baby arrives. You can tell them you're my great niece come to stay and help me now I'm getting on a bit." She grinned.

Lily smiled back as she slipped the ring onto her finger. If ever a woman didn't need help, it was Annis Clayton.

Lily enjoyed her first walk into Hawes. She remembered from her journey the previous evening how steep the hill was. She slipped through the narrow stile into the first field. Annis had told her there were four fields the farmer allowed them to walk through. They had been ancient rights of way centuries ago, allowing people to access their fields. When the land had been enclosed, the rights of way were still there.

The sheep looked on disinterestedly as she walked through. She crossed the lane and went through the next stile. The path there was much more worn. She reached the third stile and had to climb up the stone steps in order to get over it. A short, but steep, path led to the small humpbacked bridge over the river, which was quite narrow. The final field was flat now that she had dropped down into the dale. Once she was across the road, it was a short walk over the bridge, through the final field, and past the railway station where she had arrived a few short hours ago. Then she was in Hawes.

She was to go to the post office and the chemist to collect some things for Annis. When she had asked Annis for directions, the older woman had laughed and said, "Hawes isn't that big, lass. You'll soon find them." Words she hoped were true as she walked over the cobbles towards the High Street.

twenty-three

At the post office, the young woman on the counter took the two packages Annis had given Lily to post, weighed them, and stuck two stamps on each.

"That will be four shillings," she said.

Lily handed over the coins.

"I expect you'll be back tomorrow," the young woman said, taking the parcels and putting them on the shelf behind the counter with several others. "Seems to have parcels to send every day, does Mrs. Clayton," she commented, clearly curious.

"I wouldn't know," Lily replied. "I only arrived recently."

The young woman looked interested. "Oh, are you staying with Mrs. Clayton, then?"

Lily nodded. "I'm a relative," she added. "My husband is missing and believed killed. Annis invited me here to help out a little." There was some truth in there somewhere, though she was surprised at how easily she had managed to lie.

The young woman looked at her with sympathy. "I'm sorry. I hope he comes back," she said. "Three of our young lads will never come back. Daft buggers. Two of them were brothers and too young to go. Their mother is beside herself."

Lily nodded, thinking of her own brother, Tommy, and wondering where he was.

She got out the list Annis had given her and entered the chemist's shop. She had always been fascinated by chemist shops. The various bottles of coloured liquid, the small labelled wooden drawers, and endless jars of odd-looking contents along with the smell of nutmeg and cloves were in some way comforting. The bell had barely stopped ringing when a young man stepped out from the back of the shop.

"Can I help you, miss?" he asked, his voice a deep, rich baritone.

He was tall and broad shouldered underneath the white coat he wore. His hair was a dark brown, as were his eyes, which were fringed with thick, dark lashes any woman would die for. He was the handsomest man she had seen in a long time.

"I need to collect these items for Mrs. Clayton." She handed over the note Annis had given her.

He took it and looked at it for a moment or two. "It will take a few minutes. Do you have anything else to do in Hawes?"

She shook her head. "Not really. I've only just arrived, but I could have a walk around and find my bearings."

"It will take me about ten minutes to find everything on here," he said, smiling as he indicated the list.

Lily crossed the road and looked in Blythe's, the tailor and costumier. Though she doubted she'd need anything from there other than some stockings. Life with Annis wasn't going to call for the latest fashion, not that she could afford it. In any case, she was aware her body was already beginning to change. She would soon have to let out the waistbands on her skirts. But she could not resist going into Chapman's and getting a quarter of toffee, which had to be broken into small pieces with a little hammer. Popping a piece in her mouth, she walked past the grocers, butchers, and bakers as well as the small creamery where they made the famous Wensleydale cheese.

When she returned, there were two large packages on the counter. She picked up one and put it in her canvas bag.

"You'll never manage both," an amused voice said as she lifted the second one. "It won't fit in the bag, and I know that path up to Sedbusk. You'll never get over the styles."

"I can manage," she replied, knowing it wasn't going to be easy.

"I'll tell you what," the chemist went on. "If you wait a few minutes, I'll walk with you and carry that." He nodded towards the parcel.

Lily shook her head. "I can't ask you to do that."

"You didn't ask. I offered," he pointed out.

"Even so, I don't know you. Why would you want to do such a thing?"

"It's what we do around here. We help each other out," he replied. "In any case, it's my half day, and I wanted a walk anyway. Quite apart from the fact that if Mrs. Clayton's goods aren't perfect, she'll have my guts for garters."

Lily smiled. "I imagine she might be a little daunting."

"People in Wharfedale, Wensleydale, and Swaledale would climb the three peaks in an hour rather than upset Mrs. Clayton," he replied, but his smile belied his words. Annis, as Lily was fast learning, was a respected woman.

"Well, if you're sure," she said. She was grateful for his help as her bag was already weighing on her.

"I'll just get out of this," he said, indicating his white coat, "and lock up, and we can be on our way." He held out his hand. "I'm Ian, by the way. Ian Steele."

"Lily Russell."

A little over a quarter of an hour later, they were on the path out of Hawes. Ian insisted not only on taking the large package but her bag as well.

"If you're going to stay here any length of time," he said, looking at her shoes, "you'll need a stout pair of boots."

"I'll remember that," she replied as she scrambled over a stile.

"So how do you come to be staying with Mrs. Clayton?"

Lily took a breath. She didn't like the idea of lying to anyone, let alone this man, but she couldn't confess. Not yet. As Annis had said, not all people would be understanding of her predicament. Many would judge her. Although she instinctively felt she could trust Ian Steele, she didn't know for sure. So she stuck to the story she had agreed upon with Annis: the missing husband presumed dead.

"I'm sorry to hear that, Lily. This war is a terrible thing," he said quietly.

She looked up at his words. "One of my brothers lied about his age and ran away to join up. We don't know where he is or if he's even alive."

"They'll tell you soon enough if he isn't," he replied, climbing over the stile and holding his hand out for her to follow.

"You sound as though you speak from experience," she said, dropping lightly to the ground.

He shrugged. "A sniper managed to get me in his sights. His shot came within inches of my heart. Unfortunately, it somewhat damaged my lung. At one point, they thought I might lose it and the use of my arm, but for some reason, I did not. However, the British Army felt I could no longer be of use to them. Hence, here I am in Hawes. Walking around these hills has made me stronger. I'm sure of it."

"I am so sorry. I can't begin to imagine what it must have been like," Lily replied.

"No one can unless they've been there. The mud, blood, and cries of men injured and dying out in no man's land. Knowing you can't get out to rescue them..." His eyes focussed far away. "Still—" His voice became brisk. "—I came back. I was one of the lucky ones, and it falls to me, and others like me, to ensure we never forget those who didn't."

"I wouldn't say you were one of the lucky ones," she replied, her eyes misting.

"The man next to me wasn't so lucky with the sniper's next shot. I... Never mind. You don't want to know."

As they walked up the field on the last part of their journey to Sedbusk, Lily asked, "Were you a chemist before the war?"

He turned to her and smiled. "I was. My father had the shop before me. He had been apprenticed to the previous chemist, but times change, and I had to study in order to qualify. When he retired, it was the obvious thing to take over the shop."

"I've always wondered," she began. "What is in those glass bottles and jars? They were in the chemist's shop in Hope too."

"It's a trade secret." He grinned.

"Really?"

"No." His grin became a laugh. "It's just coloured water, really. I think it goes back to the days when a lot of people couldn't read. They saw the coloured bottles and knew it was somewhere they could go to get their medicine."

"Makes sense, I suppose. Though I was expecting something a little more exotic." She laughed. "Have you always lived in Hawes?"

She looked around at the stunning scenery. The hills were purple with heather as they loomed over the valley. The fields crisscrossed by the drystone walls and were dotted with sheep, stretching as far as the eye could see.

"It's amazing I come from the same county, but believe me, Hope is nothing like this."

Ian, too, looked around him. "As soon as I finished my studies, I wanted to travel and see something of the world, which I did. Then the war intervened. Now I am happy to spend my days here. I know most of the people in Hawes and nearby. There's plenty of open space, and I feel free to breathe. It's worth more than money."

"Only people who have money say that sort of thing," she replied.

He looked at her with interest. "Tell me something about yourself, Lily."

She was saved from saying much as they approached Annis's house, and the door opened.

twenty-four

"Well, come in the pair of you. I've a meat-and-potato pie in the oven. Mind you wipe your feet," Annis said before disappearing back into the house.

"I think that means you're invited for lunch." Lily grinned as she wiped her feet on the doormat.

"It's bound to be better than the cheese and bread I was going to have. Mrs. Clayton's cooking is well-known," he replied, taking off his coat and hanging it on the hook.

Within minutes, they were all sitting around the kitchen table.

"Did you have all the things I wanted?" Annis asked Ian.

"All apart from the petroleum jelly, and I'm expecting a delivery of that in a day or so," Ian replied, helping himself to a large slice of pie.

"I don't suppose a day or so matters," Annis replied, passing a white jug with gravy. "It'll mean another trip to Hawes for you," she said to Lily.

"I don't mind, Annis," she replied. "I enjoyed the walk."

"It's certainly easier getting there than walking back." Annis laughed.

"Especially with a heavy bag," Ian said. "I could drop off the jelly if you like. It'd save you the walk."

Lily smiled. "That is very kind of you. Thank you."

Annis's eyebrows raised. "And why would you want to walk all the way up here?" she asked. "Folk generally try to avoid it."

Ian smiled at the older woman. "Mrs. Crallan at Stonehouse ordered some things that should arrive with the same order as your jelly. I shall have to come up to deliver them, so it's not far out of my way," he explained.

"Well, only if you're sure it won't put you out," Lily said.

He turned his smile on her. "Not at all."

He really was a genuinely nice man, but Lily couldn't get involved. She knew that. In any case, when her condition became obvious in a few weeks, his attitude would undoubtedly change. Even if he believed the story of her lost husband, there were few men prepared to take on another man's child. Still, she could enjoy his company and friendship if they were offered.

After he had gone, she and Annis cleared the table.

"He's a fine young man is Ian," Annis commented. "It's a miracle he came back."

"Yes, he told me," Lily replied, wiping her hands.

"I wouldn't like to see him hurt," Annis went on.

"Neither would I."

"I don't expect he told you his fiancée left him virtually standing at the altar, did he?"

Lily paused, the tablecloth half-folded. "No, he didn't mention that."

"When he came back, no one thought he would survive, to be honest. For months, he was in that hospital in Harrogate. Sarah, his fiancée, went to visit every week to begin with. Then, when he was well enough to come home, he told her the engagement was over. He didn't want to be a burden, you see."

"What happened?"

"Sarah assured him she loved him anyway and that she still wanted to marry him. The invitations were sent, and the banns were read. But the morning of the wedding, she sent a message to say she couldn't go through with it."

"How terrible," Lily whispered.

"Anyway, it turns out that on one of her visits to Harrogate, she'd met someone else. A major in the army."

"But why did she say she wanted to go through with the wedding?" Lily asked.

"Guilt, I think. At the very least, she saved them both from what would no doubt have ended up being an unhappy marriage."

"What happened to her?"

"She left the Dales. Couldn't stand the gossip. I believe she married her major and lives in Beverly. It took Ian a long time to get over her. He's better now, both in body and spirit, but I shouldn't like to see his peace shattered."

"Nor would I, Annis. I like Ian, but given my situation, all I want is a friend."

Annis nodded. "Now," she went on briskly, "there's copper and brass to polish."

There was indeed a lot of copper and brass to polish. The copper fender and coal scuttle were first, then Annis's collection of copper kettles and pots. When she returned the shining brass weighing scales to the kitchen, Lily was intrigued to find Annis standing over an earthenware bowl stirring steadily, but there were no aromas of cooking. Instead, the heady scent of lavender filled the air.

"What are you doing?" Lily asked, her curiosity getting the better of her.

"A lot of the farmers' wives have chapped hands. I make them a balm that helps stop the skin from cracking. In fact, some of them have told me their husbands use it as well."

Lily came further into the room and looked over Annis's

shoulder into the bowl. As Annis stirred, the mixture began to solidify and look like a cream.

"How do you do that?" she asked.

Annis laughed. "I've been doing it for years. My grandmother taught me, as her grandmother taught her. In the old days, I would probably have been burnt as a witch. Here." She placed a small blob of cream on Lily's hand. "Rub it in," she ordered.

"That feels so soft," Lily replied. "And the scent is lovely."

"Lavender is a favourite," Annis replied as she scraped the cream out of the bowl and put it in the small glass pots on the table. "You can use rose also. Well, you can use most flowers if you know what to do."

Lily sat down, intrigued as Annis deftly scraped the last of the cream into the final pot and began to place discs of waxed paper on the top before screwing on a tin lid. The speed at which she worked suggested she had done it many times.

"What's in the balm?" she asked.

"Lanolin, mostly. Some beeswax, vegetable oil, and lavender oil," Annis replied.

"What's lanolin?" Lily asked.

"It's a kind of wax you get from a sheep's fleece. It's what protects the sheep's skin."

"And ours too?"

"And ours too."

"How do you get it from the fleece?"

"It's a bit of a job, that's for sure. The fleece has to be boiled for a few hours. Then the lanolin rises to the top when it cools and you scrape it off. I do that out in the washhouse," Annis explained. "There are a lot of sheep around here, so fleeces are easy enough to come by. Most of the farmers' wives are happy with the balm and persuade their husbands to give me a good price."

"So you sell the balm?" Lily asked.

"Well, I don't give them away," Annis replied. "It puts food on this table. Though, I could always sell more than I can make."

"We used to try to make perfume by putting petals in water," Lily volunteered, smiling at the memory.

"And all you ended up with was brown, nasty-smelling water I imagine," Annis replied.

Lily nodded. "Every time."

"I think all little girls try that. The petals just rot. You need the oil."

There was a pause before Lily asked, "Do you make other things besides the balm?"

"Sometimes I make medicines using the recipes my grandmother gave me, hence the herb garden, the beehives at the back, and the flower garden at the front. Doctors are expensive, but if you know what to do, herbs can help with any number of ailments. But the lotions and creams are what sell well."

"Annis," Lily began hesitantly, "do you think I could help? It looks fascinating. I want to learn, and I won't get in the way. Please."

twenty-five

Lily held her breath. She had never been particularly interested in cooking or sewing, but this she was interested in. Helping Annis with the chores wasn't going to take up much of her time, and she needed to feel useful. She had never been one to sit around. The life of a maid didn't allow for that. Seeing Annis working had awakened her thirst for knowledge. She wanted to know everything. She almost shrank under Annis's steady gaze.

"All right," the older woman finally said. "I'll teach you. There's a lot to learn, mind, and I expect you to do as you're told without question. I've no time to be arguing the toss with you."

"Agreed." Lily grinned.

"You'll have to learn about the herb garden, and there'll be plenty of walking to make deliveries as well as making the items."

"That's fine. I've never minded walking."

Annis's eyes narrowed. "How are you with your numbers and letters?"

Lily shrugged. "I liked school. I can read and write with a neat hand, and I enjoyed mathematics."

"Good. You can do the paperwork. There's ordering and accounts to be done." She indicated a wooden chest in the corner. "All the paperwork's in there. I have neglected it a bit of late," she admitted.

"I'll be happy to sort it out."

"Well, then. It looks as though we're in business." Annis held out her hand and they shook.

Annis had been right. There was much to learn. Lily found she enjoyed being in the garden tending to the plants as well as picking and hanging them over the range to dry. She was amazed at how much lavender it took to make a small phial of oil. She enjoyed the flower garden, but the herbs had their own beauty. She was fascinated by the processes by which Annis turned the natural ingredients into a variety of cosmetics and medicines. She bought a notebook so she could write everything down.

"I know you learned this as you grew up," she explained when Annis raised an eyebrow, "but I'm new to this, and I don't want to forget a thing."

Some days were devoted to delivering products to the farmers' wives, which meant long walks. But Lily didn't mind. She enjoyed being out in the fresh air and felt it was doing both her and the new life inside her good. Sometimes she even forgot she was pregnant and felt guilty that she thought less and less about Jonathon. The women were always glad to see her, and her delivery bag often came back filled with butter, cheese, and a few potatoes as well as the few coins in payment for their products.

In only a few weeks, she had learned to boil a fleece to extract the lanolin and to make oil from lavender. Annis had even allowed her to take part in making a lotion, closely supervising so that Lily used the right quantities of lanolin, liquid paraffin, petroleum jelly, and lavender oil.

In the evenings, Lily sat at the kitchen table with a cup of tea to sort through the chest. It took several evenings to sort the papers into order and enter the figures into the large ledger, but she was beginning to see that there was potential for more profit.

"How do you get your customers, Annis?" she asked one evening when they were ladling lotion into glass bottles.

Annis looked up. "Word of mouth, I suppose. The first time I made balm, it was for Mrs. Thwaite at Hilltop Farm. I'd seen her in Hawes on market day, and we got to chatting. She said her hands were bad, and they were. She showed me. They were so dry the skin had cracked. I told her I might have something that would help. I came home and made some balm and gave it to her the next market day. By the end of the month, I had half a dozen women asking for some. It just went from there."

"What about the other things you make?" Lily asked.

"Well, someone asked if I knew of anything that might settle their stomach, and someone else was having trouble sleeping. Before long, I had a steady stream of customers. I must be getting something right because they keep coming back." Annis laughed. "And it's making a difference, having someone to help," she added. "We've been able to make more and build up a bit of stock. Before, it was getting to be a bit of a struggle to cope at times."

Lily nodded, noting with pride the fact Annis had said, "We've been able." She took a deep breath. "I was wondering whether you'd ever thought of perhaps taking a stall in Hawes market and selling your things there," she ventured.

Annis stood still, her spoon poised over the large pan. "I've never thought about that," she admitted. "It's all I could do to make enough for my regular customers."

"Well, there are two of us now," Lily replied.

"But do you think anyone'll want to buy it? Making some balms and a few tinctures for women I've known for years is one thing, but selling them to other folk? I'm not so sure."

"I'm sure," Lily replied. "Look how many people want to buy your products now, and that's just by word of mouth. If women here want to buy your things, why wouldn't others want to buy them? Think of it this way," she went on, noticing Annis's doubtful look. "The farmers' wives buy your hand balm because the work they do makes their hands chapped and dry. In the winter, they get cracks in their skin. Well, housemaids and housewives do the same. My mum used to suffer terribly in the winter with cracks in her hands. It's not just farmers' wives who'd buy it. It's, well, any woman who does housework, for a start."

Annis slowly nodded. "You might be right. But I don't know anything about selling at the market."

"Neither do I," Lily replied. "But we can learn. Do you think we've enough stock to start next month if we can get a stall?"

Annis looked at the jars and bottles of all shapes and sizes scattered throughout the kitchen. They were on the table, the windowsill, in every cupboard and shelf, and in the little scullery at the back. "I should think so. In fact, it'll be good to get rid of a few."

"I'll call in at the office in the Market House and see what we need to do."

———

The following Tuesday, Lily walked up the steps to the Market House and looked in. There were stalls selling all sorts of things, from bed linens and towels to leatherwork, pots and pans, and knitting wool. She noted there were no stalls selling anything like the creams and balms Annis made. The market supervisor was only too happy for them to have a stall, but there were none available at the moment. Though, she was told there may be something coming up soon in Leyburn on Fridays. She was advised to enquire there. In the meantime, there was to be a bazaar at the Market House at the end of the month, and he'd just had a cancellation. Lily handed over the money without delay.

As she left the hall, she bumped into Ian.

"You're looking very serious," he said. "I was just about to go to take a walk up to The Green Dragon at Hardraw for a spot of lunch. Would you like to join me?"

"I would. Thanks," she replied with a smile. "As it happens, I have a couple of deliveries to make up that way." They walked in companionable silence, and as he always did, Ian took Lily's bag for her.

There was a roaring fire in The Green Dragon. Its wooden panelling hadn't been changed for centuries. It was one of the oldest inns in the dale, and the owner proudly boasted that the artist JMW Turner had stayed there. The rooms were small and cosy. At this time of day, there were few others around to overhear their conversation.

Over a hearty meal of pie, mashed potatoes, and carrots washed down with lemonade, Lily explained the new venture.

"I think it's a splendid idea." He took a sip of beer. "Might I make a suggestion?"

"Of course."

"If you're going to sell to the public, you need to think about the packaging. What Annis does now is fine, but if you want to sell to people who don't know her or her products, you need to make them look more attractive. I found it's often the packaging that attracts customers to look at the item and then buy it."

"I hadn't thought of that," Lily exclaimed. It had always been the cost rather than the look that had determined her purchases. Her hand went to her mouth. "Oh, I've just had a thought. You sell creams and the like. Are you all right with Annis and I setting up in competition?" She held her breath.

"As a matter of fact, yes." He smiled. "I imagine we won't be competing for the same customers. If you're really interested in setting up a cosmetic business, you might consider taking me as a partner."

Lily's eyebrows shot up. "A partner? You? But you're a chemist."

"Exactly," he replied.

twenty-six

Annis required little persuading that Ian joining them would be a good idea. He already provided a lot of the ingredients as it was, and if he came on board, they would no doubt be able to purchase things at cost.

They had little time to get things ready for the bazaar and no time to get labels and boxes professionally made, so Lily took it upon herself to draw labels. Annis found her an old box of watercolours, and to her surprise, Lily found she could produce something that wasn't an embarrassment. She didn't attempt realism as she hadn't the skill, but her stylised drawings of the plants the products were made from were simple and effective. Her handwriting had always been commended by Miss Hodgeson, and the flowing letters contrasted nicely with the simple drawings. She and Annis were glueing them onto the jars when Ian arrived. He had brought with him a couple of items Lily couldn't carry the last time she visited the shop.

"Very good." He smiled as he looked at Lily's drawings. "Next time, we'll have time to get them printed."

They were in the habit of taking a walk on Sunday afternoons. Lily looked forward to them. Having lived all her life in a town, she could never get bored with the beautiful scenery that now surrounded her. She would never tire of seeing so many shades of green. The fields in the dale were a rich emerald but became less vivid as the fields trailed up and over the hillsides before blending with the gold and purple of the gorse and heather as they reached the top.

Today, Ian suggested they walk over Stags Fell and down towards Simonstone. The lane became steep, and Lily was glad when they turned off. Although they were still climbing, the slope was less steep, and walking on the soft turf was much more pleasant even though the recent showers had created several streams they had to jump over. When Ian held out his hand for her to hold as she jumped, Lily felt her insides tighten. He seemed to hold it a moment longer than was necessary, but he said nothing, and they walked on.

"Not everyone knows about these paths," he commented as they clambered over a stile. "There used to be lead mining up here not so long ago. That's how Sedbusk came into being, apart from the farm having been there for generations. They built some of the cottages for the miners. It's all gone now, though, apart from a few stones where the buildings used to be. You'd hardly know it had ever been here."

"Why did it stop?" she asked.

He shrugged. "The usual, I suppose. Basically, they extracted all they could, and this was only ever an extension of the seam over in Swaledale. I don't think it was ever profitable enough. When the price of lead fell, that was the end."

"It must have put a lot of men out of work," she said, thinking of the time her family had struggled when her father couldn't work after the accident.

"Most of the men here worked in farming and did the mining alongside, so it wasn't the same problem it was over in Swaledale. Whole villages disappeared there when the mines closed. Apparently, over here in Wensleydale, they produced more butter and cheese than they ever produced lead."

They both laughed.

"And knitting, of course."

"Knitting?"

"A hundred or so years ago, Hawes was known for its knitters. Before the factories opened in Leeds and Bradford, every man, woman, and child in Hawes walked about the place, knitting caps, mittens, gloves, jerseys, and socks to earn extra money. You could hear the clicking of their knitting needles on the streets."

"You are a mine of information." She smiled.

"That's what comes of generations of family living in the same place," he replied.

As the hill got steeper, they walked in silence until they reached the top.

"That's what I wanted you to see."

The whole dale seemed to be laid out in front of them like a carpet. The town of Hawes was nestled in the valley with the river running through it like a stream of silver. The church stood proud in the centre of the town. Appersett was to the right. Across the valley, she could see Burtersett at the foot of Wethergill.

"There's a Roman road across the top of Wethergill," Ian said. "If the Romans wanted to build a road, they didn't waste time going round a hill. It was straight all the way. They always say of Burtersett that this side of the dale gets the sunshine, but that side has the money." He laughed.

He took a rug out of his knapsack. They sat close to the edge, eating the apples he produced.

"I can see Annis's cottage," she exclaimed.

"Speaking of Annis, is she really all right with becoming a partner in the business?" he asked.

Lily turned to look at him. "Of course. She thinks you'll be able to bring some scientific knowledge to our work as well as get ingredients at cost."

He laughed. "Ever the Yorkshirewoman." He paused.

"What of you, Lily? It can't have escaped your notice that I enjoy being in your company."

"And I yours," she replied, scarcely daring to breathe. She was afraid to look at him. There were things she had to tell him, things that, once they were spoken, would change any relationship.

He took her hand in his. " May I hope that you and I might be friends? Well...more than friends?" he asked. "I know your husband is... God, this is difficult." He ran his hand through his hair. "I know your husband is missing, and most likely killed, and I could never hope to replace him, nor would I want to, but should he not come back from this terrible, terrible war, I should like to look after you. In short, I should like you to be my wife."

Lily looked first at their linked hands and then at his face. "Oh, Ian. You know nothing about me, and this talk of my husband—"

"I know you will never love me as you loved him," he interrupted. "But I think we both deserve the chance at some happiness. I think we could do that together."

Lily took a breath. "There is one thing I must tell you before we go any further in this conversation. It will be obvious, in any case, in a few weeks. Before he disappeared, Jonathon left me expecting a child. He didn't know—doesn't know," she corrected herself. She hadn't told a lie, though she knew Ian would assume Jonathon was her husband.

He frowned. "What of Jonathon's parents? Or yours?"

She took a deep breath. "My mother died recently, and Jonathon's parents were...not happy about our relationship." Again, she was being economical with the truth and hated herself for doing it. Ian was a good man, and he deserved better than half-truths and insinuations. She gently removed her hand from his. "This changes everything, I know," she said quietly and stood. "Shall we go down now?"

He nodded, and they picked their way carefully down the

path before it met the Buttertubs road, which went over to Swaledale. They talked of the weather and the earl's hunting lodge, the shooting season and the view, anything that wasn't connected with the bombshell Lily had dropped.

When they had passed Simonstone Hall, Lily said, "I won't trouble you to walk me back to Sedbusk. It won't take me long to walk down the lane. I'm sure you want to get back to Hawes before it's dark."

"It's fine. I don't like to think of you walking down there alone."

"I'm perfectly able to look after myself," she replied, suddenly irritated. "I assure you, growing up in Hope and working as a maid has made me tougher than the sort of woman you usually associate with. If that's too difficult for you to deal with, then so be it."

She turned on her heel and walked off. It was obvious that he assumed she was respectable. But he now knew she wasn't some simpering virgin because he thought she had been married. If he couldn't cope with that fact when he viewed her as a "widow" bearing her husband's child, he certainly wouldn't cope with the fact that she was never married to the father of her baby.

A tear slowly trickled down her cheek, and she brushed it away. She would not cry over a man again. Jonathon had let her down, and Ian would, she reasoned, probably want nothing further to do with her. She would concentrate on the business with Annis, on that aspect of her life. At least she had some control in that area, and she would have to be content, if not happy, with that. Happiness, she was coming to believe, was not something she was going to have a great deal of.

twenty-seven

Both Lily and Annis were nervous as they set up their table for the bazaar. But as Annis said, it would be a good indicator of whether, other than a few farmers' wives, people would be interested in what they had made. Lily was also pleased Ian had turned up early that morning with a small pony and trap to help them get the goods to Hawes. She had seen little of him since her revelation and had begun to wonder if he would want anything to do with her. It seemed, if nothing else, he was still keen to be a business partner. She hoped he would still be a friend.

As the doors opened, there was a rush of mostly women into the hall to take advantage of the goods that were rarely available in the Dales. One stall had leather goods, fancy purses, belts, and wallets. Another had hand-embroidered pillowcases, tablecloths, and handkerchiefs. There was a stall selling handmade jewellery and another with carved wooden toys. Yet another had children's clothes, and there was a stall selling hats and scarves. One stall was selling paper flowers, feathers, and ribbons for women to decorate their own hats. There was a delicious smell of baked goods coming from the kitchen where the ladies of the Women's Institute were providing teas.

Lily was relieved their stall was attracting a fair deal of attention. Many women were looking at the products with interest, but none were buying. Lily took the lid off a pot and asked them to try the hand cream. The idea turned out to be inspired. Within minutes, Lily was thrilled to make the first sale. After that, the goods flew off the stall. Fortunately, Annis had brought a small notebook and pencil and was busily taking orders. Although the rest of the day didn't bring in quite the same number of customers, there was a steady flow. By the end of the day, all they had left were two bottles of cough linctus and the almost-empty pot.

"Well," Lily said as she packed away the sign and empty boxes, "I think we can say that was a success."

"So it would seem," replied Annis, putting on her coat and pinning her hat in place. "We have orders to prepare as well as making stock for the market in Leyburn. In short, we have a lot to do."

"We'll manage." Lily smiled. "One thing we know now is that women want this sort of thing."

They were both grateful when Ian returned with the pony and trap to take them home. It had been a long day.

"Would you care for a little walk, Lily?" he asked as they packed the empty boxes away. "Just a short one. I'd like to talk to you, if I might."

"You two go. By the time you get back, there'll be supper on the table," Annis said, fishing out some potatoes from the bin in the scullery.

They walked along Sedbusk Lane.

"I wanted to apologise," Ian began.

"There's no need," Lily replied.

"There's every need," he went on. "I behaved like an ass, firstly in relation to your husband. I was insensitive to even suggest what I did, and as to my reaction to the fact you're having a baby, I apologise. I was taken by surprise, which is no excuse, I know. But I want you to know that my feelings for you haven't changed, even if all we can ever be is friends."

"I would like that," Lily replied.

"Good," he said, leaning forward and kissing her cheek.

"And whatever I can do to help when the baby comes, I will."

"Thank you. You're a good man, Ian Steele," she replied. Their friendship had meant a lot to her, and it was good to have it back.

The meal they shared with Annis was full of laughter as they related to Ian the highlights of the day. Old lady Webster had complained at the price of the sage tincture but bought it anyway as she was "a martyr to her bowels." Old man Webster said he'd pay anything if they had something that could stop his wife's talking, at which point the old lady hit him over the head with her umbrella.

"What sold out quickly?" Ian asked.

"The rose or lavender creams," Annis replied, "and I've orders for more."

"That's what we need to produce more of for the Leyburn market," Lily responded. "If the women in Hawes want them, it's fair to assume the women in Leyburn will too."

"Exactly," Ian agreed.

"I might add a rosemary one," Annis added. "The scent is just as nice."

"Whatever we do, we have only a few weeks to do it," Lily added, frowning.

"What is causing that?" Ian asked, reaching out and smoothing her forehead.

"I was thinking of how we're going to get the goods to

Leyburn. I don't fancy hauling them onto the train or omnibus. Perhaps Mr. Dinsdale might take us in his cart."

Ian smiled. "I have a better idea. I shall bring the pony and trap. It has plenty of room. So long as we set off in good time, we'll have plenty of time to set up. In fact, if all goes well, we could consider buying some sort of delivery cart with the name of the company on it."

"We don't have a name." Lily laughed.

"And we don't, as yet, have a company," Ian replied. "But if we're to do this properly, we should make it official."

"Ian's right," Annis put in. "Let's see how we get on at Leyburn. If it's likely we might have a business, we'll do it then.

"I'll get Martin Hollis to do the paperwork," Ian replied. "We were at school together. He's the solicitor in Hawes. Like me, he took over his father's business."

The rest of the evening was spent thinking up a name.

"It should be something incorporating all our names," Annis said firmly.

"How about Slyannis?" Ian suggested.

"I don't think anyone will buy anything with the word sly in it," Lily protested.

"What do you think about Nailissa?" Annis suggested.

"We could always try Sillyannis," Ian said, making them all laugh.

"What about Ilaniis?" Lily proposed. "It sounds a little exotic. I think it could be the kind of thing women might find attractive."

"That's the one," Annis decided. "It incorporates all our names and sounds like something out of a fashion magazine. Not," she added sternly, "that I have time to read such nonsense."

"Ilaniis it is," Ian agreed. "Do you think you can add it to the labels and perhaps make some kind of poster for the stall, Lily?"

"I think so."

"That's settled, then."

The days flew by. In addition to tending to the garden, which they could not afford to neglect, Lily and Annis boiled fleeces for lanolin and crushed seeds, leaves, and petals to make the creams. Ian called every day with further supplies of petroleum jelly and liquid paraffin as well as vials and pots. Lily was able to produce a design for the labels with the new name, which they all approved. Ian took it into the printers in Hawes. Lily was horrified that he'd ordered five hundred, but he laughed and told her to have faith.

"This is too much," she said, reaching around to ease the pain in her aching back. Her waist was getting thicker. Soon there would be no doubt as to her condition.

"What is?" Annis asked.

"It's not the work. I don't mind that," Lily replied.

"Then what is it?" Annis asked, her tone gentle.

"It's the money," Lily went on. "You and Ian have put so much money into this, and I can't. What happens if it's all for nothing? What happens if you lose all your money?"

"Lily, stop this," Annis ordered. "You were the one with the idea to try to sell the creams, you were the one to think of making the labels look nice, and you were the one who came up with the name. If it weren't for you, there wouldn't be the prospect of a business. You can always put in money later. You are not to carry on thinking like this, and besides," she added with a twinkle in her eye, "I haven't had this much fun in years."

twenty-eight

Fortunately, the weather remained fine, though a little cool, but as they loaded the cart, Lily realised autumn wasn't far away. She should think about getting things together for the baby. She had put it out of her mind, but now that it was becoming obvious she was pregnant, she could not put it out of her head any longer. Ian had offered to help her on the stall since he would be there with the pony and cart anyway. Annis wanted to get on with making a new batch of creams. Ian tucked a rug around her when she had settled into her seat.

"It's a longer drive than you think, and it can get cold," he explained with a smile.

As they trotted down the turnpike towards Leyburn, they were overtaken by a motor car. The horses were clearly unused to the noise and reared, but Ian quickly got them under control.

"That's Dr. Stephens," he commented. "I'd heard he'd bought a car."

"The horses didn't like it," Lily replied.

"No, but it's the future, Lily," he said. "The army is using them over in France. I believe the days of the horse are over. In fact, I'm thinking of getting one myself. Once your creams have made my fortune," he added with a grin.

They were given a stall near the Market House, which Ian declared was a good pitch as they would get lots of interest as people either arrived or left from that entrance. The new labels and poster looked good. Lily brought a white sheet and some boxes to display the bottles and jars at different levels on the stall. She hoped the display would help catch customers' eyes.

From the outset, there was a lot of interest. Like she had done at the bazaar, Lily opened a jar of cream and invited the women to try some. They needed no second bidding, and once again, the creams and lotions sold quickly. By two o'clock, they had sold all their stock, with many customers asking if they would be there the following week. There was disappointment when Lily replied it was more likely they would be back the following month. With this and the bazaar, their stock would need to be replenished. Some women wanted to know if they sold soaps and perfumes as well. Lily decided she would ask Annis to see if they could add them to their list of products.

"I thought some women would want Annis's creams and so on," Lily said thoughtfully as she climbed onto the trap for the journey home. "But it's as though a great dam has broken."

"I think a lot of women, certainly in these parts, have made their own. But there's, as you say, a clear desire for these things. Most women either don't have the time or the skill, frankly, to extract lanolin, let alone know how to use it," Ian replied.

"There's something else," Lily added. "Two women said they wanted to buy some to give as gifts. I wonder if they'd pay a little more if we put them in nicer pots and wrap them. You know...make them look a bit fancy?"

He cast a sideways glance at her. "Well, that would put up

the cost, but you might have a point. We're thinking of the farmers' wives, but what about women in towns and cities, women who have a bit of money to spend?"

Lily laughed. "Perhaps we're getting a bit ahead of ourselves. We sold a few things at a bazaar and on a market stall in the wilds of Yorkshire. It's not exactly Selfridges, is it?"

"Are you a great customer of Selfridges?" he asked with a smile.

"Of course not," she replied. "But Miss Eleanor took regular trips to London and always came back laden with bags from Selfridges and Harrods. Frankly, at times, she had more money than sense. Half the things she bought just hung in her wardrobe or were tossed into a drawer and forgotten about. I think she only went shopping because she was bored."

He looked thoughtful. "Perhaps that's who we should be aiming our products at."

"What? Women with more money than sense?"

"No, women with money to spare. They're the sort of customers who are prepared to pay well, especially if they think they're getting something that looks good."

Lily thought for a moment before replying, "You are probably right. Mrs. Grove and Miss Eleanor thought nothing of spending more than I earned in a month on a pot of cream. As far as I could tell, it was no better than anything we've made. The only difference is the fancy box with a ribbon on it. That's why I suggested making our pots look a bit fancier, but I think you're thinking a lot bigger."

"No use thinking small, Lily."

She frowned. "But isn't all this going to take more than we can manage? It was hard enough making enough product to sell today, let alone producing enough in the herb garden. Annis, although she's a strong woman, was exhausted when we left today. I know she said she was going to make more creams, but I hope she found some time to rest."

He patted her hand. "You're a good woman, Lily Russell," he said quietly and raised her hand to his lips.

They trotted on in companionable silence until they reached Hawes. Instead of turning up towards Sedbusk as they normally would, they drove down the High Street and stopped outside Cockett's.

"I think a celebratory meal is in order." Ian grinned as he helped her down from the trap.

"What about Annis?"

"I haven't invited Annis." His grin got wider. "Don't worry. I mentioned to her I would be taking you out tonight. I think we both deserve a treat."

"I don't know that I'm dressed for going out for dinner." She bit her lip.

"You look fine. Perfect, in fact," he replied, taking her arm and steering her towards the door.

"Besides, Cockett's has been here since 1668, so I imagine it's seen it all."

The room was cosy with a fire burning in the hearth. The oak panelling was newly polished. Lily could smell the lemon and beeswax, something she was familiar with from the Grove household.

For a moment, she remembered the last fateful time she had eaten out in a restaurant. Jonathon's handsome face flashed before her eyes and she stumbled. She didn't know if he was dead or alive, and she didn't even know if she could bring herself to care. Other than the fact he was a young man cut down in the prime of his life. She realised what she had thought of as love for him was nothing more than infatuation. She had allowed herself to be swept off her feet by a charming young man who had left without giving her a second thought.

"Are you all right?" Ian asked as he caught her.

"I'm fine." She smiled up at him. "I just tripped." If only she had met Ian first. But then she would still have been a maid, and Ian would still have been so far socially above her that, in all probability, he would never have even noticed her. That was just the way life was.

Ian saw to it their meal was lighthearted and kept Lily entertained with stories of his time as a student.

"It's a wonder you didn't all blow yourselves up in the laboratory." She laughed as he told her of a disastrous experiment when his friend misread one of the chemicals in a jar.

"It was close." He laughed. "Not perhaps as funny at the time, but with several years' distance, definitely funny. I believe Nigel's eyebrows should have grown back by now."

"Oh, Ian." She gasped. "I can't remember when I laughed so much."

He smiled. "It's good to laugh. Sometimes it's the only thing that gets us through tough times."

The clear sky and full moon bathed the earth in a silvery light as they made their way through Hawes and across the river. Their journey was occasionally marked by an inquisitive sheep bleating before settling back down along the limestone drystone wall. As they passed the odd farmhouse, a dog barked and an owl shrieked, seemingly complaining they were interrupting the evening's hunt. The journey up Sedbusk hill was slow, with only one or two rabbits enjoying a late feed on the grassy bank. Ian quieted the horses as they approached the village. He helped Lily down and, to her surprise, leaned forward and kissed her cheek.

"It was a great day today, Lily. Ilaniis is going to be a wonderful success. I know it."

He reached out and tucked a stray lock of hair behind her ear. The silence stretched between them. Lily could not look away, nor did she want to look away.

"Christ, Lily, don't look at me like that," he whispered. "It makes me want to do things I have no right to do."

twenty-nine

"What things?" she asked quietly, her pulse racing, knowing she wanted those same things.

"This." He groaned, pulling her into his arms and covering her lips with his.

This was not the kiss of a callow youth. It was the kiss of a man who knew exactly how to kiss a woman. When his tongue traced her lips, she could not help but open her lips for him. He needed no second invitation to explore her mouth as his hands began to explore her body. When he cupped her breast, she gasped and pulled back.

"I am sorry, Lily," he said, resting his forehead against hers. "I apologise. I had no right to do that."

"Please don't apologise, Ian. There is nothing to apologise for," she replied. "But there is something I must tell you, and I must tell you now."

"There is every need to apologise," he said, withdrawing from her. "You're a married woman with a child on the way, and I have just behaved like a cad. I need to go."

"No, Ian. You're wrong." She clutched at his sleeve. "You need to listen to me." She paused. "I haven't been entirely honest with you."

"You already told me about the baby."

"It's not that," she admitted. "This." She held up her hand. The brass curtain ring glinted in the moonlight. "This is not real."

"Go on."

"I'm not the respectable widow you and all the people in Hawes think I am," she admitted, choking back tears. "I am pregnant. That much is true. But I am unmarried."

"What do you mean?"

"Oh, Ian. It's not difficult. I was a housemaid in a grand house. The father of this child is the son of the house, who is actually missing in action and apparently wants nothing further to do with me or this child."

"Did he rape you?"

"Nothing so Gothic. In fact, he saved me from the attentions of one of his vile friends. No, he didn't rape me. He seduced me and told me he would return and marry me," she said bitterly. "Like a fool, I believed him."

He took a step back from her and dropped his hands from her arms. His hands balled into fists. "So that's why his parents didn't help you?"

"His parents refused to believe their son would do such a thing. They accused me of trying to pass off my bastard child as their grandchild, and then they threw me out. And before you ask, I told you the truth about my mother dying, but my father is still alive, and he doesn't want anything to do with me, either. Ironic, really. He was a drinker and a fighter. I know for a fact my mother was pregnant with me before they married, but now he's gone and got religion. He doesn't want an unmarried, pregnant daughter upsetting his newfound respectability."

"But why pretend to be married?" he asked.

"Oh, Ian, are you so naive?" She rolled her eyes. "Do you know what happens to women who bear children out of wedlock? What happens to the children? The stain of being illegitimate is not one that can be easily washed away. Do you think people here would have accepted me if they had known the truth? I would have been branded a scarlet woman, and my child would have had to face the threat of being called a bastard every time he stepped out of the door. I will not give this baby up. Nothing is this baby's fault, and it deserves to be wanted and loved just like every other child. That's why Annis suggested the story of the husband missing in action. I suppose we'd have eventually killed him off."

"Annis suggested this?"

"I think Annis knows more about human nature than we do," she replied, suddenly feeling weary. "I'm sorry if this has come as a shock to you, Ian. Truly, I am. If you want our relationship to be strictly that of business partners, then so be it. But for now, I'm tired. I think you should go. But now you know all there is to know. There are, I can assure you, no more secrets." She turned to go.

"Wait." Ian caught her arm. "I want you to know I don't judge you. Perhaps we can talk some more in a day or so. I need to have some time to think."

She nodded, too tired to say more but watched as he made his way to the trap and clicked the horses into motion before entering the house. Thankfully, Annis must have already gone to bed. She couldn't bear the thought of speaking anymore tonight.

Exhausted as she was, sleep did not come easily. Images of Jonathon lying broken and bloodied on the battlefield broke through her thoughts along with Ian, turning and walking away from her. Everyone seemed to have drifted away. No one knew where her brother was, Aggie had gone, Jonathon was God knows where, her mother had died, and her father wanted nothing to do with her. Was this to be her life, that everyone she loved would desert her? Was she unworthy of being loved? Then she felt the baby kick, and her mind quietened.

I have you to love, she thought as her eyes finally closed.

A low mist hung over the fields when Lily awoke the following morning. Annis, of course, wanted to know the details of their day at the market.

"You were late home," she commented.

"We stopped at Cockett's for some supper," Lily replied, hoping Annis would leave it at that.

"And?" Annis prompted, a determined look on her face. She was nothing if not a shrewd woman.

"And I told Ian about the fact that I don't have a husband, missing dead or alive, or indeed never had."

"I imagine that caused his eyebrows to raise. Why tell him now?"

Lily looked into the eyes of the older woman. "I think you've realised Ian was beginning to have feelings for me. I couldn't let him go on believing I'm something I'm not."

Annis nodded. "I see." She paused. "Do you have feelings for him?"

"He's a good man," she replied. "He deserves to know the truth, to know what he would be letting himself in for if there was a future for us, which there isn't."

Annis shook her head. "I'm not sure that's an answer to my question."

Lily sighed. "It doesn't matter. I think my relationship with Ian will be purely professional from now on. I think that's the way he'll want it, and I can cope with that."

I hope, she added silently.

Ian had become more than a friend. She looked forward to seeing him, he made her laugh, and she felt safe with him. But it was more than that. When he kissed her, she knew she hadn't wanted him to stop. He wanted her, that much she knew. And foolish as she knew it was, she wanted him.

"Now," she said, shaking her head. It was not good to be dreaming about something that could never be. "We have a lot of work to do."

She outlined the ideas she and Ian had discussed. After several moments, Annis said, "We can't do all that by ourselves. The herb garden alone can't support that amount of products and going to the market just once has shown us we must make far more than what we have been able to make so far."

"Ian seems to think we can do it," Lily replied. "And there seems to be a real need for our creams and lotions that ordinary women can afford."

"Is one bazaar and one market day enough to make that judgement?" Annis asked.

Suddenly, things became clear in Lily's mind. "Do you know what holds us back as women?" she asked.

"I've a few ideas, but go on," the older woman said wryly.

"Money, or more correctly, the control of our money," Lily replied. "We rely on our fathers and husbands for money. When I started working for the Groves, my father and Mr. Grove worked out my wages and agreed my father would have some of them. I was never consulted. In fact, it never occurred to them to consult me on anything." She took a breath. "Well, it's time we took control of our lives, and that means control of our money. This is your business, Annis. All the things we make are yours. Shouldn't you be able to make enough money to have some comfort as you get older? You could carry on making the things you love for a few women here, and that would be fine. But isn't it time we showed the world that we women can make a successful business?"

"What about Ian?" Annis asked with a smile. "In case it slipped your mind, he's not a woman."

"Ian will be an equal partner. That's what he said he wanted to be right from the outset, and credit to him, he's the one who encouraged me to think bigger than the local markets."

"I imagine he'll be the one to approach the bank for a loan. If we're going to make the amount we need, we're going to need bigger premises for a start. To be honest, I can't imagine the bank manager entertaining one very pregnant woman and one old one, even if women were allowed bank loans, which they're not." Annis laughed.

"Does that mean you're happy to go ahead?" Lily asked, her eyes shining.

Annis cocked her head to one side. "You have a silver tongue, Lily Russell. I think you had better be in charge of selling."

Lily took that as a yes.

thirty

Their second trip to the market had proved as successful as the first, with people wanting to place orders and being very complimentary about the products.

"My sister bought some hand cream. She says it's the best thing she's ever tried."

"I bought some for my mum, and she swears by it."

"It works! The cuts have gone."

"I think we're going to have to make a lot more than we thought," Lily said as they unloaded the empty boxes from the cart.

"Considerably more," Ian agreed.

As they had the first time, they counted the money and allocated money laid out by both Ian and Annis. Then they divided the rest into three. As she had done the last time, Lily took a few coins and divided her share between Ian and Annis, explaining once again that she needed to put something back into the business.

Since Ian and Lily spoke on the last market day, they had maintained a polite stream of conversation, but the fact of Lily's unmarried pregnant status stood before them like an invisible wall. It was obvious Ian wasn't ready to talk to her about it, so she did what she always did and kept busy, concentrating her thoughts on what they could do to make their business bigger by making endless notes, sketches, and writing letters—a lot of letters.

Annis and Lily were both looking at the plants on the drying rack when there was a knock on the door, and Ian walked in.

"Are you consulting the Almighty about something?" he enquired with a grin.

Annis quelled him with a look. "We're looking at what we have available for making the creams," she replied. "The growing season's almost over. We've enough lavender and rosemary, but rose petals, I needn't remind you, will be hard to come by soon."

He looked up thoughtfully. While his attention was elsewhere, Lily glanced at him. If it was his intention to keep their relationship on a purely professional level, then so be it. But it was harder than she had thought it would be. The truth was, she liked Ian—more than liked him. He was the first man who seemed to care about her, about what she thought and what she felt. He was the first man who didn't take from her. Her father had taken her childhood, and Jonathon had taken her virginity. Ian was different. He didn't take more than she was prepared to give. More than that, he gave. He was a good man, but even good men had their limits. Given how the rest of the world would judge her, he had at least not done that.

As usual, it was not long before Annis had placed a large brown teapot and a plate of freshly baked scones on the table.

"I've been thinking," Lily said, setting out her notes on the table. "I've done a little research, and I think we can buy things like rose petals and oils from bigger farms down south. The fleeces for the lanolin won't be a problem in this area. We can easily source them from the farms, though we're going to have to buy the quantity we need. We can't rely on getting enough as payment."

"We're also going to need bigger premises," Annis added. "We can't store any more than we're doing at the moment, or it will take over the whole house."

"What about the barn?" Lily asked.

"I suppose we could use that, but it hasn't been used for years," Annis replied. "It's as good a place as any to store things, I suppose."

"No," Lily went on, her eyes shining as the idea took shape. "We need somewhere bigger to make the products. Making them in the kitchen worked when it was only for the local women, but if we're to make enough for the stall, we need to make more, and we can't do it in here."

They all looked around. Every surface was covered with jars and bottles, some with the finished products and others with some of the ingredients. There was barely room on the table for the teapot.

"I think Lily's right." Ian nodded. "You need a bigger place, and you also need your home to be your home."

"You might be right," Annis conceded. "But it'll take a lot of work to get the barn into a fit state."

"Let's go and look at it now while there's still some daylight," Lily suggested.

As far as barns went, it wasn't a large one. Over the years, someone had divided it so there were three rooms downstairs and a large space on the upper floor. Lily turned on the tap in the first room. After a few moments, the water turned from brown to clear.

"Look," she said. "This room could be used to get the lanolin from the fleeces. There's plenty of room, and that old boiler, if it still works, would be ideal. It would mean we could produce far bigger quantities than we can in the scullery."

"It will need a lot of cleaning up if we're to use it for making the creams," Annis said from the bottom of the wooden staircase.

Lily laughed. "Well, I was a housemaid, so I think I know a

bit about cleaning. Mrs. Grove and Mrs. Cadeby made sure I can clean a place fit enough for the king to eat his dinner off the floor."

"I'll pitch in," Ian added. "You can't possibly expect to do all this yourself, given your condition."

Lily nodded. "That would be very helpful. Thank you."

Perhaps things could be worked out between them after all.

"This large room can be used for making and packing the products," she went on. "We shall need to put some benches in, but I think, once it's cleaned up and we put some lamps in here, we shall have plenty of room. The larger room downstairs can be used to store the stock until we need it, and the smaller room can be a little office."

"We've never needed an office," Annis said.

"I think it's a good idea," Lily replied. "If we're getting bigger, we need to keep a track of orders, stock, and accounts, things like that."

"You seem to have thought of everything," Ian said.

"For an uneducated housemaid?" she asked, an edge to her voice. She would not be underestimated again.

He sighed. "I knew you would take that the wrong way," he said. "I just think you're remarkable. That's all. You haven't had the benefits of a great education, that's true, but what you've done is far more impressive. You've educated yourself."

"It's true," Annis added, "and you've educated me. I was content with making the creams and such for the local women, but you've shown me we can be so much more. Even at my time of life, I feel excited about the future, about what we can do together."

"Oh, stop it, the pair of you," Lily replied, her face turning pink. "You both know we're all needed to make this thing work, and as far as this place goes," she indicated the shabby room, "we'd better make a start on it before we get ahead of ourselves."

The work started the following morning. Armed with a mop, bucket, and rags and dressed in an old pair of men's trousers Annis had found for her, Lily climbed the stairs to begin cleaning the barn. Truth to tell, she was wondering whether she had bitten off more than they could chew. She was prepared to work hard, of that there was no doubt, but she hadn't been brought up with the idea that she could run a business. All her knowledge so far came from her limited experience on the market stall, instinct, and the books she had borrowed from Hawes library. She recalled her mother's words as she rolled her sleeves up and put her foot on the wooden step ladder: "Aim high and have ambition."

It would take longer than she thought. There was years of dirt and dust to fight. It had taken four buckets of soap and water to clean the ceiling.

She would need a very large dollop of Annis's hand cream at the end of the day, she thought as she filled the bucket for the fifth time and took it outside.

The walls were just as bad. She was pleased to note both the roof and the walls were sound. Once they were clean and whitewashed, the barn would be a great improvement on the kitchen.

She was on the top step of the ladder, reaching into the corner, when an annoyed voice said, "What the hell do you think you're doing?"

She had not heard Ian enter the building. His voice caused her to wobble. The ladder rocked, but he steadied it.

"I'm cleaning the walls," she said through gritted teeth. "Didn't your mother ever tell you not to creep up on people, especially when they're standing on ladders?"

"You shouldn't be up a ladder," he replied, his hands gripping the sides.

"And how, pray tell, is this barn going to be made ready to use?" she replied.

"You're pregnant."

"That fact had not escaped my notice," she said, tempted to tip the bucket of water over his head.

"Pregnant women shouldn't be climbing ladders."

The bucket was getting even more tempting. "When my mother was pregnant with Betty, she climbed a ladder to clear the gutters because my father couldn't. Women, pregnant or otherwise, sometimes have to do a lot of things they shouldn't do."

He sighed. "Lily, please come down. Annis sent me over with a cup of tea, and I want to talk to you."

thirty-one

He handed her a mug of strong, steaming tea and sat beside her on a couple of old wooden crates. "I've been thinking a lot about what you told me regarding the baby. I'll be honest. You did rather take me by surprise, and it made me realise some things about myself that I'm not proud of," he paused and took a sip of his own tea. "Primarily, although I thought I wasn't the judging type, I found I was judging. I want to be honest with you, Lily. I suppose it's years of, I don't know, social conditioning. Then I thought long and hard, and the one I'm really judging is the man who did this to you."

"He didn't rape me, Ian," she said.

"No, you said he didn't, but he did take advantage of you. He was in a position of greater power, and he should have known...did know better."

Lily shook her head. "He was just a boy, Ian. He said he didn't want to die without making love to someone."

"Don't defend him, Lily. You were a virgin before, weren't you?" he ground out.

She nodded.

"Young or not, he knew what he was doing. If he wanted to sleep with someone, he could have chosen any number of women who were more experienced. Hell, he could even have paid for it."

"Stop it, Ian. You're making it sound sordid. It wasn't like that. I have to believe it wasn't like that."

His voice softened. "I just want you to be realistic. Don't paint him in a romantic glow."

She thought for a moment. "I suppose you could be right," she admitted. "The following morning, he left a note thanking me for a good time."

Ian regarded her solemnly but said nothing.

"It was the one night," she added. "One night and my whole life has been turned upside down."

He, at last, permitted himself a smile. "But look at what's happened," he said. "You met Annis, you're part of a business, and," he added, taking her hand, "you met me."

She shook her head but didn't withdraw her hand. "You're right. I would still be a housemaid, I suppose. But Ian, nothing can come of this. I'm a fallen woman, as they say—not respectable enough. Even you judged me."

"I was wrong," he said firmly. He stood and drew her towards him. "Surely you must know I have feelings for you."

She looked into his eyes. They were so dark they were almost black. "As I said, Ian..."

He lowered his head. "Lily Russell, you say too much," he whispered as his lips touched hers.

It was as though a charge of electricity flowed between them. His lips moved across hers, enticing her to open herself to him. He gathered her in his arms, holding her close as his tongue touched hers, causing her to gasp. Time seemed to slow to a standstill as the world shrank to the two of them. Lily could not have said how long they had stood there kissing each other. Finally, Ian stepped back, though he kept his arms around her.

"I think we have something special, Lily," he said. "I want to spend time with you, to get to know you more and let you get to know me," he added softly. "I want to see if we might have a future together."

She quirked an eyebrow. "Are you talking about courting me?"

He laughed. "I suppose I am. I think you deserve to be courted properly."

She could not help but laugh. "I think it's a little late for that, don't you?" she asked, looking down at her swelling belly.

He didn't return her laugh. "It may be a quick courtship, but I intend to marry you, Lily. I think you should know that. I intend to marry you. I will give this child my name, and I will raise it as if it were my own."

Lily stared at him. "Do you really mean that?'

"I would not have said it if I didn't," he replied.

"But why?" she asked. "Why would you bring up another man's child?"

"Are you trying to talk me out of it?" he asked, a gleam in his eye.

"I'm just trying to understand," she said, her eyes never leaving his face. "Most men would want nothing to do with me. Jonathon..."

"I'm not Jonathon," he cut in. He took a breath. "I want you, Lily. I think we could be good for each other, good together, and I would never want to come between you and the baby. It's taken me a long time to think about it. That's why I haven't spoken to you about it before. I had to get everything clear in my mind. But I've realised it's not only the right thing to do, but it's the only thing to do. More importantly, it's what I want to do."

She drew back slightly. "Very well, then. I shall permit you to court me." She leaned forward and kissed his cheek.

"Excellent," he laughed and kissed her soundly.

The courtship began the following Saturday when Ian announced they were going to York for the day. Lily was to be ready early to get the first train from Hawes Junction to Northallerton where they would change for the train to York.

"I've never been to York," she admitted as they settled into their seats.

"Never? It's the county town. How can you call yourself a Yorkshirewoman if you've never been?" he teased.

"There wasn't the money for outings," she replied. "Until I came to live with Annis, I'd never been out of the town I was born in," she said quietly, thinking not for the first time that the gap between her and Ian was almost as big as the one between her and Jonathon.

He was instantly contrite. "I apologise, Lily. I should have thought before I spoke." He took her hand. "It truly doesn't matter what your situation was before. It's the future that's important. Our future," he added emphatically.

Like everyone before her, Lily fell in love with York, from its sturdy walls to the magnificent minster and the narrow street called The Shambles, where it was said that neighbours could shake hands across the street from the upstairs windows.

"I've never seen anything like this," she said, her eyes shining with excitement as they looked in the shop windows at the sweets and baked goods on display. "If I lived here, I don't think I would ever want to leave. It's as though Hope is from another planet, and yet they're in the same county."

"Yes," he agreed, looking down the street. "From the Romans and Vikings to the men who built the minster, York has always been a special place. But there's somewhere else I want you to see. It's not so much the past as what might be the future," he added, mysteriously.

They walked for ten minutes before Ian stopped. "Look, Lily."

She followed his gaze and gasped. "I've never seen

anything like that before," she said as she crossed the road and stood in front of the shop.

The window display was full of pretty boxes of all shapes and sizes. Their colours ranged from the darkest red to the palest pink at one side and through to the deepest purple at the other. Each one bore the name of a perfume in silver or gold, black or white. Peering inside, Lily could see shelves laden with perfumes. There were small bottles on the counter for women to try out the scents. She looked up at the sign over the window. Burgins was written in a flowing script. The whole place had an air of luxury about it.

"This is what could be, Lily," Ian said, his hand reaching for hers, "if we dream big and work hard."

Her eyes were shining as they caught his. "Do you really think so?"

"I do," he replied. "Annis and you have created something women want, but there's nothing to stop us from branching out into perfumes as well. From what I read, cosmetics are going to be a huge market. We have the opportunity to be a part of it."

"But to do something like this, it's huge," she said. "Don't you think we'd be biting off more than we can chew? I mean, we've only just decided to work in the barn. We'd need a factory and money, a lot of money."

He laughed. "Lily, this war isn't going to last forever. At the end of it, there will be factories with plenty of spare capacity. And don't forget I'm a chemist. We know a thing or two about perfumes. Trust me, we have the skills between us, and the banks will be falling over themselves to lend us money when they see how successful we're going to be. After this war, people are going to want to forget the horror and spend their money on a little luxury."

"You seem very confident," she replied, still wary.

"I am. We have wonderful products that people want to buy. If we're to move forward, we need to do it by believing in ourselves. Of course, I have confidence, and a lot of this is down to you."

"Me?" she squeaked. "How do you work that out?"

"If you hadn't come to Sedbusk and met Annis, I wouldn't have met you, and we wouldn't have started Ilaniis. This is just the beginning. Now apart from being confident, I'm also hungry, and there's another place I want you to see."

thirty-two

Lily couldn't help the little gasp of surprise as she looked at the tea shop in front of her, the house was as crooked as a house could be before it gave in and fell over. Not one wall or window was straight.

"Oh, it's lovely," she said, her eyes shining. "It's like something out of a fairy tale."

Ian smiled back at her. "It's even better inside. That's where the food is."

It was small inside, with panelled walls, and would have been quite dark had it not been for the gas lamps being lit, even though it was only late afternoon. The light from the mullioned windows only lit the tables nearest to them. Each table was covered with a blue-and-white gingham cloth, which matched the curtains, and sparkling silverware. Ian chose the lamb cutlets, and Lily the omelette.

"Would you like some wine?" he asked.

"The one time I had wine, it didn't end well," she replied wryly. "Besides, the thought of anything alcoholic makes me feel sick at the moment," she added.

"Of course." He nodded and ordered them both tea. Once

the waitress had left them to their meal, Ian asked, "So what do you think?"

"About the business?" She chewed thoughtfully. "I'm not sure. I take it you haven't consulted Annis yet?"

"Actually, I have. It seems Annis has many more recipes, if that's the right word. Apparently, her grandmother wrote them all down. She has several notebooks she hasn't used yet."

"And what did she think of expanding?"

He took a sip of tea. "Like you, she was cautious about expanding too much too soon," he admitted.

"Then perhaps we're right." She smiled. "I'm wary of running before we can walk. After all, we haven't even signed the papers yet. Ilaniis doesn't actually exist."

"No, but Martin has drawn up the paperwork. All we need to do is sign them. I also made an appointment with Mr. Schofield at the bank to discuss a loan to transform the barn."

"Someone else you were at school with?" she asked.

"Good Lord, no. Mr. Schofield must be a hundred and three, if he's a day. But he is a good friend of my father's, and I'm hoping that counts for something."

"I should imagine he'd want a more substantial reason for granting a loan than knowing your dad," she said.

"Of course, but we'll discuss it when we meet. Now we must make tracks, or we'll miss the trains. The war has made it so there are fewer trains, so if you don't want to be stranded..." He held out a hand.

It had been a long day, and Lily was only too happy to take the weight off her feet and rest her head against Ian's shoulder as the train chugged through the countryside. Things were moving quickly, and she felt both excited and terrified at the prospect. No one in her family, as far as she knew, had ever owned a business. They'd never had the money or opportunity to do more than earn a wage through hard work, physical work at that.

Except her mother's family, she thought as she drifted off to sleep.

Perhaps they owned a business. They might be able to help.

———

Two days later, Annis, wearing her best hat with pheasant feathers, was seated with Ian and Lily in the comfortable office of Martin Hollis. The whole process took less than ten minutes for the articles of partnership to be signed and witnessed.

"And that's that," Ian said when they were outside. "Ilaniis is now officially in business. We have the market next week, and then we must focus our efforts on moving into the barn. How is Mr. Dinsdale getting on with the fitting out?" he asked.

"Nearly done, as a matter of fact," Annis replied. "The cupboards, shelves, and workbenches are done. He just has to fit out Lily's office, but that man can drink tea." She laughed.

———

Leyburn market was bustling as people were beginning to think of gifts for Christmas, and the new boxes and packages proved very popular. They had almost sold out by lunchtime when a smartly dressed woman approached the stall.

"You don't know me, but my sister, who lives in Leyburn, sent me a pot of your cream, and I loved it. My family owns a store in Leeds. We normally stock Helena Rubenstein products, but the war has made getting a regular supply somewhat difficult. We should like to have a detailed look at your stock with a view to placing an order. Perhaps you might come to Leeds with your samples, and we can discuss business in quieter surroundings than here." She indicated the market where the fruit and vegetable man was shouting out his wares in competition with the man who sold every kind of china and pottery.

"We will be delighted," Ian replied quickly, taking the woman's card. "Mrs. Madison," he read from the card, smiling. "Shall we say next Thursday at eleven o'clock?"

Mrs. Madison nodded. "That will be fine. Until then."

They watched as she climbed into a shiny black car and was driven off.

"Well," said Lily, "what was that?"

Ian grinned. "That was just the start. We won't be working on market stalls for much longer. That I can tell you."

———

Annis spilled her tea the following morning when they told her what had happened. "Well, I never," she exclaimed. "Who would have thought that Granny's recipes would get so much attention?"

"I think they're going to get a lot more," Lily said, reaching for her apron. "We had better get to work. We need to have as many things as possible to show Mrs. Madison."

They worked steadily. Fortunately, they had plenty of lanolin. The new rosemary cream worked well, but they used up the last of the rose petals.

"Does this Mrs. Madison want any of the tinctures and tisanes?" Annis asked as they packed the last box.

"I don't think so," Lily replied. "I think she's interested in the skin creams, but we saw a shop in York selling perfumes. She might be interested in those if we can produce some."

"I do have some recipes for perfumes as it happens. Granny made scents from all kinds of flowers."

"Ian was talking about cosmetics as well. He thinks people are going to want a bit of luxury when the war is over."

Annis raised an eyebrow. "Cosmetics were frowned on in Granny's day. But if it was good enough for Cleopatra, I reckon it's good enough for us."

"Don't tell me Granny knew about cosmetics as well." Lily laughed, wishing she could have met this amazing woman.

"Nothing wrong with gilding the lily, she used to say," Annis said with a wink.

The more she thought about it, the more Lily wished her mother could have met Annis. They would have gotten on well. They were both cut from the same cloth, women who made the best of whatever life threw at them and coped without complaint. She would have liked to have known more about Annis's life, but she didn't like to pry. Annis was the sort of person who spoke when she had something to say. So when Annis patted her arm as they were sitting by the fire at the end of a long day, she was surprised.

"Thank you, Lily," Annis said quietly.

"What for? I haven't done anything," Lily replied. "It's I who should be thanking you for taking me in and giving me the opportunity to be part of this business."

"For this." Annis indicated the room which was now filled with boxes. "For giving me a new lease of life. Before you came here, I was happy enough making a few jars of cream for the local women. I had no idea it could become something more. Life is exciting again, and without you and Ian, I would have just carried on until I fell off my perch."

"Annis, that isn't going to be for a long time yet." Lily winced.

"What's the matter?" Annis asked, concern in her eyes.

"Just the baby kicking," Lily replied. "I swear this little one has arms like an octopus."

"When did you say you're due?"

"Sometime around Christmas, I think."

"Let me take a look," Annis replied briskly. "I've birthed more babies than I can count."

"Do you think something might be wrong?" Lily's voice was anxious.

"Not at all, but I think there might be a surprise or two in there."

thirty-three

"Twins?" Lily's face paled. "Are you sure?"

"This," Annis indicated the small trumpet-like instrument, "doesn't lie. I can definitely hear two heartbeats, and unless I'm mistaken, there are at least three feet. So yes, I'd say you're definitely having twins."

"Oh my God," was all Lily could say.

"A double blessing."

"I'm not so sure about that."

"Do twins run in your family?" Annis asked, standing and putting the little horn instrument back in its case.

Lily thought for a moment. "I'm not sure. I don't think so on my father's side, and I don't really know much about my mother's side."

"Probably from the baby's father's side, then."

"Well, I wouldn't have a clue about that." Lily grimaced. "To be honest, the less I know about the Grove family, the better. But I must look for a cottage now. You've been more than kind to me, Annis. I should have looked for somewhere before now. When Mrs. Cadeby arranged for me to stay here, I was grateful to have somewhere to go. To be honest, I didn't think much beyond that. I can't impose on you anymore. Not with two babies."

"Nonsense," Annis said firmly. "I've thoroughly enjoyed having you here. You've given me a new lease of life, and I'm looking forward to having a baby or two to dandle on my knee. Besides, there's enough room, and you're going to need plenty of help."

Tears welled in Lily's eyes. "Oh, Annis, that means so much. Are you sure?"

"Of course, I'm sure. I learnt long ago not to say something if I didn't mean it. You'll stay here, and that's the end of the matter." Her voice was a little gruff, and Lily could see the tears gathering in her eyes.

———

A few days later, Ian and Lily took a taxi from the station in Leeds to the address Mrs. Madison had given them.

"You're very quiet, Lily. Is everything all right?" Ian asked.

"Of course," she replied. She hadn't told him the news about the twins. She needed time to gather her thoughts. "Just a little tired, I think," she explained, which was true.

The conversation was cut off as they arrived at Madison's.

"Goodness," Lily exclaimed. "When Mrs. Madison said she owned a store, I didn't think it would be anything like this."

The store stood on a corner with large windows down either side of the building. One window displayed hats, another tea dresses, a third lace and linen, and a fourth crockery and silverware. There were other windows further down the road, but Lily couldn't make out what was in them. Above the windows was a balcony with a wrought iron balustrade from which globe lamps hung. The name *Madison's* was picked out in cursive gold lettering.

This was exactly the kind of shop Mrs. Grove and Miss Eleanor would have patronised, Lily thought as she stepped towards the entrance. Ian followed with the two suitcases they had brought. A uniformed and top-hatted doorman held the door for her.

"We've an appointment to see Mrs. Madison," she said. "Which way do we go?"

"If you'll just wait here, madam, I'll send a message to her office. Someone will come down to escort you."

Lily's eyes narrowed, wondering if he thought they didn't belong here.

"If you'd like to sit here, madam," he said, indicating a plush covered chair, "it shouldn't take more than a few moments."

As Lily sat, she looked around. The store was indeed an Aladdin's cave of beautiful things. To her left were leather goods, beautiful handbags, purses, and evening bags covered with silk and little sparkling stones that caught the light. No wonder Miss Eleanor frequently returned with snags on her silk dresses. To her right were scarves in every hue. Not the heavy woollen scarves her mother had worn to cover her hair when she went shopping, but light silks and satins surely worn as decoration rather than practicality. Further on, she could see stationary, expensive writing paper. According to the poster above, one could choose to have one's address printed on them.

But it was what was directly in front of her that interested Lily the most. Here she could see the range of Helena Rubenstein cosmetics and, further along, Pond's and Rimmel. Though, she noticed none of the counters seemed to contain an abundance of stock. However, what she also noticed was that each counter had two or three women looking at the products. Her attention was drawn to the crisscross of wires above her head and the small containers whizzing by at regular intervals.

"What on earth is that?" she asked, looking up as yet another container flew past.

"It's how they pay. A lot of these department stores have this system," Ian explained. "It's a cash carrier. The assistant places the money and the docket in the container, and it zooms off to the cashier. Look up there." He pointed to a small booth above the ground floor. "The cashier takes out the money, puts in any change and a receipt, and records it in the ledgers."

As she watched the metal containers, she commented, "It's a wonder everyone gets the right change."

"I know." He laughed. "It looks chaotic, but it seems to work, and I suppose it cuts down the chance of theft."

Lily turned to him. "So the assistants basically aren't trusted to handle the money?"

He shrugged. "I suppose the idea is less people can be accused of theft if the takings don't balance at the end of the day since not many people have access to it. Don't see things that aren't there, Lily."

She opened her mouth but was interrupted by the appearance of a smartly dressed young woman in a crisp, white blouse and black skirt walking quickly towards them.

"You must be Mr. and Mrs. Russell," she said. "Please come with me. Mrs. Madison is ready to see you. Don't worry about the suitcases," she said to Ian, who had stooped to pick them up. "One of our porters will take them for you."

As they progressed further into the store, it was clear this was the place where the wives of rich mill owners come to shop. There were counters with jewellery and hats, trinket boxes and handkerchiefs. There was even a section for the most delicate lingerie. There was, as far as Lily could make out, everything a person might ever want, and all of it was of the finest quality. The thought both intrigued and terrified her. How would their collection of homemade creams and lotions possibly compete with what the store already had to offer? She wouldn't be at all surprised if they were exposed as frauds, escorted out of the building, and thrown out onto the street by the young porter striding ahead of them with their samples.

Ian took her hand. "Courage, Lily," he whispered. "She wouldn't have invited us here if she wasn't interested in what we have to sell."

Their journey took them up a grand staircase to the third floor, where double oak doors opened onto a thickly carpeted corridor well-lit by floor-to-ceiling windows with rich red-and-gold drapes and snowy-white net curtains. At the far end of the corridor stood Mrs. Madison at the door to her office.

"Welcome, welcome." She stepped forward and offered her hand. "I am so sorry to keep you waiting. Please come in."

The office was bright and airy with windows on two sides. The rich red-and-gold theme was repeated in the drapes and carpet. The walls were cream with several photographs of the store as well as two prominent ones of men from a previous generation, which Lily presumed were the store's founders. In front of one of the windows was a large oak desk, and to the side was a deep burgundy leather chesterfield with a coffee table in front. The masculine feel of the room had been softened by a few feminine touches, such as the vase of flowers on the desk and some silver-framed photographs, but the whole aura it projected was luxury and success.

"Please, do sit down," Mrs. Madison said, indicating the chesterfield. "I think we might be more comfortable over here."

In contrast with the opulence of the room, Mrs. Madison was dressed in understated elegance. She wore a fitted black skirt cut slightly above her ankles that was cinched at the waist with a narrow leather belt with a small gold buckle. Her cream blouse had a Peter Pan collar and long sleeves with stiffened cuffs. Her only adornment was a single strand of black pearls.

"I thought we might talk in here first, then you can set your samples up in the board room through there." She nodded towards the other door. "We can go through what you have and decide whether we can do business together," she finished with a smile.

She's good, Lily thought. This is the sort of woman Mrs. Grove was always trying—and failing—to be. Mrs. Grove knew how to give orders. But Mrs. Madison gives them without people knowing they've been given, and then they're carried out without a problem. I wonder if she listens to other people.

"Unless there's a better way for you to show and explain your samples to my buyers and myself." There was that smile again.

She does listen.

thirty-four

An hour later, they had explained to Mrs. Madison the nature of their products and how they were made. She was particularly interested in the fact that they were handmade with natural ingredients. "People set a great store by that kind of thing," she said. "Now do you have any questions?"

"I was wondering," Lily began, "how our products fit in with the likes of Helena Rubenstien and Rimmel. I thought Miss Rubenstein didn't sell her products outside of her salons."

"I see someone's been doing their homework." Mrs. Madison smiled. "It's true. Helena usually does everything through her salons. In fact, we're the first store to stock her products. I met her in Paris before the war, and we've always kept in touch. When she said she wanted to see how her products sold both here in Britain and in stores, I offered to take the line. We're both pleased with the way they are selling."

"I'm surprised Mr. Selfridge didn't get in first," Ian put in.

"I guess knowing Helena is the advantage I hold." Mrs. Madison laughed. "Don't be fooled into thinking that all the rich women who might buy your products shop in London, though many of them do. Leeds has more millionaires per head of the population than anywhere else, and I hate to say it, but this dreadful war has made more."

"Do you really think these people will want to buy our products?" Lily asked. "After all, we've really only sold on a market stall."

"So did Marks and Spencer, and now they have over ten stores," Mrs. Madison replied. "People want quality they can trust. Let me remind you that I heard about your creams from my sister when she tried one and sent it to me. I wouldn't have come all the way to Leyburn had I not been convinced it was something we could sell and sell well. Now I suggest we have some lunch and set out your samples so my buyers can decide exactly what they want to order to finish the deal."

They were led to a small, private dining room where several tables were laid. Mrs. Madison led them to a table in the centre of the room. Each table was laid with a white damask cloth with a crystal vase of flowers.

"I'm afraid the menu isn't as extensive as it was before the war," Mrs. Madison apologised. "Though the lamb should be very good. It is from Yorkshire, after all."

"Do all the staff get to eat in here?" Lily asked as the tables began to fill up.

"They do," Mrs. Madison replied. "Before the war, this was the directors' dining room. With all the sacrifices everyone is making, we decided to open it up. To be honest, it's been a great success. We all feel part of the same team in a much more personal way than we did before."

Lily was beginning to like Mrs. Madison more and more. "How long has Madison's been going?" she asked.

"My husband's grandfather started it in 1884, his father took it over in 1895, and my husband in 1910. Sadly, the Madison men do not tend to be blessed with longevity. My dear Harry died in 1914. Unfortunately, we had no children, and his only sister died of the measles, so I found myself at the helm."

"Did you face opposition from the directors?" Ian asked. "I can imagine a fair few of them would not be happy at the thought of a woman in charge."

Mrs. Madison smiled. "You're right, of course, but the one thing this dreadful war has given is opportunity, especially for women. What with the young men going up to fight, the older members of the board felt it would be better to have someone with the Madison name on the letterhead. As it happens, my own parents own a chain of grocery shops, Mayfairs, so it wasn't as though I was completely lacking in experience in retail. I had also helped Harry. I think—" She paused to wink at them. "—they thought that if it failed, they at least would have a ready scapegoat."

They chatted throughout the meal like old friends. Mrs. Madison, or Kathy, as she told them to call her, was interested in how they came to set up in business and expressed a great interest in meeting Annis in the future. She was particularly interested in how Lily came to be involved. Lily had decided early on that she wasn't going to hide her humble beginnings.

"Quite right, too," Kathy agreed. "There's absolutely nothing to be ashamed of. My goodness, people should admire the fact that you've pulled yourself out of poverty. Very few people would have the energy, tenacity, or ability to do so. Though, I have to warn you that there is still a great deal of snobbery you will have to face. I have been to social events in the highest places where I've overheard people talk about the 'stench of commerce' when I've walked by."

"What did you do?" Lily asked.

"I looked at their crumbling mansions with threadbare carpets and buckets collecting the rain as it came through the holes in the roof they couldn't afford to fix and thought the 'stench of commerce' smells sweeter than rotting old houses. Times are changing, and this war will make it change faster. War always does. The trouble for the idle rich is that they have yet to realise it, and if they're not careful, they'll go the way of the dinosaurs."

After lunch, it didn't take long to set out their wares in the boardroom. The buyers and Mrs. Madison went through each product, smelling them and trying it on their skin, until they were satisfied. Lily found herself holding her breath. This was a huge moment for her, one that would make the difference between them trading at market stalls or stepping up as a big business. To think that their products might be on the same shelves as those of Helena Rubenstein's, from America, was almost more than she could believe. Eventually, Mrs. Madison, after a brief, quiet conversation with her buyers, looked up and smiled.

"I think we can do business. We shall want to take all the hand, face, and body creams as well as the floral scents. The tinctures and medicines are not our sorts of things. However, there is a growing interest in cosmetics, so should you produce face powder, rouge, and something to brighten the lips, we should be interested. Now that the Hyde Park Picture House has opened, women come in wanting something to put on their lips to make them stand out like the Biograph Girl. "

"And the prices we quoted?" Ian asked.

"Perfectly acceptable." She paused before holding out her hand. Once they had all shaken hands, Mrs. Madison said, "Excellent. I shall get our lawyer to write up a contract. We shall expect delivery of the first order in time for the Christmas season."

As they travelled back to the station in Mrs. Madison's car, Ian took Lily's hand in his. "This is only the beginning, Lily. Who would have thought a few months ago that we would be doing business with the best department store in Leeds? I think we should take a trip to London and see whether or not we can sell to other stores. If Mrs. Madison thinks our goods will sell in Leeds, you can bet your boots they'll sell elsewhere."

"You're probably right," she agreed. "But what about the production? We're going to have to take on some help. We've only just cleared the barn to make more products. I'm not sure the barn is going to be big enough now, and Annis and I can only do so much, especially with the babies coming."

There was a moment before Ian said, "Babies?"

She looked up, but it was beginning to get dark. Though the lamps were lit, it was difficult to see his face. "Babies. Annis is sure I'm having twins."

"Twins?"

"I know." She could not help but smile. "That's exactly the reaction I had. But she heard two heartbeats, so twins it is."

"Well, you certainly know how to surprise a man, Lily Russell."

"If this makes a difference..." she began.

"Of course, it doesn't. Baby or no, twins or no, it's you I love, Lily. That hasn't and will not change as long as I live."

"Oh, Ian." She sighed and kissed him. If ever there was a man who deserved her love, it was Ian Steele, and, she admitted to herself, she did love him.

thirty-five

Annis was fascinated to hear about their meeting and almost choked on her tea when Lily told her how much Madison's was prepared to pay for their stock. Like Lily, she was concerned about producing sufficient stock.

"I think we'll have to take someone else on," she said. "I think young Stella Fossett might be a possibility. Her father hasn't much use for daughters. I'll ask her when she comes with the eggs."

"That'll be grand," Lily replied.

"She can't come soon enough," Annis said with a grin. "Now that you know you're having twins, you seem to have blossomed overnight."

"I know," Lily said, looking down at her stomach. "It seems to have come from nowhere."

"I once birthed a girl who didn't know she was pregnant until she virtually gave birth. Then she was back in her own clothes a week later. It's the power of the mind, you see. It's almost as though you've finally given yourself permission to acknowledge that you're having babies," Annis said, taking a sip of tea.

"Well, let's hope that's the same with me." Lily laughed.

Their conversation was interrupted by a loud knock on the door. Lily's face drained of colour when she heard the person asking, "Is Lily Russell here?"

Within minutes, Mr. and Mrs. Grove were sitting awkwardly in Annis's living room. Mrs. Grove balanced on the edge of the sofa as though something might bite her if she sat further back.

"I suppose you want to know why we're here," she said.

Lily didn't feel the need to respond but replied anyway. "I imagine it has something to do with Jonathon." Why else would they be there?

"Indeed," Mrs. Grove continued. "The thing is, Jonathon is home with us."

"That must be a great relief for you," Lily replied. She wasn't sure if she should have felt something. Jonathon was alive, after all, and he was the father of her children. Other than gratitude that another young man had survived, she felt nothing. "I am glad to hear he survived. Please give him my best regards." She stood.

"Please, there is more," Mrs. Grove went on.

It was strange to hear this woman say the word "please."

"Jonathon would like to see you."

"I don't think that's a very good idea," Lily replied, recalling how he left a note thanking her for sleeping with him as though she were a whore.

"You don't understand." Mrs. Grove twisted her wedding ring. "Jonathon is...not what he was."

Lily sat down. "Is he badly injured? Miss Eleanor said he was missing in action."

"Of course, he was injured. His plane was shot down, but he landed in a tree, thank God. What the damn fool was doing joining the Flying Corps, I don't know," Mr. Grove said, his attitude a complete change from the pride he'd had when Jonathon had signed up.

"Well, at least he's alive and back home with you," Lily replied. "But I really don't see that this has anything to do with me. You were very clear the last time we spoke that I was not to contact either you or him."

"The thing is—" Mrs. Grove paused to clear her throat. "—Jonathon knows about the child, and he wants to see you. And we—". She stopped to look at her husband. "—think it's a good idea."

"Jonathon has not been himself since he returned," Mr. Grove added, taking up the story. "We think, and his doctors think, that it might be for the best if he were to see you for a while."

"This is not a good time. Apart from the fact that I'm due soon, I have work here," Lily replied.

"You needn't stay long. Two or three weeks at the longest, that's all. But it must be soon. Now if you can. Mr. Grove will drive you, of course. The motor is parked at the end of the lane," Mrs. Grove said.

"I don't understand the rush. I could come in the new year when things have settled down." Lily was reluctant to tell them that there were two babies on the way, and she didn't want to be away from Annis when she was due to give birth.

"I'm afraid that will be too late," Mrs. Grove said, reaching in her bag and taking out a handkerchief to dab at her eyes. "Jonathon's injuries make it unlikely that he'll be with us in the new year. Please, Miss Russell, come and see him. Not for our sake, but for his. I know he meant a lot to you, and I know we were not kind to you, but he will never forgive us if we fail to take you to him before he dies."

"I don't know what to say," Lily began. "I had no idea."

"Of course, you didn't. Why would you?" Mr. Grove replied. He turned to speak to his wife. "You've made a complete hash of this, Mildred. I told you this was a bad idea. You need to be honest with the girl." He turned back to Lily. "The fact is, Miss Russell, that Jonathon is injured. Not just in his body, but his mind has been affected as well. The doctors tell us that he is unlikely to ever be able to walk again, and his lungs are almost useless. Due to the gas, you see. The thought of seeing you seems to be the one thing that is currently keeping him going. I will make it worth your while to come and spend some time with him."

Lily reared back. "Do you honestly think I want payment to sit with your dying son? That is a despicable thing to suggest."

He had the decency to look ashamed. "I apologise, Miss Russell. It's just that Mrs. Grove and I would do anything to make Jonathon's last days as comfortable and as memorable as we can."

Lily looked at the two people in front of her. They were both as well-dressed as ever, but somehow the bluster and arrogance had suddenly gone. They were parents grieving over the fact that, although their son was still with them, his life was gone. All the hopes, dreams, and expectations they had for him lay in ruins. And Jonathon? Could she really ignore the fact that a dying man needed to see her? Perhaps his conscience needed assuaging for the cavalier way in which he'd left her after having taken her virginity.

"How did Jonathon find out about the baby?" she asked.

Mrs. Grove glanced at her husband before admitting, "I told him. Eleanor threatened to tell him. She said he had a right to know that he was to be a father, but I thought it should come from me."

"What did he say?"

"He was angry, furious, that we had sent you away. He insisted we find out where you were. We went to see your father, but he had no idea where you were and was, shall we say, less than helpful. It was Eleanor who knew that Mrs. Cadeby had helped you." She paused. "I have to say, she wasn't very keen to tell us where you were. It was Jonathon who persuaded her."

"Once we knew where you were, we came straightaway," Mr. Grove put in. "We didn't want to run the risk of you leaving before we got here."

"So what do you say? Will you come, Miss Russell? Please," Mrs. Grove begged, her eyes never leaving Lily's face. "I know we treated you badly, and I don't expect you to forgive us. I know that Jonathon was less than a gentleman as well, but please, I beg you. Please come and see him one last time."

Much as she didn't want anything to do with any of the Grove family, she knew she couldn't deny a dying man. "Very well. I'll go with you."

Mrs. Grove wiped her eyes once more. "Thank you. Will you come with us now? It would be better for you in your condition, surely, to come in the motor car than make the journey on your own by train."

Lily nodded. "Not tonight. I need to prepare one or two things, but if you can wait a day, I will be happy to accompany you." In truth, the thought of the journey by train was not one she relished, and she needed to tell Ian where she was going as well as ensure that Annis would manage without her.

"Very well. There's a hotel called Cockett's in Hawes. We'll put up there for a day or so, but time is of the essence, Miss Russell." Mr. Grove stood and picked up his hat.

When they had gone, Lily went through to the kitchen where Annis was mixing a lotion.

"The Groves want me to go with them to see Jonathon," she explained.

"So I heard," Annis said, without looking up. "Are you going to go?"

"He's dying," Lily replied. "I don't think I have a choice. It's the right thing to do."

"Then you must go. But remember, there's a man here who loves you."

"What about the business?"

"We'll manage," Annis replied.

"I won't be gone long."

"Make sure you're not and take good care of yourself. Those people will do whatever it takes to get their own way."

thirty-six

There had not been time to see Ian before she left, but she had penned him a note, which Annis promised to deliver. The journey passed in almost total silence. If Mr. or Mrs. Grove spoke at all, it was only to each other. Neither of them had anything to say to her. Lily didn't mind. She really had nothing to say to them and enjoyed the relaxation of watching the scenery go by. She found the motion of the car soothing, and before long she had fallen asleep, waking only when the car pulled to a halt in front of the Grove's house. Night had fallen during the journey, and the house was in darkness, apart from a light in the window of what she knew to be Jonathon's room.

"I've arranged for you to use the blue guest room," Mrs. Grove said as they entered the cold hall. "I'll bring up a tray, then you can settle in and see Jonathon in the morning."

Lily frowned. "Shouldn't I see him now?"

"I think the morning would be best. He will no doubt have taken something to help him sleep by now. There is a nurse with him. It would be much better to see him when you're both fresh."

There was no need for Mrs. Grove to show her to the room.

After all, she had polished and dusted it many times before. Mrs. Grove made no move to do so, other than saying that her bags would be brought up shortly.

"Perhaps I might see Mrs. Cadeby?" she asked.

"I don't think we need to disturb Mrs. Cadeby tonight," came the reply. "You run along, and I'll be up shortly with a tray."

Nothing seemed to have changed. The blue room had been aired, a fire had been laid in the grate, and the bed turned down. There was even a small vase of pansies on the tallboy. She had always liked pansies. They were such cheerful flowers. Her mother had told her they symbolised loving feelings, something that was in short supply in the Grove household.

Lily took off her coat and hung it in the wardrobe. She felt like an unwelcome guest who was tolerated merely because she had something the Groves wanted, which she did. Their son wanted to know about the baby he had fathered. She sat on the edge of the bed and took off her shoes. Sitting in the car for so long had caused her ankles to swell. It was the first time her pregnancy had caused a problem since the morning sickness.

It wasn't long before Mrs. Grove herself appeared with a tray containing tea and some sandwiches. Lily wondered whether she still had maids. There had been no evidence of staff as they had come in, and the war had meant women could earn a living in other ways.

"There you are," Mrs. Grove said as she placed the tea on the small table by the window. "Get a good night's sleep, and you can see Jonathon first thing in the morning. I don't suppose I need to tell you where everything is, do I? If you would like to join Mr. Grove and myself for breakfast, we shall be in the dining room at eight." There was a slight pause before she added, "Good night."

Whether Mrs. Grove had made the sandwiches herself or she still employed a cook, Lily didn't know, but she found she was both hungry and thirsty and ate them with relish. Quite what to make of this visit, she didn't yet know.

Perhaps after she had seen Jonathon, things would be clearer, she thought as she climbed into bed and quickly fell asleep.

———

A lifetime of helping her mother with the younger children and working in this very house had made her an early riser. It was only six thirty when she walked quietly down the main stairs and towards the kitchen. As she thought, Mrs. Cadeby was already at work. There was a young woman in the uniform Lily had once worn setting a tray cloth and cups on a wooden tray to take upstairs at seven o'clock for the Groves' early morning cup of tea. A copy of *The Times* was included for Mr. Grove to read during breakfast. Lily had always believed he read during breakfast so that he didn't have to look at or talk to his wife.

"Lily." Mrs. Cadeby turned around and went towards her, enveloping her in a warm embrace. "It's so good to see you. I'm so pleased you agreed to come."

Lily returned the hug with equal warmth. "It's lovely to see you too, Mrs. Cadeby," she replied.

The older woman stepped back and looked at her. "You're blooming, Lily. Not long now, I think."

"A couple of weeks, I think. Sometime around Christmas."

Mrs. Cadeby cocked her head to one side. "It's going to be a bonny one, judging by the size of you."

Lily laughed. Mrs. Cadeby had never stood on ceremony. "Well, I had a little surprise myself a little while ago."

"Not twins?"

"Annis thinks so."

"Well, Annis has birthed most of the children in Wensley-dale, so I imagine she's right. Twins do run in Mrs. Grove's family, of course. In fact, way back, there was something of a jealous feud between twin brothers. One, of course, inherited everything due to being born a few minutes before the other."

"Well, that explains it. As far as I know, twins don't run in my family."

"Come and have a cup of tea. It's been a long time, and I'm sure there is lots to catch up on. Enid," she addressed the maid, "why don't you pour yourself a cup and sit here for a few minutes? Cook will be here shortly, and you can manage the early tea by yourself, I'm sure."

The girl nodded. "Yes, Mrs. Cadeby."

"Come, Lily. We'll go through to my sitting room where it's a bit more comfortable."

Mrs. Cadeby's sitting room was cosy with a fire burning in the grate. The curtains were still drawn as it was not yet light, and the room was lit by two gas lamps.

"So how is Annis? I hope you two get on."

When Lily described how they had started a business together, Mrs. Cadeby's eyes widened.

"I knew Annis made potions, but who would have thought they would sell? And to a grand shop in Leeds?" she said when Lily had finished.

"And that's not all. Ian thinks we should try and sell to other stores in places like Harrogate and Scarborough, even London. He and Mrs. Madison seem to think there's going to be a great demand for creams and cosmetics, especially when this war ends."

"And who is this Ian?" Mrs. Cadeby asked.

Lily blushed. "He's a chemist. He runs the pharmacy in Hawes. I got to know him when I was doing errands for Annis. He, too, suffered a terrible injury in the war. That's why he's back home. He has recovered, but there's no question of him fighting again. He's part of our business too."

"And?" The older woman raised her eyebrows.

"He's a good man," Lily admitted. "He's willing to marry

me and give the babies his name, even though the idea of twins came as a bit of a shock."

"Is willing to or wants to? There's a difference," Mrs. Cadeby stated.

"I think he loves me, and I think I love him." Lily blushed as she spoke.

"And what does Annis think? I can't imagine she doesn't have an opinion."

Lily smiled. "Annis has known him all his life. She more than approves."

"Well, I hope you know what you're doing. Think how you felt about Master Jonathon."

Lily frowned. Talk of Jonathon brought her back to reality. "I thought I loved him, and I thought he loved me. But I think it was infatuation on my side now, and he was just a frightened young man going off to war. But how is he really, Mrs. Cadeby? Mrs. Grove said he's not as he was, but she didn't go into details."

The housekeeper carefully placed her cup on the saucer and set it down on the table. "It's not really my place to say, but if the Groves haven't told you anything, it's also fair that you have some inkling of what you will find when you see him. You know his aeroplane came down and crashed into a tree which, although it probably saved his life, left him with severe physical injuries. He broke many bones. When the plane caught alight, he suffered burns that affected his lungs. Probably gas as well. How he managed to get free and get back to our side is something of a miracle. I believe he was found by a farmer who dressed the worst of his wounds, put him in his cart, covered him with sacks, and got him back to the British line."

Lily covered her mouth with her hands. "Oh my God. I hadn't realised."

"There are also other injuries, injuries we can't see." Mrs. Cadeby paused. "His mind is not what it was, Lily. He takes strong medication at night, but there are nights when he wakes up screaming. Whether it is from memories of what happened or pain, we don't know. What we do know is that the moment he was told you were coming, he became much calmer."

thirty-seven

As she remembered from her days working there, the Groves rarely took breakfast together. When they did, they barely acknowledged the other's presence. Lily began to wonder whether they actually ever spoke to each other at all. Mrs. Grove did, at least, attempt some form of conversation regarding the weather and the coming of Christmas, but she pointedly asked nothing about the baby.

After what seemed like hours, Lily finally placed her napkin on the table and said, "Might I go and see Jonathon now?"

Mr. Grove lowered his paper and looked at Mrs. Grove.

"The thing is dear," she began, "Jonathon is very different from the man you remember. He has some scarring on his face from where his aeroplane caught fire. At the moment, he needs to rest."

"It's all right, Mrs. Grove," Lily said. "Mrs. Cadeby told me. The reason I'm here is to see Jonathon, and I'd like to do it sooner rather than later so I can go back to my life in the Dales."

The couple exchanged a further look. "Let the girl go

upstairs, Mildred," Mr. Grove said. "We can talk further when she's seen him."

Lily paused at the door of Jonathon's room. Although both Mrs. Grove and Mrs. Cadeby had warned her, she was still unsure of what she would find on the other side. Eventually, she straightened her shoulders and tapped before opening the door and stepping inside. Jonathon was sitting in a chair by the window in a warm dressing gown. His legs were covered in a blanket, and he was looking out of the window. He turned at hearing her light step, and it was all she could do to keep her expression neutral. One side of his face was pitted with a red angry scar from the fire. The charred flesh had pulled on his left eye, which drooped slightly. His mouth, which had always turned up in a ready smile, was a thin line. His hands, neatly folded on his lap, had also taken the brunt of the fire.

"Lily." It seemed an effort for him to get the word out. His voice was hoarse and almost sounded rusty, as though from lack of use. "You came," he added, tears in his eyes.

"Of course, I came," she said, walking towards him and sitting on the small stool beside his chair. "As soon as your parents came to find me, I came."

"I'm so sorry, Lily." The tears were falling now.

"Shh, Jonathon. There's no need," she replied softly. "I'm here now."

"I behaved so badly towards you," he continued. "I left without a word. I was going to come back and marry you. I promise."

"It doesn't matter, Jonathon," she said.

"It does," he replied fiercely. "When my plane came down, all I could think of was getting back to you, and I didn't even know about..." He looked down at her swollen stomach. "I behaved like the worst kind of cad, something I despised in others. I seduced you and left you without considering the consequences. I didn't even know you weren't here anymore until I got back."

"Jonathon, don't upset yourself. This won't do you any good," she replied.

"But I have to say this. Please, Lily. I need to say these things, or I shall never get any peace. I was in the hospital for a long time, but eventually, the doctors agreed I could convalesce at home. I think they realised there was nothing more they could medically do for me, so my parents brought me home. When I asked where you were, they were cagey, said you'd gone to work in a factory somewhere and they'd no way of getting in touch with you. As you can see, I was not able to go see your father to ask where you were."

"It wouldn't have done you any good." Lily smiled weakly. "He has no idea where I am either."

"Your father wouldn't take you in?" he asked.

She shook her head. "My father got religion. Having an unmarried, pregnant daughter didn't fit with his newfound morals."

He sighed. "Eventually, it was Mother who told me about the baby. Eleanor told me about the shabby way my parents treated you. I'm not sure I shall ever be able to forgive them, in all honesty, and I shall never be able to forgive myself."

"Jonathon, you weren't to know," she began.

"But to leave you like that." Tears welled in his eyes again.

The door opened, and his nurse bustled in. "It's time for Mr. Grove's medication, and then he'll need to rest," she said briskly. "You need to leave, miss, and come back later."

Jonathon caught her hand as she rose. "You won't go away and leave me, will you?"

"No, Jonathon. I promise I will come back later when you've rested," she replied, dropping a kiss on his forehead.

"Thank you, Lily," he replied.

Mrs. Grove was waiting at the bottom of the stairs as Lily

came down. "How did he seem?" she asked, twisting her wedding ring round and round.

"Quite calm, I think. He explained why he hadn't been able to contact me earlier," she replied.

Mrs. Grove at least had the decency to look guilty before she straightened and took a breath. "Perhaps you would join Mr. Grove and myself in the drawing room. There are things we wish to discuss with you."

The drawing room hadn't changed since Lily had been responsible for tidying and polishing it in what seemed a lifetime ago. The curtains were open, and Lily could see evidence of an early frost on the lawn. She hadn't noticed in the dark last night, but the garden was not as neat as she remembered. Even in winter, their gardeners had always kept it neat and tidy. The fire had been lit, and so had the lamps. It was daytime, but the room was still a gloomy room with dark furniture and heavy drapes. Mr. Grove was sitting in one of the armchairs by the fire. He folded the newspaper and laid it aside as the two women entered the room.

"Now, Miss Russell, Lily," Mrs. Grove began. "We weren't kind to you when you came to us and told us of your...predicament. For that, we apologise. The thing is, circumstances have changed. As you can see, Jonathon is no longer the man he was. The doctors told us the fact that he survived at all is nothing short of miraculous, but we have to face reality. Jonathon is unlikely to live much beyond the end of the year. His lungs and heart have been badly affected."

Lily could only think that his mother had already cried all her tears because the way she spoke about her own son was completely without emotion. She could have been talking about a complete stranger.

"Surely something can be done," Lily replied.

"All that could be done has been done," Mr. Grove stated. "Our son has been sent home to die."

"I'm so sorry," Lily responded. There was nothing else to say.

The couple exchanged a glance, and Mr. Grove nodded to his wife. "The thing is, and I would like you to hear me out, we have a plan that will benefit all of us, but it very much depends on your cooperation," the older woman went on.

"I don't understand." Lily looked from one to the other.

Mrs. Grove cleared her throat. "We should like you to marry Jonathon as soon as possible so that the child is legitimate. You are our only hope of having a legitimate grandchild."

"I beg your pardon." Had she heard them correctly? This was the same couple who had denied that their son had made her pregnant just a few short months ago. They had wanted nothing to do with her and threatened her should she mention their son was the father.

"It's quite simple, girl," Mr. Grove continued impatiently. "You and Jonathon marry so the child you're carrying is born within wedlock. That being the case, the child may eventually be able to inherit my business. If it is a boy, of course."

"What about Eleanor? If she has children, you will have other grandchildren."

Mrs. Grove sighed. "I'm afraid we're rather estranged from Eleanor. She did not approve of the way we treated you or of our trying to keep Jonathon from seeing you when he came home. In any case, any son Eleanor has will be brought up to inherit the title her husband will one day hold."

She could not say she was surprised. Eleanor had been growing apart from her parents ever since she had met her, and the war had allowed her more freedom to live her life in the way she wanted. She was glad to hear that Eleanor had married her dashing young man and that he had survived so far at least.

Lily's eyes narrowed. "And what part do I play in this grand scheme when Jonathon dies?"

"You give the boy to us, of course. We will formally adopt him and see that Jonathon's child is raised to be a gentleman befitting his station. You will be recompensed, of course," Mrs. Grove replied.

"You will stay here, obviously, during your confinement, even if Jonathon is no longer with us. When the baby is born, you can go and get on with your life with sufficient money to see to your needs until you decide what you want to do. We would even give you a reference," Mr. Grove announced grandly.

"Twins," Lily said. "Actually, I'm expecting twins."

thirty-eight

"Twins?" Mrs. Grove said, placing her hand on her heart.

"Not surprising," Mr. Grove commented. "Twins run in both our families. In fact," he went on, "this could be even better, particularly if one shows more competence than the other."

Lily could scarcely believe her ears. This horrendous couple was talking about their grandchildren as though they were mere operatives. Worse, actually. It was as though they were commodities with value only if they were useful.

"What if one of them is a girl?" she asked with barely concealed contempt.

"In that case, you would keep the girl, and we would take the boy," Mr. Grove answered without hesitation.

"What if they're both girls?" Lily could not help herself asking.

"That would present more of a problem," he conceded.

"Because girls would be of no use to you, I imagine."

"Of course," Mr. Grove replied without a hint of embarrassment. "Women are not leaders of business. The men wouldn't respect them, you see. A woman's place is in the home."

"What does Jonathon think of this?" she asked, not trusting herself to reply to their request.

Once again, there was the now familiar exchange of glances.

"We haven't actually discussed it with Jonathon," Mrs. Grove admitted. "He was too ill when he first came home, but it was only when he insisted we find you and bring you here that the idea came to us."

"What do you think he will have to say about this idea?" she asked.

"I'm sure he will be amenable. After all, he would want his children to be brought up properly. The fact is that we can do far more for them than you will ever be able to. They will have the best schools, the best of everything. You will know they will want for nothing. Don't you owe it to them to give them the upbringing you didn't have? It's for the best. Surely you can see that," Mrs. Grove said.

"Jonathon will do as he is told," Mr. Grove added. "He's in no position to object."

Lily rose, keeping both her expression and her voice neutral. "You have given me a great deal to consider. I think I'll just go to my room and rest for a little while, if you don't mind."

"Of course," Mrs. Grove replied, smiling. "You need to keep healthy for the sake of the babies."

Back in her room, Lily was too angry to rest. She paced for a while but then sat down and penned letters to both Annis and Ian, which she decided she would post after lunch when Jonathon was resting. In many respects, what the Groves said was true. If she married Jonathon, her children would have the best of everything, and they wouldn't have to bear the stigma of illegitimacy. But the thought of the Groves having anything to do with the upbringing of her children filled her with dread, and the thought of giving up her children made her feel physically ill.

And what of Ian? He was a good man, and he loved her, as she loved him. He had already offered to marry her and bring the children up as his own. Few men would be prepared to raise another man's child. He would be devastated. She doubted he would ever forgive her, and why should he? Her musings were cut short by a knock on the door. Mrs. Grove entered bearing a tray with tea and biscuits.

"I thought you might need a little refreshment," she said, placing the tray next to Lily on the bed and sitting down beside her. "Have you had time to think over our proposition?" she asked.

"Not really," Lily replied.

"It really is for the best. When you marry Jonathon, you gain the protection of the Grove name. The children will not be bastards. They will be raised in wealth and comfort. Mr. Grove and I have talked about it, and even if one is a girl, we shall see to it that she marries well. You will be well paid and can get on with whatever it is you want to do with your life. You were trained well here. Perhaps you might wish to work in one of the bigger houses. Lady Brampton, for example, is a personal friend of mine, and she is always looking for staff. I could recommend you if you would like."

"And what would happen were I to refuse your offer?"

Mrs. Grove's attitude changed to something Lily was far more familiar with. Gone was the smile and soft, persuasive voice. "It's quite simple, Miss Russell. We shall go to court to gain custody of the children. You will be painted as an unfit mother. They will be taken away from you, and you will be left with nothing."

"Surely you wouldn't want the story splashed all over the newspapers," Lily replied.

"Oh, I don't think we need to be worried about that. Mr. Grove is a well-respected businessman, even more so now that he has been helping out the government. He knows people who can make this sort of thing happen without our names being involved at all. The only person to lose would be you." She smiled a sickly smile. "I urge you to think carefully and come to the right conclusion. And quickly, as time is of the essence." With that, she rose and left.

Unable to stay indoors for a moment longer, Lily donned her coat and hat and set off for the postbox at the end of the lane. Walking in the brisk winter air cleared her head and she was able to think about the so-called proposition, which was more like blackmail. If they could have gotten away without the ignominy of having her for a daughter-in-law, no matter how short a time, they would gladly do so. That was the only bargaining chip she held: the all-important legitimacy of her children. They didn't care about her, and they seemed to care very little about their own son, but they wanted the children. She didn't really understand why. They didn't appear to like children, and she had no doubt that at the earliest opportunity they would be sent away to boarding school. The only explanation she could come up with was the idea that they wanted to keep their wealth intact for another generation. Money, power, and position seemed to be the only things they were interested in, and there was no way she would consider, even for a moment, giving in to their plans.

As she posted her letters, she noticed a familiar figure walking towards her. There was no mistaking her father's gait. She waited until he drew near.

"Hello, Dad," she said. For all he hadn't been the best of fathers, he was still her dad.

"Now then, our Lily," he replied. "I'm just off to work at t' pit. I'm on afters." He indicated the snap tin he held in his hand.

Lily raised her eyebrows. "I didn't know you were working down the mine," she said. "I thought you had a job for life with Mr. Grove's business."

"I thought so an' all," he replied, "until young Mr. Grove

got yer in the family way an' they sent yer away. Once yer'd gone, I was no longer needed. 'E paid me off, but not enough to live on for long, so I'm working at the Main."

"I thought you hated the thought of going underground," Lily replied.

"I do, but I couldn't do that sort of thing now. Going down below is a young man's game. There's not many old miners. No, I'm in t' lamp room. I get t' lamps and tags ready for t' men before they start their shifts and collect them in when they come back up top."

"I see."

"I knew yer were 'ere. Yer can't fart in Hope without someone knowin'. So what do they want with yer? I thought they wanted nothin' more to do with yer."

Lily laughed. "They don't. Not really. Jonathon is back from the war."

"I'd 'eard that an' all. In a bad way, though, I 'eard."

"He won't live long, according to the doctors."

"I can't say I'm fond of the Groves by any manner of means, but war's a terrible business. There's already a lot of lads who won't be coming back to Hope. Them that do are broken. I wouldn't wish that on anybody," he said quietly.

"The thing is, they want me to marry Jonathon to make the babies legitimate. Then the children can apparently inherit from the Groves one day," Lily explained.

He looked at her steadily before saying, "And is that what you're goin' to do, lass? Marry the lad?"

She sighed. "I don't know, Dad. It would mean that the babies would never go short of anything. It might give them the best chance in life."

"Babies?" he looked pointedly at her swollen belly.

"Twins, Dad. I'm having twins, and not long now."

"Well, I'll be capped."

"And I've started a business with two friends making

beauty creams and the like. It's going well. We're just about to expand," she added.

He tipped his cap back. "Yer were always an ambitious one, our Lily. I knew Hope would never be big enough for yer. So why do yer need to marry the Groves' lad?"

She looked into the distance before replying, "Part of me thinks it would be good for the children to know I was married to their dad. If I wasn't married to their father, they would have to live with the shame of it. You know what people are like. But in all honesty, I'm not sure."

She suddenly felt the need to tell her father precisely what the Groves had offered. "The thing is, Dad, once Jonathon is gone, his parents want to adopt the children and bring them up. I wouldn't have a say. I doubt they'd let me see them."

He let out a low whistle. "I can't say I'm surprised. That sort think they can buy whatever they want. If yer want to marry t' lad, marry 'im. But do it for t' right reasons. Bairns need their mam and dad, I'd say. But yer must do what yer think is for t' best."

Lily smiled. It was not often her father had offered advice. He gave his opinions frequently, but advice, he gave rarely. "Thanks, Dad," she replied, leaning in and giving him a kiss on the cheek.

He looked surprised. "What's that for?"

"Talking to you has been helpful," she replied.

He nodded. "Just remember, lass. If they want yer kids to inherit something, all they 'as to do is write a will. P'raps yer might come down before yer go, let me know what yer decided. Besides, there's other things we need to talk about. Things that need to be said. Things that should have been said before."

"I will, Dad. I will."

He tapped his cap and carried on walking towards the long lane running to the pit that dominated the lives of so many in Hope. She watched as his figure receded into the distance. He seemed softer than she remembered. In the past, he'd either been angry and drunk or, since her mother's death, judgemental and unforgiving. Something had mellowed him, and for the first time, she began to think there might be a chance of reconciliation between them.

thirty-nine

Lily had just arrived back at the house and was just hanging up her coat when Mrs. Grove came out of the sitting room.

"There you are. No one knew where you had gone. You really must let someone know if you're going out," she admonished. "Please come with me."

Lily was surprised to see Jonathon sitting and dressed in one of the wingback chairs. She was shocked to see how ill-fitting his clothes were now that he had lost so much weight. It hadn't been so noticeable when he had been wearing his robe. His face was white, as though the effort of getting dressed and coming downstairs had taken all his energy, and she dreaded to think how he would get back upstairs.

"I wasn't expecting to see you down here," she said as she went over to him and sat on the stool next to his chair.

"It's the first time Jonathon has shown any interest in coming down," his mother said, speaking for him.

"I was worried about you," he said, his eyes searching Lily's face. "I thought you might have been frightened away."

She smiled. "I'm a Russell, remember? We stand and fight."

He returned her smile. "I should have remembered that. You aren't afraid of anything."

He turned to his parents. The smile disappeared. "As to this notion of blackmailing Lily into marrying me, how could you?"

There was a shocked pause before he went on. "I heard your conversation with Lily this morning, Mother. My room is close by. Both doors were open, and you were never able to keep your voice down."

"Now then, Jonathon. Your mother and I are only doing what we think is best for the children. They need to be legitimate if they're to be a part of our world," his father said.

Jonathon looked at his father as though he was seeing him for the first time. "I'm not sure I want my child to have anything to do with you and your world."

"Jonathon," his mother replied in a shocked voice. "We only want to do what's best."

Slowly, Jonathon raised his hand and brushed it through his hair. "Would you and Father leave Lily and I alone, please?"

When they had gone, Lily stood and closed the door. *This was going to be a difficult conversation*, she thought as she returned to her seat.

"I'm so sorry, Lily. I had no idea when I asked to see you that my parents would suggest such a thing."

"It's all right, Jonathon. I don't blame you," she replied before taking a deep breath and adding, "It's only fair to tell you that there is no chance I would give up my children to your parents."

"I don't blame you," he replied with a sad smile. "Look at the mess they made of bringing up Eleanor and me." He paused for a moment as a thought struck him. "Children, my parents and you said children."

Lily smiled at him. "As if this couldn't get any more dramatic, I'm having twins."

"Twins?"

"That's right. Annis, who I live with, is an experienced midwife. She heard two heartbeats. I should hope it's twins, or this baby is the size of an elephant," she said, looking down at her stomach.

He laughed. "You could always make me laugh, Lily. That's what I love about you." He became serious. "The thing is, dearest Lily, if I could go down on one knee and propose properly, I would. Regardless of my parents' plotting, it would make me the happiest man if you would agree to marry me."

"Oh, Jonathon," she replied. "I really don't think it's such a good idea. I know it was only a few months ago, but we're both very different people now."

His face hardened. "Is it because I'm like this?" He indicated his body.

Lily reared back. "Of course not. How could you think such a thing?"

"I knew chaps in the hospital who were engaged to be married, but their girls just couldn't bear the sight of them and ended it, usually by a letter," he said quietly.

She traced a pattern on her skirt. "The feelings I have for you, Jonathon, are not the same as they were when..." She trailed off, unable to finish the sentence.

"When we made love?"

She nodded. "I was halfway to being in love with you. I will always love you in some way, Jonathon, but it's not in the way a wife loves her husband," she finished.

He looked at her for a long time before asking quietly, "Is there someone else?"

She looked at the flames in the fireplace. "Your silence would suggest there is."

Finally, she raised her head. "I met someone. A good man. He has offered to marry me and raise the children as his own. There are not many men who would do such a thing."

"I see." He, too, looked at the flames.

"I'm sorry, Jonathon." She took his hand in hers. "I'm truly sorry."

"When I came back, I couldn't stand to be near a fire," he said quietly. "It reminded me, you see, of being in the crash and smelling my own burning flesh. The pain of shattered bones is nothing to the pain of burning. I'm not the same man I was. Far from it. I have seen and done things I will never be able to forget. War is not a grand adventure. It's not bunting and parades. It's mud and blood and terror and men crying out in agony for their mothers and sweethearts. It's a hungry beast that steals men's lives and minds."

Lily said nothing, knowing he had to say these things.

"And yet," he went on, almost unaware she was there, "in all the chaos and confusion, there are acts of kindness that remind you of the essential goodness of humanity. The farmer who rescued me took a great risk in getting me back to our line. He didn't know me. He just knew I was an English airman. I needed help and he gave it." He turned to her. "I want to do the right thing by you, Lily." He raised a hand as she took a breath.

"I know I don't have long left. I won't make old bones as they say. I would say I have a few weeks left. Months, at most. The crash damaged things inside, you see. My parents know. They keep talking about what I'll do when I'm recovered, but they know and I know it isn't going to happen. So what I'm asking, and I know I'm being selfish and asking a lot, is will you marry me, Lily? Let the babies bear my name. It's the only thing I can give them. You have probably guessed that there is no possibility of me being a proper husband to you in the bedroom, but it would make my last hours on the earth bearable, especially if I live to see the little ones born."

"But what about your parents? I will not let them raise our children," she said fiercely.

"I will make sure they understand that they are the grandparents and nothing more. They will have as much or as little contact with them as you decide," he said with some of the old firmness in his voice.

"I don't know, Jonathon…"

"They are my children as well as yours," he said quietly. "I'm not saying that to blackmail or to make you feel guilty, but as their father, I would like to know I provided for them and gave them my name. It would give me some dignity, at least. And I will provide for them, Lily, as well as you."

Lily looked around the room before she spoke. It was a room designed to impress and show off the Groves' wealth, like the rest of the house. Yet that wealth had made none of them happy. The Groves' marriage, as far as she could tell, had been an unmitigated disaster. Neither of them even liked the other. As far as she could see, neither of them had ever loved the other nor had any expectations to do so. Their daughter was estranged from them, and their only son, the apple of their eye, was dying.

She felt sympathy for Jonathon. It would be a heartless woman who didn't feel for his situation, cut down in the prime of his life and dying inch by inch. But she didn't love him. Was it right to agree to marry him for the sake of the babies and to give a dying man his last wish? And if she did, what would happen to her relationship with Ian? He had been more than understanding, and his love had been generous, but there was surely a limit to what he might tolerate. The thought of her marrying another man, no matter how brief and convenient that marriage might be, might just be more than he was prepared to tolerate.

She felt Jonathon take her hand. "I love you, Lily. I know you don't love me, but I can live with that. Damn, I hadn't intended to beg, but I will. Please marry me. For the sake of our children." He paused before adding, "It won't last long."

"Oh, Jonathon" was all she could say through the tears. "I will marry you. For the sake of the children."

His eyes were brimming with unshed tears. "Thank God. I promise you, Lily. You won't regret it."

I hope not.

forty

"I know yer said yer'd marry the lad but are yer really sure?" her father asked as he poured out cups of tea for both of them.

The house hadn't changed much since she had said goodbye to him a few months before. She noticed it was neat and tidy with gleaming copper pans hanging above the range and crockery stacked on the shelves above the sink. There was no dust on the dresser, and the floor had been fairly recently washed. Even the front doorstep had been whitened.

"To be honest, Dad. I'm not sure. I feel sorry for Jonathon. He's in a bad way, and he told me himself that he doesn't expect to live much longer. He wants to give the children his name. It's the least and only thing I can do for him now," she replied, taking a sip of the strong brew.

"But is it enough, lass?" he asked. "Yer mum and I were married for years, and I know I didn't treat 'er as I should. For that, I shall always be ashamed. But we did love each other. Gettin' wed's the easy part. It's the marriage that's difficult."

"I don't think you understand. It's the beginning of December now. It'll take at least three weeks to sort out a special licence and such if you give your permission. That takes us to Christmas. Jonathon is not expecting to see much beyond the new year. It's that desperate. I only hope he gets the chance to see his babies." Tears gathered at the corners of her eyes. "There won't be much of a marriage," she finished.

He took another drink of tea. "What about after?" he asked.

"I'll go back to the Dales. I like it there, and it's a good place for the kiddies to grow up. Lots of fresh air and places for them to run about. That's where the business is. I have friends there as well. It's where I belong now, Dad."

"And this business, is it going to keep yer? Bairns cost a lot."

"The business is going well. We've started selling to a big store in Leeds, and Ian is going to see other stores in Harrogate and Scarborough. He thinks we might be able to sell to the big stores in London, especially after the war."

There was a pause before he asked, "Who is this Ian?"

She couldn't help the blush that flushed her cheeks. "He's one of the partners in the business."

Her dad raised his eyebrows. "Look, our Lily, I wasn't born under the cabbage patch. I don't think yer'd be blushing like a beetroot if he was just one of t' partners."

She took a breath. "Ian's the chemist in Hawes. I met him when I was collecting ingredients for Annis, the other partner in the business. We started working together. At first, Annis and I told people I had a husband who was missing in action, which as it happens was sort of true. To be honest, it was difficult. Ian came to have feelings for me, but he wouldn't act on them because he thought I was married. Eventually, I told him the truth. I didn't know at that time that Jonathon would come back. The thing is, Ian is willing to marry me and raise the children as his own. Ian loves me, and I love him," she finished.

"And does this Ian know that Master Grove has come back, let alone that you're planning to marry him?"

She shook her head. "I sent him a note before I set off

saying I had to return to Hope on urgent family business. When we met at the postbox the other day, I was posting a letter to him telling him about Jonathon."

"But not that you're about to wed?" her father pressed.

She shook her head again. "No, I couldn't think of the right words."

"I don't think there are any right words. Not for this."

"He's going to hate me, isn't he?" she said quietly.

Her father crossed his arms and looked into the fire. "I don't know if hate is the right word. If he loves yer as yer say he does, but 'e's bound to feel angry at first. Of course, 'e will. After 'e's offered to do the right thing by yer, it'll come as a kick in the teeth. 'E'll probably be jealous as well. It's what men do."

"Do you think he will understand and forgive me?" she asked, dreading to hear the answer.

He took the poker and poked at the coals, making a flame burst into life. "I don't know the man, so I can't really answer for 'im."

"What would you do?"

He laughed. "Well, in my younger days, I would probably 'ave taken a few pints of beer and attempted to rearrange young Groves' face. I'd 'ave done things that are stupid and shameful, but that's the fool I was back then."

"And now?"

"It doesn't matter what I think now. It's what yer young man thinks. Though I imagine you've chosen one that's a lot more sensible than me," he replied.

"That's the trouble." She sighed. "I don't know what will happen. He might forgive me and wait for me, or he might want nothing to do with me. He might think I was using him to give my children a name until something better came along."

"Well, if 'e's any kind of a man, I should think 'e'll let yer know soon enough."

"The house is looking good, Dad. Obviously, Alice and Dorothy have got you sorted out," she said, looking around. "Are those new curtains?"

"Aye," he replied. "But I sent yer aunties back. They were constantly mithering me about something. I pay a woman down the road to come and do for me. Nice woman. Beryl Ellis. Yer might remember 'er. She was widowed when there was that disaster down t' mine back in '11. She made them curtains. Said the old ones looked like rags. To be honest, I'd never noticed."

Lily smiled. It was nice to have a conversation about everyday things. "Well, I take my hat off to her if she got you to make a few changes."

"She's changed a few things for me," he admitted. "I know it's not long since yer mother died, our Lily, but me and Beryl are walking out. I'll always love yer mother, make no mistake about that, but I'm t' sort o' man who doesn't like being on 'is own, and that's a fact."

Lily could not say she was surprised. She had seen him go to pieces when her mother died, and she couldn't find it in herself to condemn him. "It's all right, Dad. Life's too short. If you and Beryl are happy, then that's fine."

"She won't replace yer mother," he said fiercely, tapping his chest. "Not in 'ere, but we're more companions, like. Something I should 'ave done with yer mother a long time ago."

"I'd like to meet her," Lily replied.

"Come for dinner on Sunday. Cooks a grand piece of beef, does Beryl."

"I should like that," she replied. She hadn't seen her father look so happy and contented for a long time.

"I don't suppose young Grove will be able to come, will 'e?"

"No. He can only walk a few steps, and that's with someone helping him. He came downstairs the other day to talk to me, and he's had to stay in bed ever since. I think we're going to have to have the wedding at the house. Mr. Grove is taking me to the registrar to see if we can get dispensation to do that. Apparently, they let soldiers get married in the hospital if they can't get to church, and Jonathon is as sick as many in the hospital."

"Well, give me the piece of paper, and I'll sign my permission." They both moved to the scrubbed table. Her father brought over a pen and ink. "There," he said. "It's done."

Lily looked at the well-scrubbed table. How many times had she sat there with her brothers and sisters as her mother ladled out some kind of stew she had conjured up from an onion, a carrot, and a few cabbage leaves with precious little else? "Have you heard from Aunt Polly about the children?" she asked.

He shook his head. "Not since they left. To be honest, I'm more than a little ashamed of 'ow I treated yer mum's sister. I don't think I was quite in my right mind when yer mum... Yer know. I was wondering if you knew owt about them."

"No, but that's partly my fault. I was too raw when I first got to the Dales. Then we started the business, and I haven't had the time. Or more to the point, I haven't made the time to write. But I will. I promise. I don't suppose you know anything about our Tommy?"

He shook his head. "Nothing, but as they say, no news is good news. 'E's a scallywag is our Tommy. Whatever 'appens, 'e'll come right. If 'e fell in 'orseshit, 'e'd come up smelling of roses."

"Well, thanks for signing this, Dad," she replied, standing up and putting the paper in her handbag before retrieving her coat and hat.

"Come back again soon, our Lily. I've missed yer."

"Me too, Dad. Me too."

forty-one

The meeting with the registrar was more than "just the formality" Mr. Grove had promised her. They sat in the small, stark registrar's office as the woman went to consult the chief registrar about whether it was possible for Lily and Jonathon to be married at the Groves' house. Since his proposal, Jonathon had barely been able to get out of bed, and his breathing was worse. Lily would often sit and read to him, which he liked.

The door opened, and a man Lily assumed to be the chief registrar entered. He was a tall, thin man with bushy eyebrows and a moustache.

"Your request is rather irregular," he began. "Marriage ceremonies in private homes were made illegal many years ago. According to the law, a wedding must be a public affair."

"So I understand," Mr. Grove said in what Lily assumed was the voice he used when he was negotiating a business deal. "But under the circumstances..."

The registrar pointedly looked at Lily. "I'm afraid those circumstances are not sufficient to merit a relaxation of the law." He sniffed.

"Not those circumstances, man," Mr. Grove replied, irritated. "My son has fought for king and country and is severely injured. He will be unable to make the journey to church for the wedding, let alone stand through a service. Most likely, he won't be able to get out of bed. That's the reason we need a special licence and permission for the wedding to take place at home."

The man steepled his fingers. "As it happens, there has been a letter from Whitehall telling us that, in certain circumstances, we may take a more relaxed view. Wounded soldiers have been married in hospitals. That sort of thing. Possibly because of that sort of thing." He looked pointedly once again at Lily.

Lily felt her temper rising. "I'll thank you to treat me with respect. This—" She pointed to her stomach. "—takes two to make, or did you think it came about through immaculate conception?"

"There's no need to take that tone, young lady," he bristled.

"I'm sure she meant no offence," Mr. Grove interjected quickly, patting Lily's hand while sending her a warning look. "The thing is," he went on, "my son, speaking frankly, will not live long enough possibly to even see the birth of his child. The least he can do is give it his name. That's all we're asking. The vicar is willing to perform the ceremony, and there will be more than enough people to witness it."

The man looked from one to the other. Lily returned his gaze, determined not to be intimidated and thinking he was deliberately taking his time in order to underline his power.

"Very well," he said finally. "I'll ensure the paperwork is completed correctly. It's a Church of England vicar, I assume?"

Mr. Grove nodded.

"That makes things simpler. They are all registrars, so he will be able to complete the marriage certificate on the day." Now that it was happening, Lily quickly penned notes to Annis and Ian, telling them of her impending marriage.

Once the special licence was granted, Mrs. Grove went into action arranging the wedding, much to Lily's amusement.

"You must have something new to wear," she told Lily. "Though I can't for the life of me think of any style that will make you look less…"

"Pregnant?" Lily provided helpfully. "Perhaps a couple of curtains joined together?"

Mrs. Grove gave a tight smile. "I don't suppose it matters what you wear. It's hardly a society wedding, is it?"

In the end, Mrs. Cadeby came to the rescue and ran up a dress in navy blue with cream piping at the cuffs and neckline, cleverly cutting it to disguise much of Lily's bump.

"A decent-sized bouquet should do the rest," she said as she finished the final fitting.

They were just sitting down to a cup of tea when the doorbell rang. Lily almost automatically stood to answer it.

Mrs. Cadeby laughed. "Sit down, Lily. Young Ruby will answer it. She's not been here long, and she's nothing like as good as you, but she's learning and willing to work. I doubt she'll stay long, though. They pay better, and the hours are shorter everywhere else."

Within a few minutes, Ruby appeared in the doorway. "It's a gentleman for you, miss." She nodded to Lily.

Mrs. Cadeby raised her eyebrows. "Were you expecting someone, Lily?"

She shook her head. "I don't think so. Unless it's my dad."

"It's a Mr. Steele, miss, and he wants to see you. I've put 'im in the drawing room. Mr. and Mrs. Grove have gone out, so you should be all right in there."

Ian was standing by the fireplace, twisting the band of his hat in his hand when she walked in.

Ruby should have hung that up, Lily thought absently.

"Ian, I wasn't expecting you, but it's a wonderful surprise."

"What did you expect after sending your note saying you are getting married?" he asked.

"I explained what was happening," she replied.

He ran a hand through his hair. "I need to hear it from you, Lily. Not in a note. How do you think I feel learning that the woman that I love, the woman that I intended to marry and give her children my name, is now going to marry someone else?"

"He is the father of the children," she replied quietly.

"Who abandoned you without a second thought," he shot back.

"It wasn't like that, Ian. He went to war. He didn't know I was pregnant until he came back injured. As soon as he found out, he demanded his parents find me."

"And you came back because all this—" He gestured around the room. "—this is what you want, is it?"

"That's not fair, Ian," she said. "I came back because Jonathon is dying, and he wanted to see me. Don't you see? He wanted to put things right between us. He can't be a true father to his children. The only thing he can give them is his name. As a matter of fact, I hate all this. Believe me, Mr. and Mrs. Grove would be delighted were I not here at all."

He sat down on the chesterfield. "I didn't come here to fight."

"I know you didn't," she replied.

He turned to face her. "Do you love him? This Jonathon?"

"Not in the way I love you, Ian. You have to believe that. The love I thought I felt for Jonathon was infatuation. That's all," she replied, her eyes never leaving his. "What I feel for him now is sympathy and pity that his life is ebbing away almost before it's begun. Every time I see him, he's a little weaker. I only hope he lives long enough to see the babies born, and that's all he is hoping for as well."

"And what if it's not? What if he has a sudden rally? It can happen. Look what happened to me. I wasn't supposed to survive, and I did. What happens then?"

"I don't think that's likely to happen. Jonathon's heart and lungs are injured from the gas and fire," she replied. "Apart from that, his mind isn't strong either, if I'm being honest."

"And yet you're willing to tie yourself to him." His tone was harsh.

"What do you expect me to do, Ian?" Her voice was sharp. "I can't turn my back on the dying man who is the father of my children."

He stood up. "Well, that says everything I need to know, doesn't it, Lily? My love isn't enough. I can't compete with a dying man, and I won't be second best. Or did you expect me to wait around patiently until you really are the widow you claimed to be when we met?"

"Ian, you're being unfair, but in a way, I did think you would be willing to give me and the children a second chance," she admitted.

He clamped his hat on his head. "You are quite unbelievable."

"And you are letting your masculine pride get in the way," she shot back. "I'm trying to do what's best for everyone, for Jonathon and the children. I thought you would understand. I don't love Jonathon. I love you."

"We're legally bound together through our business contract, and I will honour that. The business will go on. In the few weeks since you've been away, it has already moved on, but I think it's best if we keep our relationship strictly business from here on. Goodbye, Lily. I hope your marriage brings you all you hope for."

She waited to hear the front door slam before she dissolved into angry tears.

forty-two

"I heard you had a visitor," Jonathon said softly, as though every word was something of an effort.

He was sitting in the chair by the window with a rug over his knees. Since going downstairs to confront his parents, he had not left his room. Every time Lily saw him, he seemed a little paler and thinner, as though he was fading before her eyes. In fact, he was determined to wear the morning suit hanging in his wardrobe, but Lily doubted he could withstand the effort of getting into it. They had already decided the wedding would have to take place in his bedroom rather than the library, to the disappointment of his mother. Much as she didn't approve of Lily, she certainly didn't like the thought of what she called "a hole-in-the-corner affair."

"Ian visited," she replied. "He's very angry about this wedding." There was no point in denying it.

Jonathon closed his eyes for a moment. "You explained to him why, I trust."

She nodded. "I think he feels, in some way, betrayed after he offered to marry me and raise the children, that I have flung his kindness and his love back in his face."

"He'll come round."

"I don't think so. I have never seen him so angry, and there's the matter of his male pride, that I chose you over him." She sighed.

"Male pride has a lot to answer for," Jonathon replied with a small smile. "Would it help if I spoke to him?"

She shook her head. "I don't think so. Not at the moment at any rate."

"Well, write to him directly after the wedding and ask him to come back. I'll talk to him then. I know you don't love me, Lily, and that you're doing this for the sake of the children, but you deserve to love and be loved. If I can do something to assist when I'm gone, then I'll do whatever I can. That I promise."

Tears brimmed in her eyes. "Thank you, Jonathon. You're a good man. And who knows? If things had been different..."

"One of the things I have learned, Lily, due to all this—" He waved his hand."—is that we must live for the moment. I don't have the luxury of time. There's no point in thinking I do. I have to make the most of the little time I have. I want to put right the things I have done wrong if I can."

"And that includes me?"

"It includes you. I was an arrogant fool, and you deserve better. You deserve this Ian, and if I can make him see reason, I will," he finished, his voice almost a whisper.

"You were always a good man, Jonathon. Better than you think," she said quietly, but he was already asleep.

––––––––

"There you are. Done," Mrs. Cadeby said as she fixed the cream silk flowers in Lily's hair. "You make a beautiful bride."

"If you discount the fact that I am the size of a small house," Lily replied.

"Even considering that." Mrs. Cadeby smiled. "And as I said, the bouquet will hide a multitude of sins."

"Sins indeed," Lily replied, grimacing.

"I didn't mean..." Mrs. Cadeby began.

"I know you didn't," Lily replied. "I just got a twinge of backache. It must be what comes of sitting around doing nothing."

"I hope that's all it is," the older woman replied.

"Of course. The babies aren't due for another day or so, if that's what you mean."

"Babies come in their own time. Let's just hope they wait until after the reception. Cook will be most unhappy if there's no one here to eat the wedding cake." Mrs. Cadeby smiled and handed Lily the bouquet of cream roses and lilies. "Are you ready?"

Last Christmas, Lily would have never believed the path her life had taken. She was in the same house, but instead of serving the guests, she would soon be a part of the family. The house was decorated with streamers and the usual tree in the hall. Evergreens had been placed on the mantelpieces, and she knew Jonathon's room, where the wedding was to take place, had been decorated with holly, ivy, and red ribbons. It was hard to feel festive, but for Jonathon's sake, she was going to try. It would be Christmas Eve in two days, after all.

Jonathon's room was large but felt crowded with the wedding party. His parents were there, of course. She was delighted to see Eleanor and her husband as well as Annis and her father. A cloth had been placed over the tallboy with two candlesticks to form a makeshift altar. Jonathon's chair was in front of it.

With the help of his nurse, he rose to his feet as she entered the room. He wore a morning suit, though as she suspected, it was now far too big for him. The vicar wasted no time in starting the service as they all knew Jonathon would not be able to stand for long. They said their vows.

There were no readings, and the ceremony took ten minutes before they were pronounced man and wife. Jonathon leaned forward and kissed her cheek before sinking onto his chair. The register was signed, and the certificate was given to Lily.

"It's a tradition that the wife receives the marriage lines," the vicar explained. "It ensures that the man can't deny it," he added with a chuckle.

It was a very strange wedding breakfast in the dining room. The bridegroom was unable to attend as the service had taken too much out of him and he had to rest. Mr. Grove made a short speech, thanking people for coming. He made little reference to either his son or his new daughter-in-law. Mrs. Grove maintained her social smile.

"Well, as the parents are clearly not going to mention it, welcome to the family," Eleanor said to Lily as they sat together on the sofa enjoying a cup of tea after the meal.

"Thank you," Lily replied, "and thank you for coming. I know things have not been good between you and your parents."

Eleanor glanced to where her parents were sitting away from their guests. "Yes, I rather think this is the last time I shall see them, at least for some time. Would you believe they have not said a word to me or Barty since we arrived? In fact, it was only that Jonathon wrote and asked us to come. We didn't even know about the wedding as they didn't bother to tell us, as though they thought I wouldn't want to attend my own brother's wedding," she said with disgust. "A pity, because they won't be meeting their grandchildren on this side of the family, and I strongly advise you to keep your children from them."

"Actually, they wanted me to marry Jonathon, have the babies, and disappear so they could adopt them," Lily admitted.

"God, they are truly awful! I'm so sorry." She patted Lily's hand. "If there's anything I can do, you know, when the time comes…"

"Thank you, but I'll be fine. I am in business now, so I shall be perfectly able to take care of the children."

Eleanor smiled. "I can't say I'm surprised, Lily. You were always going to stand out from the crowd. What business are you in? I thought you'd gone to live in the wilds of Yorkshire."

Lily returned the smile. "I did, and it was the best thing I could have done. You see the woman over there talking to Mrs. Cadeby?" She inclined her head. "She's actually Mrs. Cadeby's aunt. She's been making natural creams and lotions for farmers' wives for years and has taught me. To cut a long story short, we took some to market, and now we're making them for Madison's."

"Madison's? The department store in Leeds?" Eleanor raised her eyebrows.

Lily nodded. "Not only that, but our other partner is in the process of showing our goods to similar stores in Harrogate, Scarborough, and even London. Mrs. Madison thinks there's going to be a big demand for all kinds of cosmetics, especially after the war is over."

"My goodness, Lily. You sound as though you're definitely on the up and up. A woman of business… That's wonderful. I am both pleased for you and proud of you," she said, adding, "And who is this third partner? Are they here?"

Lily dropped her eyes. "No, Ian couldn't be here."

Eleanor raised an elegant eyebrow. "Ian? Is there something else I should know?"

Lily shook her head. "No, Ian is a chemist and a good addition to the business, but that's all," she said firmly.

"If you say so," the other woman replied. She stood up. "Well, Barty and I must be going. It's a long drive, and there's snow forecast. Don't forget, darling, if I can do anything, I will."

Eleanor had not long gone when Annis plopped herself down next to Lily.

"Well, you've done it now," she said.

"I know," Lily replied. " I think it's the right thing to do, don't you?"

"Of course," Annis said. "For the sake of the kiddies and the lad upstairs, but I only hope it turns out to be the right thing for you as well."

"It will have to be," Lily answered. "I will make the best of it."

The older woman caught her hand. "I don't doubt that you will, but I can't help feeling that you've lost an opportunity with Ian."

"I know," Lily admitted sadly. "The thing is, I love Ian, but I was trying to be fair to Jonathon, whose life was stolen from him. He should have some rights as the father, and I thought I was being fair."

"And you expected Ian to fall in with your plans?"

Lily nodded. "I suppose I did. I thought he would be prepared to marry me once...you know."

Annis shook her head. "I think you have something to learn about men, love. A man has his pride, but he also has his insecurities. Ian is hurt, upset, and angry that you chose Jonathon over him. He probably feels that you're still in love with the poor lad and that he can't compete with a dead man."

"Do you think he will come around?" Lily asked.

The older woman shrugged. "He may. At the moment, he's gone off on what he calls a 'selling trip' around the country, partly because he wants to get away from thinking about you. While you've been away, he's thrown himself into the business, looking for other barns and premises so that we can produce more. To be honest, it's getting a bit much for me."

"I'll come back as soon as I can," Lily promised.

"Don't look so down in the mouth." Annis winked. "I said

he'd gone on a trip around the country, not that he'd joined the Foreign Legion."

Lily laughed, then gave a gasp.

"What is it?" her friend asked.

"The babies. I think they've decided to make an appearance." Lily grimaced.

forty-three

"Thank God you're here," Lily said through gritted teeth.

"Aye, it's a good job I am," Annis replied, applying a damp cloth to Lily's brow. "That young doctor looked wet behind the ears. I doubt he's seen a baby born, let alone helped birth it. I sent him to look at young Jonathon instead."

"Is Jonathon all right?" Lily asked, clenching her teeth as another spasm hit her.

Annis waited for the pain to subside before she replied. "I think the wedding took more out of him than he showed. But," she added, "the important thing for you is to concentrate on getting those babies out. Your husband has plenty of people helping him."

"How much longer do you think it will be?" Lily asked.

Annis shook her head. "Babies have a habit of coming when they're ready, but I would say it won't be long now. You're nearly ready to push. It's important you don't do it until I tell you. Otherwise, you'll exhaust yourself."

"I didn't know it would hurt this much." Lily grimaced.

Annis laughed. "If they did, no woman would have a baby, and they would certainly never have more than one, but you'll forget it as soon as they're here. Trust me."

Mrs. Cadeby entered with fresh towels and hot water. "How are you doing?" she asked.

"Well, it's not something I would care to do every day," Lily replied drily.

"At least you've not lost your sense of humour." Mrs. Cadeby laughed.

"Indeed," Annis put in. "Some women use language that would make a sailor blush."

"I can see why." Lily grunted as another spasm of pain hit.

"Almost there now, Lily," Annis said, checking the clock on the bedside table. "The contractions are only a few minutes apart. These babies seem eager to make your acquaintance."

For an hour, the contractions continued at a steady rate.

"I think the babies have decided to stay where they are," Lily said quietly.

"They're just getting themselves ready for the big push," Annis replied. "They'll be here within the hour."

As she spoke, Lily's face contorted. "I have to push." She gasped.

"Yes, it's time." Annis stood up. "Mary, you take her hand." She turned back to Lily. "This is where the hard work begins. It's not called labour for nothing."

Annis was true to her word. Within the hour, both babies had entered the world crying lustily, a boy and a girl, the girl being the elder by two minutes. Between them, Mrs. Cadeby and Annis had the babies cleaned and weighed on the kitchen scales. They also cleaned and set the room to rights. There was a knock on the door, and Mrs. Grove entered.

"Is everything all right?" she asked. "I thought I heard a baby cry."

"All went well," Annis answered. "Lily is fine, if a little sore and tired. The babies are small. Twins usually are, but they have all their fingers and toes and are healthy as far as I can see."

Mrs. Grove came further into the room, her eyes darting to

the two babies nestled in Lily's arms. "Should we get Dr. Burgess to look at them to check?"

"That won't be necessary, Mrs. Grove," Lily replied. "Annis has plenty of experience in these matters."

Mrs. Grove looked at the older woman with distaste and said, "As you wish. What are they? Are they both boys?"

"One of each," Lily replied, looking down at the two bundles in her arms.

"You'll call the boy Hubert, of course, after his grandfather, and you may name the girl Mildred, after me," Mrs. Grove stepped closer.

"Jonathon and I haven't discussed names yet, Mrs. Grove," Lily replied. Mrs. Grove was her mother-in-law, but she would always be Mrs. Grove, the lady of the house. Furthermore, there was no chance on earth she would name her children after the two people who wanted her out of their lives and made no attempt to hide the fact.

"May I tell Jonathon his children have arrived?" she asked.

"Of course," Lily replied, "and as soon as I can, I'll bring them for him to see."

Mrs. Grove nodded and left.

"Not quite the wedding night you were expecting, I imagine," Annis said as she sat down and helped herself to a cup of tea and a biscuit.

"No." Lily laughed. "Though, you might say we somewhat jumped the gun on that one. I don't even have cots ready or anything."

"I shouldn't worry about that," Mrs. Cadeby said. "There are two Moses baskets in the attic from Master Jonathon and Miss Eleanor. I'll get them directly, and there are plenty of sheets we can cut down. I believe Mrs. Grove has done a bit of shopping for you, so I don't think these babies are going to want for anything."

"Apart from a father they're never going to know," Lily replied sadly.

"There's no use thinking like that," Annis said. "It's a tragic shame what's happened to that young man. I don't deny it. But there are many babies who are never going to meet their fathers at all."

"I suppose you're right." Lily sighed.

There was another knock on the door, and her father appeared. "I 'ope it's all right to come in. Mrs. Grove said I might." He twisted his cap around. It was clear he was not comfortable in the company of so many women, particularly after childbirth. "Can I see the bairns?" he asked.

"Of course, Dad," Lily replied with a smile. "You can hold one of them if you want."

"Oh, I don't think so, lass. They're so tiny, I might break one," he replied, moving closer. "My but they're a bonnie pair. Yer mum would be proud."

"It's hard to think of you and Mum as grandparents."

"Aye, Grandad Joey, that's what I'll be," he replied, smiling down at the two infants, his smile growing broader as one of them curled their tiny hand around one of his fingers. "Look at that," he said in wonder. " 'E must know it's me." He leaned in towards the child. "When yer a bit older, lad, I'll take yer to t' football on a Saturday."

"Well, you're welcome to do that, Dad, but that one's the girl." Lily laughed.

"Well, I'll look after yer lass. Better than I did yer mum," he said softly.

"Thanks, Dad. I hope you see them as much as you can." Lily's eyes filled with tears.

"I'll see them whenever I can, if yer'll let me." His eyes too were moist.

"Of course. They'll want to see their Grandad Joey," Lily replied. She knew he felt he had failed as a father, but she had a feeling he would try very hard to be a good grandfather.

"I'd best leave yer now, lass. Mrs. Grove said I 'adn't to tire yer." He put his cap in his pocket. "I'll be gettin' along now. I 'ope to see yer afore yer go back up north."

"I'll bring the babies down before I go," she promised.

When he had gone, Annis asked, "When are you planning on coming home?"

She liked the sound of that. Sedbusk had indeed become home. She couldn't imagine living anywhere else. "It will rather depend on what happens here," she replied. None of them said anything, for they all knew that it truly depended on how long Jonathon had to live. She knew she wouldn't leave while he was still alive. That had been the unspoken agreement between them. She owed it to the twins to let them have as much time with their father as possible.

———

It was two days before Jonathon was well enough to see either Lily or the babies. Annis had once again proved to be a Godsend, teaching her how to breastfeed with patience.

"It's best for the babies, and it'll help you to get your figure back," she said, adding, "Though you're young, so I imagine you'll be back to normal in no time."

"Thank you for all you've done for me, Annis. I'll never be able to repay you," Lily said, giving the older woman a hug.

"Go on with you," she replied. "It's time these two met their daddy."

forty-four

Jonathon was sitting in the chair by the window with a rug over his knees. He turned around as she entered and smiled at the two bundles in her arms.

"I was beginning to think I'd never see those two," he said, his voice thick with emotion. "Bring them closer please so I can see them."

Lily walked forward and bent down so he could see their faces. "It's like looking at two peas in a pod," he said.

Lily laughed. "Well, they're already showing their personalities. When he's hungry, he quickly gets into a rage, while she's a little more patient."

"May I hold them?" he asked.

"Of course," she replied without hesitation. "You're their daddy. Let's put a pillow on your lap."

"Because I'm too weak to hold them?" he asked, a hint of bitterness in his voice.

"Of course not," Lily replied. "It will just lift them a little so you can see their faces better." She took a pillow off the bed and laid it on his lap before placing a child in his arms. "There," she said. "Meet your daughter."

As if on cue, the baby opened her eyes and looked steadily at Jonathon.

"Hello, baby girl," he said huskily. "You won't remember me, but always know that I love you." He looked up. "It's almost as though she knows me," he whispered.

"Of course, she does. You're her father. Nothing can ever take that away from you—or her."

"What have you decided to name them?" he asked.

"I thought we might do that together." She smiled. "Though I have to tell you I won't be naming her after your mother."

He smiled. "I don't blame you." He was silent for a moment before adding, "She's beautiful, like a little rosebud."

"That's it, then. Let's call her Rose. Are you happy with that? It's a lovely name, and it shouldn't offend anyone. There's no one in my family called Rose."

"I think it's perfect," he replied. "What do you think, little Rose?" He smiled down at the child as she responded with a huge yawn. He looked up at Lily. "I think she likes it." He paused for a moment. "Could we add Ruby? A precious jewel, and a beautiful flower."

Lily thought for a moment. "Rose Ruby Groves or Ruby Rose Groves. I think the second sounds better, but whatever happens, we'll call her Rose. With names like that, she'll have a lot to live up to. I hadn't realised that you were such a romantic." She laughed.

He returned her smile. "May I hold my son now, please?"

Lily laid Rose on the bed and settled her brother on Jonathon's lap. He stirred a little but didn't wake.

Jonathon looked up at her. "Have you thought of a name for this one?"

She shook her head. "I've always liked the name Edward," she replied. "I think Edward Jonathon would suit him."

"Edward's a bit of a mouthful for a little one," he replied, his eyes turning back to the sleeping infant in his arms. "How about we call him Teddy while he's young? If he wants to change it when he's older, he can."

"That's settled, then. Edward Jonathon and Ruby Rose." She smiled, suddenly happy and glad that Jonathon had been there to choose their names. It was one thing she could tell them about their father when they were old enough to understand.

"Thank you." His gaze held hers.

"What for?"

"For adding Jonathon to Teddy's name. In that way, he'll always carry a part of me with him."

"Oh, Jonathon." She sighed. "You'll always be their father. Nothing can ever take that away from them, and I promise," she added. "I promise I'll make sure they know all about their father." She paused. "Well, the good bits," she added with a smile.

"Oh, Lily, if only I could be there to be a proper father to them and a husband to you." A lone tear spilled from his eye and slid slowly down his cheek.

Lily stopped it with her finger. "It's no use thinking like that, Jonathon. The important thing is to make the most of the time we have left together."

Jonathon seemed to rally. Whether it was the birth of his children, or whether it would have happened anyway, Lily couldn't say. He took an interest in his appearance and insisted on getting dressed every day. His appetite improved, so he began to lose some of the gauntness and gained some colour in his cheeks. He spent as much time as he could with the children, and Lily found herself looking forward to sitting with him as he held his son and daughter, insisting on reading stories to them.

"You do know they don't understand a word," she said one day at the end of *Hansel and Gretel*.

"Of course, they do," he replied with a grin. "They are extremely intelligent children. And even if they don't, I want you to be able to tell them one day that's what I did."

"I'll tell them everything about you," she assured him, "including the fact you tried to change their nappies and managed to stick the pin in your finger."

"At least I tried. I honestly don't know how you women do it without injuring yourselves or the child." He laughed.

It was good to see him laughing again, and some of the lines of pain etched around his mouth seemed to have faded.

"Lots of practise," she replied crisply, remembering that it was always she who had been pressed into helping with her younger brothers and sisters as none of the boys had ever been expected to do anything.

"I was wondering how you feel about taking the children out for some fresh air. They're obviously thriving, and Mother has bought a special pram. If we wrap them up warm, it will do them good. I could come too. It's been an age since I felt the sun on my face." He looked wistfully out of the window where spring had come early, causing the cherry tree to already be laden with blossom. "Jonathon, are you sure?" she asked.

"Just a little walk down the drive. I'm sure I can manage that. I can always push the pram if need be," he assured her. "It will do me good as well," he added, seeing her worried face.

"If you're sure..." she replied.

Although the sun was shining and the day was bright, there was little warmth in it, but they were soon bundled in coats and scarves and slowly making their way down the drive. The motion of the pram quickly sent the twins to sleep. After a few steps, Jonathon took hold of the pram.

"Are you all right?" Lily asked anxiously.

"Never better," he replied, though his breaths were coming in short gasps.

"Perhaps we should turn back," she suggested.

"Damn it all, Lily. I intend to at least get to the end of the drive."

Their pace slowed as each step was an effort for Jonathon.

"Please, Jonathon, let's go back. You've done really well, much better than we could have hoped a few days ago."

"I will get to the end of the drive," he repeated.

"You're being ridiculous," she snapped. "What does it matter if you don't get to the end?"

"It matters to me."

She could see the sweat beading on his forehead. "What are you trying to prove?"

"That something of the old me is still in here somewhere," he replied.

"Your pride will be the death of you."

"Quite possibly." He gave her a weak smile. "But look, Lily. The gates are in sight. I made it," he said before sliding to the ground.

"Jonathon!" she screamed. "Jonathon, get up!"

There was nothing for it but to run back to the house as fast as she could with the twins and get help. Within minutes, Mr. and Mrs. Grove, Mrs. Cadeby, and the nurse came running down the drive with Jonathon's wheelchair, which they managed to lever him into and push back to the house. Once inside, Mrs. Grove immediately telephoned for Doctor Burgess while the others settled him on the sofa.

"What were you thinking?" Mrs. Grove spat as she hung up the receiver. "He's not strong enough to be gallivanting out."

"He wanted to go outside," Lily replied. "It was just a little walk to the end of the drive."

"If you had any feelings for him, which I doubt, you would

have stopped him," the older woman's voice was tight with fury.

"He thought it would do him good," Lily explained.

"He doesn't know what is good for him."

Lily could feel the anger—the anger she had kept in check until now—bubbling up inside her. "Perhaps what Jonathon needs is to be treated like a man. Not like a child or a piece of china wrapped up in cotton wool."

"How dare you?" Mrs. Grove shot back. "Jonathon is my son. I know what's best for him. I've always known what's best for him."

"And he's my husband, and he's a man who wants to be in control of his own life, no matter how little there's left of it. If he wants to go outside instead of being cooped up in his room, then that's what he'll do," Lily said, looking the older woman directly in the eye.

"If Jonathon dies because of this stupid jaunt, I'll never forgive you." Mrs. Grove turned and left the room.

"I don't think I'll ever forgive myself either," Lily murmured.

forty-five

Her fears on this occasion were unfounded. After a few days in bed, Jonathon declared himself fully recovered, though the chill had left him with a persistent cough. The birth of his children and his wedding to Lily seemed to have a positive effect on Jonathon. He saw the children every day and was even well enough to be dressed and sit in the sitting room in the afternoons. His appetite improved once more, and he began to lose the gaunt look that had shocked Lily when she first saw him. He declared he was well enough to go out for a drive in the motor car, though Lily had her doubts. His mother was firmly against the idea.

"Don't be ridiculous, Jonathon," she said. "It's far too cold for you. Look what happened the last time. We can't risk you catching another chill on top of everything else."

"I'll wrap up warm, Mother. I promise. Perhaps you could look after the children for an hour while Lily and I take a short drive," he suggested, knowing full well that his mother could not resist the opportunity of sitting with her grandchildren, something he was sure she had avoided with her own children.

"Wait a minute," Lily exclaimed. "Who will drive us? You aren't able to, and I can't."

"Then it's time you learned," Jonathon replied. "I'll teach you."

"In an hour?"

"An hour today, an hour tomorrow, and by next week, you'll have the hang of it." He grinned. "Besides, a business-woman needs to be able to get around independently, doesn't she?"

As ever, Jonathon got his own way. They were soon sitting in the car on the driveway with Jonathon suitably muffled up in a hat, thick overcoat, scarf, and gloves, sitting in the passenger seat explaining to Lily the basics of the internal combustion engine.

"Are you sure about this?" she asked nervously.

"Of course. It will be a breeze," he replied. "If Eleanor can do it, you certainly can. Trust me, the hardest part will be getting the thing started."

As it happened, years of physical work helped Lily. The crank turned, and after a couple of slight grinding noises, they were off down the drive, though not in a straight line.

"We'll stick to the quiet lanes until you get the hang of it," Jonathon said, though it didn't escape Lily's notice that he was holding on to the strap at his side.

Forty minutes later, he declared, "Well, bless me, you're something of a natural, Lily."

"I am enjoying it," she replied, laughing. "I imagine it's like the feeling you must get when you're flying." She stopped abruptly. "I'm so sorry, Jonathon. I didn't think."

"It's all right, Lily, and yes, you're right. There's an exhila-ration that's similar, but we'd be fooling ourselves if we thought I'd ever experience flying again," he said calmly.

Lily glanced at him. He had gone pale and his hands were shaking. "I think we must go home, Jonathon. You're getting cold."

"Very well," he agreed, more readily than she had expected. "But we shall try again tomorrow. Now that you've mastered the basics on the quiet lanes, you need to practise on bigger roads."

"Only if you feel up to it," she replied.

"I most certainly will be. I haven't had so much fun since... Well, I don't know when."

It was all too easy to allow herself to believe this was her life. The twins were almost six weeks old, and she had fallen into a routine with the help of Mrs. Cadeby. Annis had left after two weeks, needing to get back to the Dales. The new barn was up and running, and Ian's selling trip had been more successful than they could have imagined. They now had orders from stores all over the north of England. It was likely they would have to increase their production yet again.

"We're going to have to take on more girls," Annis commented as they both looked at his most recent cable. "There's no chance we can fulfil all those orders without more help, especially now that your life is here."

"My life isn't here, Annis. Not forever. Once things change, I'll be back. I promise."

"If that's what you want. I wondered whether, once the babies were born, you might change your mind. Motherhood can change a woman," Annis said quietly. "But if you're coming back, don't leave it too long. Things seem to be changing at a pace. I don't know if I can keep up."

"I'll be back as soon as I can," Lily assured her.

The new young doctor, Dr. Lawrence, still called every two or three days, though any information about her husband's condition was directed towards his parents. So when Lily met him on the landing, she was pleased to see he was on his own.

"Dr. Lawrence, may I have a word?" she asked, opening the door to her room.

The young man hesitated before entering. "I don't have much time, Mrs. Grove," he said, putting on his coat. "I have three more house calls to make and another surgery this afternoon."

"I appreciate that, Doctor, but I would like to know what Jonathon's health is really like. His parents are reluctant to share anything you say, either with him or me."

Dr. Lawrence looked at her for a moment. "What do you want to know?"

Lily took a breath. "Well, I would say he has improved over the last few weeks. His colour is better, and he's eating more. We've been going for drives in the car. Well, he taught me how to drive, actually. Jonathon just seems more interested in life now."

"I'm not going to give you false hope, Mrs. Grove. Mr. Grove is never going to recover. His injuries are too severe. I would agree that there have been some improvements, but from my experience, I would say that men in his position often have a rally before the end."

Lily's eyes widened. "Then what you're saying is that we should prepare for the worst?"

"I'm afraid so. The improvements over the last few weeks are temporary, possibly due to his marriage to you and the birth of his children having had a positive effect on his spirits. The human spirit is quite a remarkable thing, but it cannot overcome everything." His words were harsh, but his tone was gentle.

"What will happen?" she asked simply.

"At the end, do you mean?"

She nodded.

"He will fade away, his breathing will become shallow, he will be confined to bed, and he will gradually become weaker as he will be unable to eat. But rest assured, Mrs. Grove, I shall ensure he suffers no pain. There are marvellous drugs now to control pain. I shall see to it that he is comfortable."

"How much time do you think we have left?" She could not help but ask.

"I would say a few weeks at most." He patted her arm. "I'm sorry."

She smiled. "Thank you for being honest with me, Doctor. At least now I know. There's nothing worse than false hope."

He nodded. "I have tried to explain this to Mrs. Grove senior, but she refuses to accept it. Perhaps you might be able to convince her."

"I very much doubt that, Doctor, but I will try."

Lily watched from the window as the doctor got into his car and drove away. He had given her much to think about. She would always be fond of Jonathon and loved him as the father of her children. That would never change. But she was not in love with him. She knew in her heart that she was in love with Ian, even though they had parted ways in anger. Emotions fought within her. She didn't want Jonathon to die, but she knew he hated being an invalid. Many times he had told her that were it not for her and the children, he would rather have died in the crash than become a shadow of the man he had once been.

forty-six

Lily had taken the children to see her father and meet his lady friend, whom she liked immediately. Her father had admitted he wasn't the sort of man who could be on his own, but Beryl seemed to have the measure of him. Clearly, there was affection between the two of them, but it was clear that Beryl wouldn't stand for any sort of nonsense, and that's what her father needed. Joey had enjoyed pushing the twins around the streets in their new pram, and Lily had stayed longer than she had intended.

As she approached the house, she could see Dr. Lawrence's car parked in the drive near the house. As she drew nearer, the front door was flung open.

"Where in God's name have you been?" Mrs. Grove shouted. "Never mind," she said as Lily began to answer. "Come in quickly. It's Jonathon."

Jonathon was lying on the chesterfield in the drawing room with a rug over him. She could see from the doorway that his complexion was deathly pale and his breathing shallow. For a moment, she had thought he wasn't breathing at all until, suddenly, he gasped. Dr. Lawrence stood nearby drawing a liquid into a hypodermic syringe. Jonathon opened his eyes and seemed to focus on her.

"Lily," he rasped, "I thought you'd left me."

"No, Jonathon," she said, sitting on the edge of the sofa. "I just went to visit my father."

"I forgot. Things are getting a little hazy. Don't leave me," he said, his hand reaching for hers.

"I won't, Jonathon. I promise," she replied, squeezing his hand lightly. "What happened?"

"Jonathon woke from his rest and panicked that you weren't here. Somehow he got himself out of bed and to the top of the landing. We heard a crash and found him at the foot of the stairs having some sort of seizure," his mother replied. "We managed to get him in here, and Dr. Lawrence came immediately. Jonathon would not settle until you arrived back." There was definitely an accusatory tone to her voice.

"Would you all leave Lily and me for a moment?" Jonathon asked, his eyes never leaving hers.

Dr. Lawrence put down the hypodermic. "Just for a moment."

When they had gone, Jonathon struggled to sit up. "Don't stop me, Lily. I need to say this because, having seen it happen to so many others, I know what's coming, and it's coming soon. I want you to know that I love you, Lily. I have loved you for a long time, almost since the moment you opened the door to me. That moment seems like a lifetime ago. I regret not having the courage to do anything about it until it was too late. I know you don't love me in the same way, but that doesn't matter now. When I'm gone..."

"Oh, Jonathon."

"When I'm gone, I want you to contact a solicitor, Mr. Walker. He has an office in Hope near the town hall. I made a will. It's important you speak to him. It's not the solicitor my father uses, because I don't trust him. Promise me you'll do that."

"I promise." She said as she nodded.

He smiled the ghost of a smile. "Good. There's just one more thing, Lily. I can't live the life I should have had, but I want you to live for the both of us. Do it for me, Lily." He sank back against the cushions and closed his eyes, exhausted. They were the last words he said.

When the doctor came back in, he gave Jonathon an injection of morphine. "He will feel no pain," he said.

"What will happen?" she asked.

He drew her to one side and spoke quietly. "He will sleep, his breathing will get shallow, and eventually, it will stop. There really is nothing more I, or anyone else, can do for him. The damage to his heart and lungs was too great. I suspect he now has some kind of infection, which is causing the decline rather than the fall. Frankly, it's a miracle he's kept going this long."

"But he's seemed so well these last few weeks. He taught me to drive, and we even had a little walk not long ago," Lily said, her eyes on the sleeping figure.

"As I told you, people sometimes have a rally before the end," the doctor said, following her gaze. "My belief is that the thought of his wedding and children kept him going longer than any of us thought possible. But it's best he goes now. Otherwise, the pain would get worse, and he would be dying inch by inch."

"He would hate that."

"Yes, he would," Dr. Lawrence agreed.

Lily's eyes suddenly shot to his. "Can he hear us, do you think?"

"Not from here. That's why I took you to the side. Though some believe hearing is the last sense to go. Nurses have reported that dying soldiers seem calmer if they talk to them, even at the point of death. So by all means, talk to him. It might ease his passage from this world to the next." He paused. "I shall leave you to sit with him and say your goodbyes, but I shall not be far."

"Thank you, Doctor," she replied. "Would you do me a favour?"

"I shall try."

"Would you please entertain Mrs. Grove? I believe her presence would upset Jonathon."

He looked at her with a gentle smile. "I shall go and sit with her. It's a wife's place to be with her husband at this time."

She sat beside him and took his hand. "I won't forget you, Jonathon. I promise, and I won't let the children forget you either," she whispered, brushing a stray lock of hair from his forehead. "I shall tell them of the night we danced at The Queen's and that you taught me to drive. I shall tell them about your time at university and about your flying. They will know that their daddy was a hero. I promise I won't let you down. We'll all live for you, Jonathon, and our children will always know that you loved them."

Eventually, as Dr. Lawrence had said, Jonathon's breathing became shallower and shallower until his chest rose and fell no more.

"Be at peace, Jonathon," Lily whispered, pressing a last kiss on his brow.

As soon as she opened the door, Mrs. Grove rushed in, collapsing at the side of the sofa, her grief overwhelming. She took Jonathon in her arms and wept. For a woman, whose life was bound by the rules of etiquette and dignity, there was no dignity now. Her howls of pain and anger could, no doubt, be heard all over the house.

Suddenly, she caught sight of Lily. "This is your fault. None of this would have happened if it weren't for you."

"Come, Mrs. Grove," the doctor said. "You're overwrought. Perhaps you should go and rest."

"I don't need to rest," she spat. "I just want that woman out of my house. Get her out!" she screamed.

"Mildred," Mr. Grove spoke as he entered the room, still wearing his overcoat. "Mildred, what is the matter? Why are you taking on so?"

"It's Jonathon." She slumped to the floor. "He's gone. She killed him."

"Mrs. Grove—" Dr. Lawrence hurried over to the distraught woman. "—Jonathon died from his wounds and an infection. He didn't die because of his wife. In fact, he probably lived a little longer than we thought possible because of her. You must put these thoughts out of your head." He turned to Mr. Grove. "Your wife needs to rest. We need to get her to her room. I shall give her something to make her sleep and come and see her tomorrow when I am sure she will be more in her right mind."

Between them, the two men managed to carry the weeping woman upstairs. After a few moments, the doctor came down.

"I have to complete a death certificate," he said to Lily, who hadn't moved from the fireplace. "There is no need to wait to call the funeral director," he said gently.

"Funeral director?" she asked.

"You are his widow. I imagine you will be arranging the funeral."

"I hadn't thought about it," she admitted.

"Very few people do until they have to," he replied. "As far as I know, the family uses Charlesworthy in Hope, if that's of any help."

"Yes," she replied. "Thank you."

forty-seven

There was no starker contrast between Lily's and Jonathon's upbringing than the funeral. Where her mother's had been as cheap as possible, no expense was spared for Jonathon. In spite of what the doctor had said, Lily was happy to hand over the planning to Mrs. Grove, who, once she had recovered from the shock of Jonathon's death, set about the task with determination. It gave her focus during the dark days after Jonathon's death. Although they had all known that Jonathon would not live long, the permanence of his death, like all deaths, still came as something of a shock.

Eleanor arrived two days afterwards and was some comfort to her mother. Mr. Grove didn't know what to do with his grieving wife and seemed to withdraw into himself. Lily spent time with Mrs. Cadeby, leaving Jonathon's family to grieve together. She was still the outsider, and though Eleanor made every attempt to include her, she knew Mr. and Mrs. Grove would have erased her from their lives if they could. Fortunately, she had the twins to keep her busy. Their gurgles and smiles were a sharp contrast to the silence and weeping in the rest of the house.

On the day of the funeral, Lily dressed carefully in the new crepe black dress she had bought, another contrast with the borrowed hat she wore at her mother's funeral. Everything she wore was new, and she was grateful for the little veil on her hat to hide half her face. Her father and Beryl arrived to look after the twins while she went to the service.

It was only when she saw the hearse arrive, pulled by four black horses with black plumes, that Jonathon's death became real. She took her seat in the funeral car with the rest of the family. As they approached the town, she heard the muffled church bells tolling, and as the cortège passed, there were quite a number of Hope's townsfolk in the street. The Groves were one of the biggest employers in the town, and Jonathon had been well-liked. The service passed by in a blur. There were hymns and a eulogy, but Lily couldn't have said what was spoken or sung. All her attention was on Jonathon. The coffin was draped with a Royal Flying Corps flag, and his cap was on top.

They had been brought together through the chaos of war and were it not for the fact that she had fallen pregnant, their lives would never have been so intertwined. And now he was gone. A single tear slid down her cheek. She grieved for Jonathon and the life he should have had and thought of all the other wives, sweethearts, mothers, and sisters who had lost their young men to the cruelty of war.

At the cemetery, Mrs. Grove had to be supported as they approached the grave for the committal. Lily wondered if she would ever get over her loss. As they all threw in a handful of dirt, she also dropped the white lilies and roses she had ordered.

"Something to remember me by. Goodbye. Rest easy, Jonathon," she whispered. She walked back to the waiting funeral car with Eleanor.

"What will you do now?" her sister-in-law asked, linking her arm through Lily's.

"I'll go back to the Dales," she replied firmly. "There's

nothing for me here now, and I have to get back to the business. Ian and Annis have been very good, but I can't let them go on carrying me in the business."

"I think Mother was rather hoping you might stay on a little longer here. The little ones might prove a good distraction for her."

"Your parents are welcome to visit Rose and Teddy at any time," she replied. "They are their grandchildren after all, but their home will be in Sedbusk with me."

"I understand," Eleanor squeezed her arm, "but I don't want to lose touch. They're my niece and nephew, after all."

Lily patted her hand. "Then it's up to us to make sure we don't. I'm sure Jonathon would want the children to know their Aunt Eleanor and Uncle Barty."

"Barty has been one of the lucky ones." Eleanor smiled. "He's found he has quite the talent for what I believe they now call logistics, though it does mean he spends a great deal of time in London at the War Office. Perhaps that expensive education wasn't wasted after all."

When they returned to the house, a meal had been prepared for the mourners. People, most of whom Lily didn't know, stood around in groups chatting quietly. Many of them seemed to be friends of the Groves, who had come to offer their support. Lily found herself unable to do more than nibble at the food as she watched Mrs. Grove circulate among her guests. Years of social training had come to the fore. She pasted a smile on her and carried on as normal. Yet she seemed to have aged ten years in the last week. Occasionally, Lily heard a laugh as someone shared a story about one of Jonathon's escapades at school or university. Eventually, the sounds of the room receded as people began to drift away and only the family were left.

Mr. Grove stood up and cleared his throat. "I think it's time we moved into the library," he said.

"Come along," Eleanor said. "It's time for the reading of the will."

Lily remembered the conversation she'd had with Jonathon a few short weeks ago. "Of course," she replied, "though I can't imagine a man of his age would have much to leave."

"You'd be surprised," Eleanor said wryly.

The solicitor, Mr. Walker, was already sitting at the large desk in the library when they arrived. He was younger than Lily expected. She had always thought of lawyers as old men in spats, though there was no reason why she should. She had only met two lawyers, and they were both only a little older than she.

When they were all settled, Mr. Walker began. There were a few personal bequests to Mrs. Cadeby and the gardener as well as a donation to a fund for wounded soldiers. Eventually, the solicitor paused and said, "All my worldly goods, money, shares both in the Grove company and any others, and income from the trust fund—everything in fact—I leave to my wife, Lily Grove."

Mr. Grove leapt to his feet. "That is outrageous. Shares in Groves... It was not intended that those shares should leave the immediate family."

"And the income from the trust fund," Mrs. Grove added. "How could he? That fund was set up by the earl for his great-grandson, not for the daughter of a common labourer."

"Be quiet, you stupid woman," Mr. Grove roared. "Do you know what this means? I put half of the shares in Jonathon's name. It means she—" He pointed an accusing finger at Lily. "—owns half of the company."

"Then we must challenge this will. Jonathon was clearly not of sound mind when he made it." Mrs. Grove turned to the solicitor. "How could you take advantage of a man who was clearly not thinking straight? You ought to be struck off."

"I can assure you, madam and sir, that Mr. Grove was of

completely sound mind. The will was written, witnessed, and is completely legal. Feel free to challenge it, by all means, but I very much doubt you will succeed. If you will excuse me, might I have a word with the young Mrs. Grove?"

Lily stood up. "Certainly, Mr. Walker. I'll see you to the door."

"I'm not sure I understand," Lily said once the door to the library closed.

"It means, Mrs. Grove, that by any standards, you are now a very wealthy young woman. Jonathon was very keen to ensure both you and the children were very well provided for. As well as the shares in the Grove business, there are other investments he had made, which have been very successful. If you would care to come by my office tomorrow, I can go into more detail with you of what happens next and what you need to do."

"What about Mr. and Mrs. Grove?" she asked.

He smiled. "Don't worry about them. The will is water-tight. Jonathon made sure of it." He reached into his pocket. "Here." He held out a white envelope. "I was instructed to give you this. Until tomorrow, Mrs. Grove. Shall we say eleven?"

Lily nodded, and the young solicitor strode off.

The door to the library flung open. Mr. Grove strode out, his face florid and his breathing heavy. "You!" He pointed at her. "I don't know what hold you had over my son, but I will not let you ruin this family, do you hear?" he roared. "He had no right to give them to you, no right at all!"

forty-eight

Her father had once again been happy to look after the children with Beryl so Lily could attend the appointment with the solicitor.

"Don't let them Groves cheat you out of owt. The lad wanted to see yer right," were his parting words.

Rose was in his arms as he waved her off from the doorstep. She left the car outside his house and made the short walk into Hope. It somehow seemed smaller and greyer than she remembered. There was no market, and the market-place looked sad and abandoned when the stalls were bare. There were a few women looking in the windows, but by this time of the week, there would be little chance of them buying anything until payday on Friday. In any case, it was Wednesday, the day most women would be at home black leading their ranges. She smiled at the memory of her mother whose days were determined, as most of the women like her, by the chores they did. Monday was washing day; Tuesdays, ironing; Wednesdays, cleaning and black leading; Thursdays, baking—her mother had always joked that it was to clean their hands of the black lead—and Fridays and Saturdays, shopping at the markets.

Mr. Walker's office had his name emblazoned on a brass plaque by the side of the door. Through the glass, she could see a girl she knew from school at a desk, typing. She pushed the door open and entered, her feet sinking into the deep carpet.

"Hello, Janine," she said. "I've an appointment with Mr. Walker."

"Hello, Lily. It's nice to see you. I'll tell Mr. Walker you're here," the other woman said, walking towards the inner door. "I'll just be a minute. Please take a seat."

In less than a minute, she returned, and Mr. Walker appeared at the door to his office.

"Come in, Mrs. Grove." He smiled.

His office was larger than she imagined. Three walls were covered with bookshelves, bearing what she imagined to be legal tomes. The other wall had a window overlooking the High Street and filing cabinets. In the centre of the room was a large oak desk containing a large blotter, pens, a calendar, and a telephone, but little else. On the blotter rested a large manilla folder, which Lily assumed to be the focus of their meeting. She sat in one of the leather chairs facing the desk.

"How are you bearing up, Mrs. Grove?" the solicitor asked. "A sad loss. One among so many due to this blasted war."

"I'm fine, thank you," she replied, not feeling comfortable playing the role of the devastated widow when she knew there were so many who were truly devastated. "Jonathon and I were not..."

"A conventional couple?" he suggested. "Jonathon was very honest with me, Mrs. Grove," he added.

"I'm not quite sure why I'm here," she said.

He opened the manilla folder. "There are several things in here you will need to sign for the transfer of shares, the trust fund, and other such items, which Janine will witness. Then I'll explain what happens next."

The next half an hour or so, Lily signed each document as

Mr. Walker explained what it was before handing over a chequebook. "This is yours, Mrs. Grove. Jonathon opened a bank account in your name and arranged to have the money from his own account transferred in the event of his death. There is—" He consulted a piece of paper. "—currently around £2,000 deposited there for you to use immediately and an investment account with £5,000, which would be the account to use should you need to buy a house, for example. A monthly sum of £200 will go into your current account from the trust, and more will also go into the investment account. Dividends from the shares you own will also be paid into the investment account. There is rental income from various properties, and I believe there are some works of art in storage. As you can see, Jonathon also set up a separate trust for your children, which you, as their guardian, will administer."

"I had no idea." She shook her head.

The solicitor smiled. "Jonathon was not one to blow his own trumpet, but he was extremely financially astute. Some would say gifted. I don't believe his parents had any idea of the wealth he had managed to create—until yesterday." He pressed a button on his desk, and they watched in silence as Janine came in and witnessed the remaining documents.

"What should I do about the shares in Mr. Grove's business? He was very angry," she asked when Janine had left.

"He was bloody furious." Mr. Walker grinned. "Apologies," he added. "Jonathon was very clear that you are to retain them. I believe it's something he may have covered in his letter."

"I haven't read it yet," she admitted.

"Mr. Grove senior transferred the shares to Jonathon as a way of avoiding paying some sort of tax. I believe he did it using some 'connexion' of his without discussing it with Jonathon. When Jonathon found out, he was furious and refused to return the shares, which his father had assumed would happen as soon as he asked. It's my opinion you should keep the shares. I believe that's what Jonathon wanted, especially given the shabby way his parents have always treated you. Natural justice, if you will."

"You have certainly given me a lot to think about," Lily replied as she rose.

He held out the manilla envelope. "Here are your copies of everything we have dealt with this morning. You are now a very wealthy woman, Mrs. Grove. In many ways, it will make your life much easier, but it will also bring a different set of problems. Just be aware of that. Should you need it in the future, I will always be happy to offer my assistance."

"Thank you," she replied. "I appreciate your honesty."

There was nothing more to keep her in Hope, and the atmosphere at Grove House was chillier than the north pole. Lily managed to avoid the Groves by eating with Mrs. Cadeby. Once Eleanor had left, she began packing for her return to the Dales. She would drive the car left to her by Jonathon. The rest of the things would come by removal van the following week. The twins were still small enough for their bassinets to fit snugly on the back seat of the car. Mrs. Cadeby would accompany her and stay with her aunt for a few days. She was in the library writing a list for the removers when Mrs. Grove appeared.

"I suppose now that you have everything, you're leaving," she said.

"I'm going home, certainly," Lily replied.

"You haven't heard the last of this," the older woman hissed. "We, his parents, are his next of kin. What were you to him? You were nothing but a single night of shame."

"I was his wife," Lily said quietly.

"Only because he didn't know what he was doing. Mr. Grove has already spoken to his lawyer, who is sure the will is invalid. We shall see you in court. Everything you have taken from us will be returned. Furthermore, we shall see to it that the children are placed in our care."

Lily reared back. "You would drag the babies into this?"

The older woman laughed. "We shall use everything we have to get those children here where they belong. We shall have you declared an unfit mother. It will be easy enough. You were stupid, entertaining your fancy man while poor Jonathon lay dying upstairs. By the time we've finished with you, you won't be able to show your face in any city, town, or village in the country."

Lily rose with more composure than she felt. "I always envied people like you when I was small, people who seemed to have it all, with your grand house and fine clothes. What I didn't realise, Mrs. Grove, is that there is one thing you do not have, and that is a heart. You don't want your grandchildren because you love them. You want them so you can have power over them. You may have loved Jonathon, but it was a suffo-cating love, and you couldn't forgive him for loving someone else. I thought it was just me you couldn't forgive, thinking I took your son away. But it would have been the same for any woman. Perhaps when he joined the Flying Corps, part of it was to find release from you."

"You think I was jealous of you," the older woman spat. "You? What are you? A gold digger. A vulture who thought she'd got lucky when she got her claws into my son."

"At least we know where we stand," Lily replied as she walked towards the door. "I thought I would hate you after all you have just said, but that's not true. I pity you."

She closed the door quietly behind her.

forty-nine

Lily had been back a week before she took the white envelope out and carefully opened it. The twins were sleeping, and it was the first time she'd had time alone without interruption. It was also the first time she had felt able to read it. The paper was thick and covered in Jonathon's black scrawl.

Dearest Lily,

I think we both know that if you're reading this, I shall have shuffled off this mortal coil. There are things I wanted to say to you but never seemed to get the chance or the time. Firstly, let me say that I love you, Lily. I know you don't love me, not in the same way, and I can't blame you for that. I behaved like an arrogant fool. I will never forgive myself for that. But please believe me, Lily, when I say that I loved you long before our magical night together. I only hope that one day you might find it in your heart to forgive me. If we had a little more time together, I hoped I might prove my love for you and that you might come to love me. Either way, you made me a father, and I thank you humbly for our son and daughter, who will, I hope, keep a part of me alive.

As to the will, I have no doubt my parents are displeased, but you are to keep every last penny. My father thought to hide some of his money by putting shares in my name, thinking he would be able to retrieve them whenever he wished. As usual, he thought to bully and threaten me to get them back, but he made them legally mine, and now they are legally yours. Whatever threats he makes, he can do nothing. Once everything is taken into account, you should have around £750,000 and continuing income from the property, shares, and the trust fund. Everything has been done to ensure the will is watertight. You will be the only person who can make the decisions, and from what you told me about your business, I believe you will do very well. I spoke to one or two chums, and they believe the cosmetic industry is set to grow hugely, especially after the war is over. I don't think it will last much longer.

I have the impression that my parents will try to gain control of our children. You must fight that for both of us. Sadly, I know my father is not above using any ways or means to get what he wants, and he is desperate for an heir to his business as part of his grand plan for a dynasty bearing his name. Eleanor will have little to do with him, and neither will her children. Their destiny lies with Barty's family. I hate to say this about my own father, but his values and morals are not those I want our children to be influenced by. I suspect you don't either. If it comes to it, get help from Dickie Walker, the solicitor who gave you this letter. He's an honest and trustworthy individual. He'll fight on our behalf.

I imagine you'll be going back to the Dales. I can't blame you. Who would want to live among the dirt and stink of Hope when you can live in the beauty and fresh air of the Dales? I am also happy to know that our children will grow up there. They will get to know Annis, who will teach them, along with you, about what's important in life. I'm also happy to know that our children won't have to struggle in life as you have had to. Yet your early struggles made you what you are, Lily, and I wouldn't change any part of you. You are a strong, beautiful woman and

*deserve to be loved by a man who deserves you. What I'm trying
to say is, when the chance of love comes along again, as it already
seems to have done with the young man who visited you, take it
with both hands—live again, love again, marry again, and most
importantly, be happy. I said this to you, and I'll repeat it: live
for the both of us and try to remember me fondly from time to
time.*

Always yours,
   Jonathon

Tears ran down her cheeks as she finished reading, carefully refolded the letter, and put it back in the envelope. Had things been different, perhaps she and Jonathon might have had a chance, but they were on the wrong side of history and society's rules. She would never have been accepted by Jonathon's friends. She would always have been "just the maid," and Jonathon would always have been the man who married the maid. However, he had left her and the children well provided for. In the morning, she would go and look for a house and begin to pick up the threads of the business. Annis had been more than understanding, but she had to begin pulling her weight. She also wanted to get back to work, needed to get back to work. She needed to make the business a success, to prove that a girl from the backstreets of Hope could achieve something.

It seemed like fate when she visited Cope's, the estate agents in Hawes, and they told her the cottage near Annis's home had come onto the market the day before. A quick visit confirmed it was perfect. There were four bedrooms and a good-sized sitting and dining room with a bathroom upstairs, which the previous owner had put in. The kitchen was a fair size. There was a cold room at the back. It even came with its own small barn. There was plenty of room for the children to grow, and she would be near Annis. Mr. Cope could scarcely believe it when she said, "I'll take it," and offered him a cheque on the spot.

When she went around to Annis's house to tell her, Ian was there. It was the first time they'd met since his abrupt departure. So much had happened.

"Look who's here, Lily," Annis said, reaching for another cup and pouring her notoriously strong brew of tea.

"Hello, Lily," Ian said. "You're looking well."

"Thank you," she replied, adding, "So are you."

He smiled the familiar lopsided smile she had come to love and had missed. "But I haven't married and had a set of twins in the last few weeks."

"No." She smiled back. "But you have had to do a lot of work while I've been gone, and I thank you for that."

He shrugged. "It had to be done, but now that you're back, we have some decisions to make."

While she had been in Hope, things had moved on apace. Madison's had doubled their order, while orders were placed from several stores in London, including Marshall and Snelgrove and Derry and Toms—names which meant nothing to Lily. Ian clearly knew them well. From his tone, she knew they should be able to supply them, and in doing so, their business would go to a higher level than they had imagined.

"Clearly we will have to increase production if we're to meet the demand," Ian said, adding, "I know this isn't what we planned, but we're going to have to mechanise some of the process, things like retrieving the lanolin, which can be done quicker. And we all know it's not the most enjoyable part of the process."

"That's all very well," Annis countered, "but we've not long moved into our barn, and there's no room in there for machines."

"You're right, Annis," Ian agreed. "We're going to have to move production to a larger building."

"You mean a factory?" Annis asked. "Absolutely not. I've

seen those in Lancashire and Yorkshire. No one should have to work in one of those. The women in Lancashire can't hear each other speak. The machines are so loud, and in all those factories, there are things in the air that get in a person's lungs."

"No, Annis," Ian replied. "Our factory would be nothing like that. There would be no loud machines where people are working, and we won't be producing anything that gets in people's lungs."

"But where would this factory be?" Lily asked. "The idea of the barns was great because we could employ people right here in the Dales. What set us apart was the fact the creams are handmade and produced from local ingredients. We can't suddenly buy a factory in Leeds or somewhere. It wouldn't be what we say we're about."

Ian ran a hand through his hair. "I understand, but it's my intention that the factory will be here in Hawes. It's important to give employment here where there's so little opportunity between farming, lead mining, and none at all for women. That kills two birds with one stone. Local people will have the employment, the local farmers will still provide the fleeces for the lanolin, and most of the ingredients will be local as far as possible."

"But there's nowhere in Hawes. Are you planning to build a factory?" Annis asked, her eyebrows raised. "Because I have to tell you that the last building to be built here was probably the Methodist church, and that was fifty years ago."

"No, Annis." Ian laughed for the first time, his eyes crinkling at the corners. "As it happens, I think I've found the perfect building, which won't take too much to make it into what we need. I'd like to take you there to see it this afternoon, if you've time."

"Take Lily," Annis replied. "I'll look after the twins. If Lily agrees, we'll see what we can do."

Lily and Ian drove to Hawes in his motor. As they turned

up the road to Kettlewell, Ian said, "We're here. Look to your left."

At the top of the hill was a long, white-painted building within a large yard. Although she couldn't see how far it stretched back, Lily could see that it was a fair distance.

"It's huge," she breathed.

"There's plenty of room, which we'll need. There's even room on this site to expand when we need to," Ian replied. "I'm serious, Lily. In the few weeks since you've been gone, things have changed drastically. After Madison's took such a big order, it occurred to me that other department stores in other cities might want to do the same, so I set off. They all want what we have, Lily. All of them."

"This seems such a big step," Lily said as they walked towards the entrance.

"There's more," Ian admitted, sliding the key into the lock. "One of my university friends went to live in New York. There's a new company there called Maybelline. They make something called mascara, which women put on their eyelashes to enhance them. Women are going crazy for it because it makes them look like Mary Pickford, Lilian Gish, or Theda Bara. Cosmetics are going to be an enormous market, and we should be in it right from the start."

"So are you saying that, as well as the creams and lotions, we should be making this mascara?" Lily asked.

"Mascara, powder, rouge, lip colour—whatever women want, we need to be selling it. Otherwise, they will buy it from America or France."

He pushed open the door, and they stepped inside.

fifty

It was a cavernous space, bigger than Lily had imagined from the outside. The walls were white, and numerous windows made the vast room feel light and airy.

"The farmer who built it intended to make dairy products here. Unfortunately, he died before he could bring his dream to reality, his children have no interest and want to sell as quickly as possible," Ian explained as their footsteps echoed around the hollow space. He gestured to the ceiling. "I thought we could put in a second floor for design rooms and offices. There's another building round the back that we can turn into labs to experiment on new products and refine old ones. There's also plenty of buildings for storage."

She looked at him, mindful of the fact that he had been careful to ensure there had been no physical contact between them since she had arrived back. "You've really thought about this, haven't you?"

"When I realised we could be onto something, I knew we had to expand to make it happen. The fact that this place came on the market at the same time seemed like fate."

"How much do you think it will take?" she asked.

"The buildings are for sale at £2,000. It will probably take a similar amount to do the alterations and put in the equipment. Fortunately, the old farmer was forward thinking and had electricity and water put in." He paused. "It's a good business plan. I've no doubt about that. The only concern will be raising the funds to buy and equip it."

She looked around. "I think I may be able to help there," she said quietly.

He stopped midstride. "What do you mean?"

When she explained the money Jonathon had left her, he whistled. "No wonder you married him."

She turned to face him, her hands on her hips. "Is that what you think, Ian Steele? That I married Jonathon in order to get his money? Well, I'll tell you this: I'm fed up with people thinking I'm a gold digger. I married Jonathon because I thought his children should bear his name. I felt sorry that a young father wouldn't live to see them grow up. I did what I thought was right by him and by them. So we'll buy this place and build the business so I have some kind of legacy to leave them as well."

She turned on her heel and left Ian standing, walking swiftly down the road and into Hawes. She ignored Ian as he wound down the window and called to her. He caught up with her in Cope's as she was signing a cheque for £1,750.

"There," she said, brandishing the receipt. "It's ours, and I think I'd better negotiate with the suppliers in the future."

"Lily, please," he said as he strode after her along the High Street. "Let's talk about this."

"About what? About you calling me a gold digger—not only just now, but the last time we met?" she said scornfully.

He caught her arm. "I'm sorry, Lily. I shouldn't have said it, and I certainly didn't mean it."

"I thought you knew me, and I thought I knew you," she replied. "Now I'm not so sure."

"You do know me, and I know you. I know you're not that sort of woman. It's just that—" He paused and ran a hand through his hair. "Can we go somewhere more private to have this conversation?"

They went into the White Hart and quickly found a table by the fire. It was early, so there were no other customers. Ian went to the bar and brought back two glasses of foaming ale, setting them down on the polished table.

"Well?" Lily asked.

"The money came as a shock," he replied.

Lily frowned. "The money? Is this just about the money?"

"All right." He took a drink of ale. "I was shocked and angry when you went off to marry Jonathon when you knew how I felt about you, but I guess when I calmed down, I understood why you did it. That comment I made back there... I apologise. It shouldn't have come out the way it did. I hadn't realised quite how rich he was."

"Neither had I," she replied drily. "The thing is, Ian, Jonathon wanted to leave me well provided for so that I could live an independent life. He had faith in me to make the right decisions, and he was proud of my going into business. He wanted us, you and I, to have a future together. He wanted to tell you personally, but he ran out of time."

"I had no idea," Ian said simply.

"No, because you went off like one of those whizzbangs they talk about," she shot back. She stood up. "All my life, I have had to deal with men like you, men who flare up at the slightest thing without thinking of the consequences. First, it was my father, who thought he could settle every argument with his fists. Then it was Jonathon, who behaved without a thought for what might happen to me. Although, to his credit, he did try to put things right at the end. Then it was Mr. Grove, who would use any means to get his own way. I thought you were different. I really did. I think, from now on, we'll do what we said before. We'll work as colleagues, and that is all."

"Lily, wait," he said, following her. "Please."

She turned. "That's all I can offer you, Ian. I'm tired of it all."

"Does that mean forever?" he asked.

"It's all I can offer," she repeated and walked away.

"I can't help noticing that Ian doesn't seem to visit," Annis said as they unpacked Lily's new belongings in her new home.

"No," Lily replied, wiping the last of the china teacups and placing them carefully in the dresser. "He and I had a disagreement the day we bought the building for the factory."

"About what?" Annis pressed.

Lily paused, her hand midair as she unwrapped the cut glass vase that had been one of her mother's possessions. "Well, it started about the money for the factory, but it ended about Ian's opinion of me."

Annis said nothing but raised an eyebrow.

"Basically, Ian thinks I'm a gold digger. He said it when he came to Hope to stop me marrying Jonathon, and he more or less said the same thing the other day."

"He doesn't really think that," Annis replied.

"I think he made himself fairly clear," Lily shot back. "And I told him a few home truths myself."

"Which were?" Annis asked.

"I've had enough, Annis. I've had enough of men thinking they have some sort of control over my life. First my father. Then Mr. Grove. Jonathon and Ian's judgement was the last straw."

"He wasn't judging, love," the older woman replied. "He was jealous."

Lily's eyes widened. "Jealous?"

"It seems you have a lot to learn about the male ego." Annis smiled. "No matter what Ian says or does, in his mind he will never be able to compete with the memory of a dead war hero. That's what he's afraid of, that Jonathon will eventually become a saint-like figure in your mind and Ian can't possibly measure up."

"But that's ridiculous!" Lily exclaimed. "In any case, Ian knows what Jonathon and I had wasn't love. He knows I married him to give the twins his name, and I pitied Jonathon. That's all."

Annis nodded. "He knows that in his head, but his heart tells a different story."

"He's being an idiot," Lily said firmly.

"Oh, he most certainly is," Annis agreed. "The question is, what are you going to do about it? I've lived long enough to see what love looks like, and I see it between you two. If you're not careful, Lily love, it will slip through your fingers like quicksilver, and both of you will regret it."

Lily sat down on the new sofa. "I don't know what to do, Annis. The last two times I've seen Ian, we've quarrelled. I've tried to explain things to him, but he doesn't seem to want to listen. He's been avoiding me altogether since our last argument. It's as though he can't stand the sight of me."

"Do you love him?"

She paused as Lily nodded.

"Then try again. Sometimes men need to have things explained more than once." The older woman smiled. "If that doesn't work, a swift blow to the head might." She laughed.

fifty-one

Lily patted her hair and made sure her hat was straight before she raised the knocker and rapped on the oak door. The sound seemed to echo around the street. Ian lived in one of the larger stone houses overlooking the dale. She waited a few moments and had begun to turn away when she heard the sound of footsteps in the hall. Ian opened the door. He was dressed in flannel trousers with his shirtsleeves rolled up. As usual, a stray lock of hair fell over his eye.

"Lily," he said in surprise. "I wasn't expecting you. Is there something wrong?"

"I thought you might be out if I warned you I was coming," she replied with a small smile, wondering if he was going to make her ask to come in.

"Of course not. Please come in." He stepped back and gestured for her to enter.

He led her down the hallway into a comfortable sitting room. Two sofas sat opposite each other with two armchairs completing the set. There were several occasional tables bearing lit lamps. A log fire burned in the large marble fireplace. Several papers were scattered around one of the armchairs.

"I don't want to disturb you," Lily began.

He ran a hand through his hair. "Lily, you have been disturbing me from the moment we met. Please have a seat." They both took a seat. "Now what can I do for you?"

Lily took a breath and tightly laced her fingers together to stop them from shaking. " I wanted to say that I don't want to fight with you, Ian. I said some things I regret the last time we met, and I want us to go back to the way we were."

His eyes caught hers. "I said some awful things to you the last time we met and the time before as well," he admitted.

"I didn't know about Jonathon's money until after he died," she explained.

Ian closed his eyes briefly before looking at her once again. "I apologise, Lily. I know you. You're the last person who would marry someone for their money. I was jealous. I know there's no excuse, but I wanted you to hurt because I was hurting. I was afraid you'd somehow fall in love with Jonathon, and I wanted you for myself."

"But you knew Jonathon was dying, and I'd already told you my reasons for marrying him."

He smiled. "I was a bloody fool. What can I say? You would always have the twins to remind you of him, and he will always remain the dashing young war hero."

She looked at him and smiled. He had just confirmed all that Annis had said. "You are a fool, Ian Steele. What we had was a chance to build something real together. Not just in business, but between us. We had the chance to build something between us."

"You're talking in the past tense, Lily," he replied.

She stood up. "Perhaps we both need more time."

He stood in front of her. "More time be damned."

He drew her into his arms, cupping the back of her head with one hand and covering her lips with his. The minute his lips touched hers, it was as though a firework had gone off between them. He raised his head.

"The last time we had more time, you went off and married someone else," he murmured before kissing her again, his tongue gently coaxing her lips open before he plunged into her mouth.

She could not have said how long they stood. It could have been minutes or hours. She lost track of time. The world melted away. In that moment, there was nothing but the two of them. Finally, breathlessly, she stepped back, but Ian's arms remained around her.

"What happens now?" she asked.

"I rather think we're going to have to get married." He smiled, his eyes crinkling at the corners. "If we don't do it soon, you might marry someone else," he teased, his eyes darkening. "I don't think I can wait much longer, Lily. You must know how much I want you."

"It's the same for me," she admitted. "I feel that we are meant to be together. In spite of everything, something brought me here—God or fate or whatever—and I'm meant to be with you. I have never felt like this before."

"Me either." He gently stroked her cheek. "I told you I was engaged, and she broke it off. But even before, when I thought I was in love, it was nothing like this."

"Thank you, Ian." She laughed. "That's exactly what a woman wants to hear, a comparison between your ex-fiancée and your new one."

He shook his head. "It's because I want you to understand how much I love you. Comparing you and Sarah is like comparing water with the finest champagne." He paused. "Just to clarify, you're the champagne." He kissed her jaw. "Definitely the champagne." He found the sensitive spot behind her ear, whispering, "Vintage champagne." He swept her close and plundered her mouth again until they were both breathless.

Finally, he drew back. "We need to stop, Lily, before

neither of us have the will to do so, and I want to do this right."

Lily could feel tears forming.

"What's the matter?" he asked. "What have I done?"

"Nothing," she replied. "It's just that no one before has ever shown me such respect and love."

"Lily, I promise I will love and respect you for the rest of my life, even if it kills me." He smiled and released her but kept hold of her hand. "Look," he added, pulling her towards the papers. "Let me show you the plans for the factory and the lists of equipment I've drawn up."

Lily started to laugh. This time, the tears were tears of mirth. "Oh, Ian, nothing speaks more of romance than looking at blueprints." She gasped through her giggles.

He joined in her laughter. "I thought we needed a distraction. Otherwise, regardless of my fine words a few minutes ago, we would be in my bedroom with me removing every inch of clothing you're wearing and making love to you for the rest of the day."

Lily's laughter stopped. There was nothing she wanted more from Ian, but she knew how much he wanted to do the honourable thing. "Very well," she replied. "The romantic blueprints it is."

Several moments later, she sat back on her heels. The factory would be state of the art. Nothing had been left to chance. There were changing rooms for the workers, who would have to change into white uniforms to work in. The offices at the top of the building would house clerks and secretaries as well as Lily's office and the design department. Ian and Annis would have an office in one of the outer buildings, where they would be closer to the laboratory to experiment with new products. Ian had even included a small canteen and eating area for the staff.

"What's this?" she asked, pointing at a room that opened onto the field at the back of the building.

"I thought we could have a crèche," he said quietly. "I imagine you won't be the only woman working here who has children."

"Ian—" She flung her arms around him. "—that is such a wonderful idea." She indicated the field before adding, "And look, the children could play out there when it's fine."

"I thought we could put in some swings and a sand pit or some such in the corner." He smiled down at her.

"You have thought of everything."

"I don't know about that, but I do think we're going to have quite a few women working with us now. The war has changed everything. When I was in London, women were driving buses and trams, and I know they were driving ambulances at the front. I know the men are going to come back and need jobs, but I think we're going to have a labour shortage. This damned war has almost lost us a generation of working men, and women are not only going to be able to make up the shortfall, but they're going to want to do it." His eyes glowed.

"We're a new industry, making products for women. Who better than women themselves to know what women want?" Lily said, adding, "And it's true. Until now there have been few opportunities for women outside the home, just service and factories in the big cities. We've shown what we can do, and we want a fairer share."

"You sound like a suffragette," he teased.

She looked up at him. "I've never really thought about it before, but yes, I suppose I am. Why should women be excluded from making decisions that are going to affect them? After all, we're half of the population. We can't even have bank accounts without a male's permission," she added, warming to the theme. "In fact, the more I think about it, the angrier I am."

"Just so long as you don't chain yourself to the railings." He dropped a kiss on her nose.

"Well, maybe not that, but I can't promise I won't get involved somehow," she replied thoughtfully.

"Oh, dear." He sighed dramatically. "You've got that determined look about you. Men had better beware when Lily Russell has that look on her face."

Lily laughed and poked him in the shoulder. "I think the way I'll choose is to become one of the best-known business-women in the country and then..."

"What?" He could not help asking.

"Then who knows." She laughed again. "I might become prime minister."

Ian threw back his head and laughed. "You know, I wouldn't be at all surprised."

fifty-two

As summer slipped into autumn, Lily felt more content than she had in a long time. The twins were thriving, sitting up, and smiling at everyone they met. Their happy gurgles filled whichever room they were in. She and Ian were enjoying getting to know each other as their relationship developed. They both knew there were problems they needed to solve, but for the moment, they were happy to spend time with each other, walking on the moors or clambering up the hillsides. Lily had settled into her little cottage and Ian was a regular visitor, often coming for supper and spending the evening as they talked through their plans and dreams for the future of the business. They avoided talking about where their relationship might lead for the time being as they both felt it was too soon to make plans.

Throughout the summer, they had managed to increase production in the barn and had employed three women, who had taken to the work like ducks to water. They knew of others who wanted to work for them when the factory was up and running. Orders were being completed, but each month, it became more of a struggle as the number of orders continually increased. There were enquiries from shops as far afield as London, Bath, and Birmingham.

November was cold and dull as Lily and Ian stood outside near the entrance to the crèche, discussing where the swing and sandpit might go, when they were both silenced by church bells. For the first time in four years, they heard the sound of the bells of St. Margaret's ring out. Lily's eyes flew to Ian's.

"What do you think it means?" she asked.

He looked up to heaven. "I believe it means that this damned war is finally over," he said, unable to keep the emotion from his voice. "It's finished, finally. Thank God."

She took his hand. "Do you really think it was the war to end all wars?" she asked.

He shook his head. "I would like to think so, but in all honesty, I doubt it. Politicians will always manage to find a way to send young men to fight, sometimes for a reason and sometimes for a patch of land. And young men will always go. Again, some for a reason, and others because they think it will be a grand adventure. They'll come back changed. That's for sure. If they come back at all."

There was no great celebration in Hawes. They read the stories in the newspapers of people thronging the streets of London, but in Hawes, people went about their business quietly, conscious of the loss and sacrifice of some of their close-knit community. Some families had lost one son, others had lost many sons and cousins whose names were well-known to everyone. Cockett, Metcalfe, Stavely, Calvert, Dinsdale, and Iveson were all well-known families in the area. There was no feeling of elation, only relief the war was over and that some of their young men would be coming back.

By the end of November, the factory was almost completed, with the last of the machinery being fitted and new staff being interviewed and trained. Annis, Ian, and Lily had decided they would take on twenty staff members to begin with. Two would be needed for the crèche, four in the labs, another two for the lanolin process, six to operate the mixing and pressing machines, four to pack the products, and two to work on the paperwork in the office. It would be a bold start, but the site could expand if needed to increase production. Ian explained this to Lily and Annis as they all sat around Lily's small table after supper. They planned to open the new factory just before Christmas. That way, if there were any snags, they could be sorted out before the real push began in January.

"Who would have thought I'd be working in an office at my age?" Annis laughed as she helped herself to a second cup of tea.

"I know what you mean," Lily replied. "This time last year, we had a market stall, an idea, and a lot of... Well, either nerve or stupidity."

"It was that nerve that got us where we are," Ian put in, "and this is only the beginning. It's exciting to be in at the beginning of something."

"It's certainly exciting." Lily laughed.

"If you ask me, it's bloody terrifying," Annis added, "but I have faith in you two and the difference we can make in the lives of both the women who buy our products and the women who make them."

Ian nodded. "It's true. It was a good idea to have women as half our workforce. As Lily said, we've easy access to the kinds of things they want us to make."

"It's caused a bit of a rumpus in some households." Annis laughed. "I've been stopped at least three times in the High Street by farmers who think their daughters should be at home helping with the sheep."

"They won't be complaining when their daughters bring home their pay packets," Lily replied.

"That's what I told them," Annis agreed. "That took the wind out of their sails."

"Just so long as they get to keep most of what they earn," Lily said, remembering the agreement her father had made with Mr. Grove.

"I imagine the farmers would rather tussle with their sheep than their daughters." Annis laughed, standing and putting on her coat.

When both her guests had departed, it didn't take long for Lily to clear away the remnants of their meal and tidy the kitchen. She always left it tidy. Like her mother, she hated coming down to a mess the following morning.

It was only when she was getting ready for bed that she found the letter that had arrived by the second post. She'd put it in her pocket and had forgotten about it as she'd been about to interview one of the women to take charge of the crèche. She drew it out and opened it, with some degree of trepidation, recognising the name of the Groves solicitor at the bottom of the single sheet.

To Mrs. Grove,

I have been instructed by Mr. H. Grove to inform you of his intention to contest the will of your husband, his late son, Mr. Jonathon Grove, as well as to inform you that he intends to pursue guardianship of his grandchildren. Should you wish to avoid a costly and public court case, and settle out of court, please contact this office before the end of the year.

Yours etc.,
Randolph Coleface

She started at the knocking on the door, subconsciously expecting it to be Mr. Grove demanding she give over the children immediately.

Ian entered. "Sorry, love, but I think I left my... Lily, what's the matter? You look as though you've seen a ghost."

Silently, her hands shaking, she handed him the letter.

"What am I to do?" she whispered as he drew her into his arms. "They won't stop until they've ruined me."

"You'll fight it," he said simply, stroking her back gently as shudders rippled through her. "Jonathon knew what he was doing. There's no way they'll get away with this. This letter is intended to scare you into giving in to them."

"They once said they'd have me declared an unfit mother. They're going to rip my reputation to shreds," her voice trembled.

"Well, for a start, anyone who has seen you with Teddy and Rose would know how good a mother you are, and we don't live in Victorian times. A woman can't be ruined."

She stepped back and looked up at him. "They will use you against me. They cast aspersions on that time you came to see me just before I married Jonathon," she reminded him. "They will tell it as though I was already carrying on with you even though I was about to get married. I know them, Ian. They'll stop at nothing to get what they want. The only reason I've heard nothing from them for so long is that they were no doubt planning what to do."

He drew her back into his arms and kissed the top of her head. "Just remember, Lily. You've faced them down before, and this time you won't be doing it alone."

For the first time since he'd returned, she relaxed against him. "Thank you," she said quietly. "Tomorrow, I'll telephone Mr. Walker, Jonathon's solicitor."

"That's my girl." Ian smiled into her hair.

"Please don't go," she whispered. "I don't want to be on my own tonight."

fifty-three

Ian sucked in a breath. "Lily, what are you asking?"

She looked into his dark eyes. "I think you know, but if you need me to say it, I want you to stay here with me tonight, Ian. I want you to make love to me, but if you don't want to..."

His arms tightened around her, pulling her close so that she couldn't fail to notice his arousal. "Lily, my sweet, I have been wanting to make love to you since we met. Keeping from you has been torture. Even when I was angry with you and you were angry with me, I have never stopped wanting you. But I need to know, are you sure you're not just sad and afraid? Because I don't want us to have any regrets in the morning."

"I won't have regrets," she promised and rose on her toes to press her mouth to his.

The kiss was light at first but became intense swiftly as he teased her lips apart to plunge his tongue into her mouth. When she touched it with the tip of her tongue, one arm slid around her back and held her against his hips.

"See what you do to me, Lily," he whispered in her ear, sending shivers of excitement down her neck.

Once more, she looked into those deep eyes. He was the man she had waited her whole life for. Not only had he treated her as an equal in business, but he had been prepared to give her the protection of his name and raise her children as his own. Life with Ian wouldn't be without problems. No life was. But together, they would have the best of each other.

"Come," was all she said as she took his hand and led him to the stairs.

"Your bedroom suits you," he said looking round and taking in the pink peonies in the wallpaper and the rose carpet that contrasted with the dark wood of the tallboy and wardrobe. The double iron bedstead was softened by the rose eiderdown and white sheets.

Lily blushed at his impression of her decoration of the room. "Oh my God, what must you think of me?" she said quietly.

He walked towards her and tipped her chin up with a finger. "I think you're a beautiful, sensual woman, Lily, and I can't wait to make love to you. Just as I can't wait to marry you. Tonight is for us and us alone. I intend to make it a night neither of us will ever want to or be able to forget."

"And tomorrow?" A moment of doubt washed over her, and she could not help asking. "Tomorrow, what will you think?"

"I will thank God you're mine, Lily, to love until the day I die," he replied, catching her to him in a searing kiss. Raising his head, he whispered, "You look beautiful in this dress, but I would much rather see you out of it."

She nodded as his hands went to unfasten the buttons at the front. He eased the sleeves from her shoulders, kissing each inch of flesh as it was revealed, and she stood in her slip before him.

"So beautiful," he murmured, easing the thin straps of her slip and unhooking her bra and sliding both from her shoulders until she was naked from the waist up. "So very, very beautiful," he repeated, running a thumb around each nipple, causing them to harden instantly. "Oh, God," he groaned, dipping his head and closing his lips around one rosy tip and then the other.

It was all Lily could do to stand as his tongue and teeth teased her breasts.

"I have to see all of you," he whispered, sliding the rest of her clothing to the floor until it lay in a puddle at her feet, leaving her in only her stockings and suspenders.

Her instinct was to cover herself with her hands, but he gently pulled them away, his eyes roaming the length of her body.

"I'm sorry," she said. "Pregnancy and childbirth change a woman's body."

He looked into her eyes. "You are beautiful, Lily. Don't ever think you're not. If you say bearing children has changed your body, then I can only imagine it has changed it for the better. Now..." His eyes gleamed. "Delightful as those silk stockings are, I want to remove them." He unhooked the suspenders and slid the stockings slowly down her legs, then the suspender belt joined the other garments on the floor. "Sit on the edge of the bed, my darling." Lily sat, her eyes never leaving his as he knelt before her. "I want to please and pleasure you, Lily, for the rest of my life," he murmured, taking her foot and caressing it, kissing her calf and the back of her knee. It was only when he kissed the inside of her thigh that she realised what he was about to do.

"Ian!" She gasped as his tongue found her entrance and slid over her lips. "Oh God," she cried out as his tongue swept inside her, withdrew, and plunged again, over and over. He used his fingers to widen her so he could plunge deeper into her warmth.

"See how you open for me like a beautiful flower," he whispered, blowing softly, then concentrating on the bud he knew would give her the greatest pleasure.

Her head dropped back as she gave in to the exquisite sensations that were beginning to flow over her. She could scarcely breathe as Ian pushed her towards a climax that pulsed through her entire body, and sparks exploded behind her eyes.

When she found the strength to open her eyes, Ian was sitting back on his heels looking at her. "Ian, that was... I never knew... Oh my God."

"Good beginnings of sentences, Lily." He laughed. "But you need to get to the end of them."

"How can you... When you've just..."

"Again, I'm going to need more details."

She cocked her head to one side and took a breath. "Now that I'm able to think, there is a slight problem."

"And what might that be?"

"Well, it's quite obvious. I seem to have no clothes on whilst you are fully dressed."

He stood up. "A problem that's easily solved." His hand went to the button of his shirt.

Lily stood. "No, let me," she said. "It's only fair." she stood on her toes and started to unbutton his shirt. "After all," she whispered into his ear, "you were kind enough to help me."

She admitted to herself that there was something about being naked in front of a fully clothed man that made her feel a little wild. Ian stood passively whilst she unfastened his shirt and pulled it apart. She could tell by his hiss of breath when she ran her hands over the planes of his chest and tentatively touched her tongue to his flat male nipples that he was not as passive as he seemed. His shirt quickly joined the jumble of clothes at their feet, and her hands went to the fastening of his trousers with infinite slowness.

"For God's sake, Lily, what are you trying to do to me?" he ground out.

She raised her head, her eyes full of mischief. "Just helping you," she said softly as she drew his trousers and underpants slowly down, releasing his cock.

He quickly kicked his clothes away. "Jesus, Lily," he said as she sank to her knees in front of him. "You don't have to. Christ."

He gasped as she took him into her mouth. She put her hands on his buttocks to steady herself as she took him fully into her mouth, licking and sucking. When she ran her tongue around the rim, he put his hands on her head.

"Stop, Lily, I need to be inside you now."

With a fluid motion, he swept Lily into his arms, laid her on the bed, and joined her, his fingers searching the tight curls at the juncture of her thighs.

"See how wet and ready you are, Lily?" He took her hand and placed it on his cock. "See how hard I am for you?" he added, leaning over her and nudging her legs apart.

He began to push into her, slowly at first, but as she began to move with him, his pace became faster and deeper until the lights exploded behind Lily's eyes once more, brighter this time. She cried out his name as he groaned and pulled out, spilling onto her stomach. It was several minutes before Lily spoke.

"Thank you," she said simply.

Ian reached down and pulled a spotless white handkerchief from his pocket, cleaning Lily first and then himself before lying back and tucking her into his shoulder.

"That was unbelievable," he said, stroking her hair. "You didn't need to thank me." He chuckled.

"I was thanking you for making sure I didn't make the same mistake again," she whispered.

He turned his head and caught her chin in his hand. "Lily," he said, looking into her eyes. "If, and when, we have more children, it will be your choice."

There were tears in her eyes as she once again whispered, "Thank you."

fifty-four

The journey back to Hope was quiet. The call to the solicitor the week before had been brief, but Mr. Walker had arranged a meeting with both the Groves, their solicitor, and themselves in order to try to settle matters without the need for an expensive and public court case. It was only a week before the factory was due to open. Neither of them could afford to spare the time, but Lily was grateful for Ian's offer to come with her. She felt the need for moral support. Annis, as ever, had volunteered to take care of Rose and Teddy. She knew the Groves would be disappointed, and no doubt angry, to not see them, but she just couldn't bring herself to trust that they wouldn't try to take them away from her there and then.

They were shown into a large room in Mr. Walker's offices, which was dominated by an oval oak table and ten leather-bound chairs. There were net curtains at the windows, through which Lily could see the busy market with the people of Hope going about their daily business. The Groves and their solicitor, Mr. Coleface, were already present. Lily was shocked to see the changes in her former in-laws. Mr. Grove seemed to have diminished. His suit hung on his body, and some of his bluster seemed to have left him. Mrs. Grove's hair had turned quite white under the black hat she wore. Her black coat was one Lily recognised from Jonathon's funeral, relieved only by a pearl brooch on her left lapel. She knew Jonathon's death had hit Mrs. Grove hard, but now, many months afterwards, she still seemed to be in deepest mourning.

Mr. Walker took his place at the opposite end of the table to Mr. Coleface. "As we are all present, I believe we should begin."

"Who's that?" Mr. Grove said, jerking his head in Ian's direction.

"That's her fancy man," Mrs. Grove said bitterly. "He's the one she was carrying on with while poor Jonathon lay dying." She reached into her handbag, brought out a lacy handkerchief, and proceeded to dry her eyes.

"In that case," Mr. Grove replied with some of his old bluster, "he has no right to be here, no right at all."

"If we could please stick to the facts, Mrs. Grove," Mr. Walker said. "Mr. Steele is in fact Mrs. Grove's fiancé and is here to support her."

"Fiancé? Is that what we're calling it now?" Mrs. Grove said.

"Mrs. Grove," Mr. Walker said firmly, "I must ask you to desist with these derogatory comments about my client, or we shall get nowhere in trying to settle this case."

Lily shot him a grateful glance.

"There are two issues of dispute regarding your late son's wishes as outlined in his will: one being the custody of his children and the other being the disposal of his wealth. I propose we deal with the second aspect first, which is simpler than the first. According to his wishes, all of Mr. Jonathon Grove's wealth and income were quite clearly willed to his wife."

"It is my client's contention that, at the time of the writing of the will, their son, Jonathon, was not of sound mind due to the medication he was prescribed," Mr. Coleface declared. "I have here documents from a doctor stating that the aforementioned medications are able, and indeed likely, to cause hallucinations, memory loss, and various other mental issues. That being the case, the will would, in fact, be invalid." He slapped a sheaf of papers on the table.

Mr. Walker did not reach for the papers but extracted one of his own from his briefcase. "I am aware of the theory. However, here is a letter from Mr. Jonathon Grove's personal physician stating that, in his opinion, Mr. Grove was not suffering from any of the conditions you suggest."

Mr. Coleface tapped the papers in front of him. "These are from the most eminent men in their field."

"And this," Mr. Walker tapped the paper in front of him, "is from the physician who was actually treating Mr. Grove up to, and at, the time of his death. Furthermore, Dr. Lawrence is no ordinary doctor. Part of his research at Cambridge was concerning the development and testing of new drugs. I believe it fair to say that he has more than a working knowledge of the conditions you are referring to, and he found none in Mr. Jonathon Grove." He looked around the silent room.

"With regard to the shares in my business," Mr. Grove began, "it was only ever intended that they should be in Jonathon's name for a limited time. The fact that they are now controlled by that woman is making business hard."

"I don't see why," Lily stated, speaking up. "Surely you are still running the business, Mr. Grove. Apart from the change in ownership of the shares, business must be going on as usual."

Mr. Grove looked at her with a degree of surprise. "Of course, my dear. I don't expect you to understand. You have little education and no understanding of business."

"I think I might have a little more than you think, Mr. Grove," Lily replied evenly. "So shall I tell you what I believe to be the case?"

The older man sat back in his chair. "Please do."

"Jonathon made it clear that you had transferred the

shares to his name in order to avoid some sort of tax. I think you need to have the shares back in your name so that your business can be valued more highly, either because you are thinking of selling it or so you have greater collateral in order to borrow more money from the bank. There is, as I understand it, going to be a huge increase in the building of homes now that the war is over. I imagine it's the latter so you may bid on the building contracts for the building of council houses. Though," she added, "I have lived in one of the homes built by your company, and I wouldn't recommend it."

Ian leaned forward. "Well done," he whispered.

"I've had enough of this!" Mr. Grove shouted. He stood up and turned to leave. "Come along, Mildred. I refuse to be lectured to by that little tart."

"Sit down, Hubert," Mrs. Grove said, speaking for the first time. "I don't give a damn about the blasted shares, but I do care about my grandchildren."

Again, Mr. Walker spoke. "Jonathon was very definite in his wishes. Mrs. Grove is to have sole custody, and it will be up to her to allow visitation rights."

"But we are their grandparents. Surely we have some rights," Mrs. Grove said, darting a look at her solicitor, who suddenly took a great interest in the grain of the oak.

"As the law stands, Mrs. Grove, the answer is no. As grandparents you have no legal rights regarding your grandchildren," Mr. Walker explained.

Mrs. Grove turned to Lily. "Please, I beg of you, Lily. Let us see our grandchildren. I will accept any conditions you may put in place. I know we weren't the best of parents and we have been far from kind to you, but I beg of you to let us see them, even if we are only able to see them in your presence. We'll do anything at all, but please don't cut us from their lives. They are all we have left of Jonathon."

Lily paused. All that Mrs. Grove said was true, but her mind slid back to her own mother, whose parents had cut her off from her family. She had grandparents, aunts, uncles, and cousins she had never met. Would it be fair to do that to Rose and Teddy? How would she feel if they one day stopped her from seeing their children? What kind of person used children as a weapon? Not the sort of person she wanted to be. Jonathon had clearly left it up to her to make the decision.

She took a deep breath. "Very well. Shall we start with a visit every month and see how it goes? Perhaps Mr. Walker might draw up an agreement so that we all know where we stand."

"I'd be happy to do so," he replied.

"Oh, thank you, thank you," Mrs. Grove clutched Lily's hand, tears streaming down her cheeks. "I promise you won't regret it."

"And there is to be no more talk of court cases," Lily said.

"Of course not," the older woman replied, leaning forward and surprising Lily by enveloping her in a hug.

"What about my shares?" Mr. Grove asked quietly.

"I'll hang on to them for now, Mr. Grove," Lily replied. "But should I decide to sell them, I shall give you the first option."

The older man leaned in closer. "If you think this is over, you're a fool," he hissed. "I'll go along with it now, for Mildred's sake, but there'll be a reckoning. Have no doubt about that."

fifty-five

Ian was still laughing as he started the car. "I can't believe you just calmly told old Grove that you might, and only might, sell him his shares back."

"I might at that, but I'll hang onto them for a while—as insurance."

"Insurance?" He raised an eyebrow.

"For all their gratitude about seeing Rose and Teddy, I shouldn't be surprised if there isn't another battle about that in the future. If you noticed, it was Mrs. Grove who was grateful. He didn't say anything. He feels more strongly about his shares than he does about his grandchildren. He isn't finished, not by a long chalk. Mr. Grove was doing what he always did," she replied.

"And what's that?"

"Underestimating every female who crosses his path," she explained. "Eleanor was desperate to go to university, but he wouldn't let her as he thinks educating women is a waste of time. I've no doubt Mrs. Grove could have helped him with the business, but like all women of her class, she was brought up to have babies and arrange flowers."

"You're right, of course, but I believe things will change," he said.

"Perhaps the only good thing to come out of this war is the fact that women have shown they can do far more than they have ever been given the opportunity for, regardless of having been denied adequate education for those opportunities."

He risked a quick look at her. "You're very passionate about this."

She nodded. "I had a wonderful teacher, Miss Hodgeson. She persuaded my father to let me stay on at school as a pupil teacher. If things had been different, I would have gone to the grammar school, and possibly on to university, but there wasn't the money for the uniform. Quite apart from the fact that my own father's attitude to education wasn't so dissimilar to Mr. Grove's. But I know that's what she was hoping for me. I just feel…"

"What?" he prompted.

"I just feel I would be better able to contribute to the business if I'd had a better education."

Ian said nothing, but after a minute, he pulled the car off the road and turned off the engine. "Look at me, Lily," he said, taking her hands in his.

"Without you, there would be no business. Sure, Annis would still be making her creams and lotions and selling them to the local women, and I would still be running the local pharmacy. But it was you who had the vision of what the company could be, it was you who had the idea that there is a bigger market out there, it was you who realised that what we are making is a luxury product that needs proper packaging, and it goes without saying that, when it comes to the company's finances, you know it down to the last halfpenny. It's your drive and ambition that have gotten us so far, and I've absolutely no doubt this is only the beginning. You may not have had a university education, but by God, you have educated yourself, and you're one of the most intelligent women—no, people—I know."

She smiled back at him. "Do you really believe all that?" she asked.

He nodded. "I do, and it needed to be said."

"Thank you," she replied quietly. "Now let's get on. We've a factory opening to organise."

"This is quite a sight," Mrs. Madison said as she observed the lines of product running smoothly along the conveyor belt.

The items were smoothly and quickly picked up and packed into pink-and-black boxes with the Ilaniis name and signature gold rose. The workers also proudly wore white uniforms with the name and rose on the breast pocket. "As for the crèche—" She turned to Lily. "—that's an inspired idea and one I shall be copying at Madison's."

"Now that the war is over, I believe there will be more women with children who have to go out to work," Lily replied. "It's helpful, of course, but it's good business sense."

Mrs. Madison cocked her head to one side. "I knew the moment I met you, Lily, that you would shake up the business world."

"Well, I don't know about that." Lily laughed and then picked up a small cut glass bottle. "What do you think of this?" she asked, taking off the stopper and handing it to Mrs. Madison.

The other woman held it to her nose and inhaled. "That is divine," she murmured, tipping the bottle and applying some to her wrists. "What is it?"

"It's Annis's latest scent, made from lily of the valley," Lily replied. "We decided we need a signature scent, and we think this might have potential."

"It's just the ticket," Mrs. Madison said. "Every scent maker is doing roses and lavender. This will stand out." She paused. "You should just call it Lily."

"Why?" Lily asked.

"Helena Rubenstein and Elizabeth Arden are identified with their products. You should be too. After all, we both know this company would never have been formed without you, and women want to buy products that have been developed for women by women."

"But Annis is the one who knows how to make the products," Lily replied. "She and Ian develop the products. I just design the packages and get them to market."

"Your loyalty is admirable, Lily. But I ask you, without your business acumen, what would Annis be doing now? I suspect she'd still be working in her kitchen. You mustn't diminish your contribution to this business."

Lily laughed. "That's almost exactly what Ian said."

"There you go." Mrs. Madison smiled. "I imagine it's exactly what Annis would say as well."

"Excuse me, miss," a young man said as he approached the pair of them. "I'm from the *Yorkshire Illustrated*. Could you spare a few minutes to answer some questions and have your photograph taken?"

Mrs. Madison gave Lily a little nudge. "Go," she whispered. "You'll never get free publicity again."

The next half hour was taken up with showing the young reporter around the building and posing for photographs with her workers, at her desk, and with the children in the crèche. Eventually, they settled in her office for the interview.

When she had given him a brief history of the company, she was taken aback when he asked, "Tell me, Mrs. Grove, what exactly is the nature of your relationship with your fellow director, Mr. Steele? There's a rumour that wedding bells may be about to ring."

"I don't know where you got that idea," she replied, keeping her voice as even as she could.

"There's another rumour that you and Mr. Steele have

known each other, were close in fact, since before you were so tragically widowed."

"What exactly are you implying?" she asked.

The young man smiled. "I'm not implying anything, Mrs. Grove. When we get information like this, it's important to investigate. We wouldn't want to print anything that's untrue."

"I'd be very interested to know where this information came from," she shot back.

He smiled again. "Ah, I can't reveal my sources."

"In which case, I have no comment to make about them."

He leaned back and steepled his fingers. "Mrs. Grove, this is the way it works. I am giving you the opportunity to tell your side of the story, a story we will print whether you cooperate or not. People are interested in the thought of a woman succeeding in a man's world of business, of course, but they're also interested in the character of the woman who does so. It will be interesting to see what they make of you."

"I imagine, given your line of questioning, that they will see me as you are about to paint me: as a woman who lacks morals and who has slept her way to the top," Lily began, noting, with wry amusement, his reaction to her candid answer. "So let me tell you, I don't care what you print because I wasn't brought up to be a genteel young woman whose purpose was to decorate a man's arm and home before providing him with an heir. This—" She gestured around the room. "—came about because I have worked hard and used my brain. Something that you and countless other men seem to consider beyond us." She stood up. "If you're any sort of journalist, I would expect you to go back and check your source in the interest of producing an accurate article. As I said, print what you like. I don't care. However, if I find anything in the article that is untrue, you may be assured I will take action. Now, I believe this interview is over," she said as she gestured to the door.

fifty-six

"I just passed that reporter chappie on the stairs. He was looking a little green around the gills," Ian said as he came into the office.

"I think he got rather more than he expected," Lily replied. "From the way he was asking questions, I would say he'd had a conversation with Mr. Grove."

"He wasn't here to give us some good publicity, then?" Ian handed her a glass of champagne.

She took a sip. "I would say not. I told you we hadn't heard the last of Mr. Grove."

"Well, I refuse to think of him today, especially as I want to do this," Ian replied, going down on one knee and taking a small box out of his pocket. "Lily Grove, would you do me the honour of marrying me?"

Lily's eyes widened. "Ian," she whispered. "Are you sure?"

"Of course I'm sure. I've never been surer of anything in my life. I want to spend the rest of my life with Teddy, Rose, and you, Lily." He paused for a moment with a grin on his face before adding, "I would appreciate an answer soon because my knee is about to give out."

"Of course, I'll marry you!" Lily laughed, holding her hand out to help him up.

"Then let's get this on your finger so everyone will know you're mine," he replied, opening the box and slipping the ruby-and-diamond ring on her finger. "There," he added. "A perfect fit."

Lily turned her hand this way and that to see the ring. "I can't believe it," she murmured.

Ian's arms wrapped around her. "Believe it," he whispered, kissing her. "I have to tell you, Lily, I don't want a long engagement. If this war has taught us anything, it's that life is too short to waste it dilly-dallying."

"I agree," she said, kissing him back.

"Then shall we agree on a date?"

"I should think three months at the most, unless you want a big wedding."

"We're not having a big wedding. Neither of us has much in the way of family."

"Excellent. Two months, it is." He laughed, kissing her again.

The article in the *Yorkshire Illustrated* wasn't the hatchet job Lily expected. Either the young reporter had considered very carefully what he had been told or Lily's words had given him pause for thought. In fact, the idea of a young woman in business caught the attention of the *Manchester Guardian*, *The Daily Telegraph*, and the *Illustrated London News*, all of which gave valuable publicity. The name Ilaniis was rapidly gaining attention, and sales were increasing at a phenomenal rate. They had orders from department stores from York to London.

"We shall have to take on more workers," she said as she, Annis, and Ian met in the meeting room.

"Can we afford it?" Annis asked.

"We can't afford not to," Lily replied. "We have more orders than we can currently fill, but we can't disappoint our customers just when we're beginning to make a name for ourselves."

"But no one else is making the products we're making," Annis said.

"Not yet," Lily agreed. "But once they see how big the market is, they will be, and we need to make a name for quality and being able to deliver what we've promised before someone else comes into the market."

"I agree," Ian put in. "And there will be a lot of factories silent now that the country's focus has moved away from the war effort. That means factories with workers who can be switched to producing other things."

"If that's what you think we need to do, then that's what we must do," Annis replied.

"The production process can be speeded up with no issue," Ian said. "We built that into the process. It's the packaging and dispatching that needs to be sped up."

"We also need to have extra help in the office," Lily put in. "With all the extra orders, we need more people to reply to customers and do the relevant paperwork."

"Fair point." Ian nodded. "It would be wise to have another sales rep. I'll struggle to help Annis in the lab and be out on the road as well."

Lily nodded. "It would seem we are going to have to expand quicker than we anticipated. From looking at the numbers, I would say we need to double our workforce."

"Are we going to be able to pay for them?" Annis asked.

"That's a fair question, Annis," Lily replied. "After reading books on business, this is where businesses often fail—when they become too big too soon. Fortunately, I can afford to put more money into the business, and it can pay me back as a dividend when time allows."

"You shouldn't risk your own money," Ian said. "We

should go to the bank for a loan."

"No," Lily replied firmly. "Banks don't deal with women. They would only deal with me before because you were there. I have the money, and what better investment than in our business?"

"Then it's settled," Annis said, standing up. "It's no use, Ian," she said, looking at him with a smile. "I think we both know by now that if Lily has an idea, there's no stopping her until she's made it happen, and if that new ring on her finger is anything to go by, you'd better learn that about her before you add the other one." She chuckled.

The meeting was interrupted by the arrival of Lily's secretary. "I'm sorry to bother you, Mrs. Grove, but there are two gentlemen to see you. They said it was urgent and that you'd be willing to see them straightaway. They're waiting in reception."

"That's fine, Susan. We were just about finished here anyway." Lily smiled. "Did these two mysterious gentlemen give their names?"

"No, I'm afraid not," Susan replied. "I'm sorry, Mrs. Grove."

Lily patted her arm. "Don't worry, Susan. I'm just going back to my office. Please show them in."

Lily paused briefly as she entered her office. Everything was as she and Ian had designed it. The large window gave a wonderful view of the dale and made the office light and airy. Her desk was a light wood with a large blotter, her pens and pencils in easy reach along with a desk lamp. Wooden filing cabinets stood along the rear wall. As well as the two chairs in front of her desk, there was a leather sofa and coffee table for informal meetings. Everything was neatly arranged, a throwback from her time as a maid. Each time she entered it, she was reminded of how far she had come from a two-bedroom terrace house in Hope.

"Well, lass, yer seem to 'ave done all right for yerself," a familiar voice said from the doorway.

"Dad?" She turned and smiled. "What are you doing here? And who's this?" she asked, looking from her father to the younger man still standing in the doorway.

The young man laughed. "It's a bit much when your own sister doesn't recognise you," he said in a deep, rich voice.

Lily paused for a moment, taking in the features of the young man, which were largely disguised by a black beard and moustache. "Tommy?" she said. "Tommy, is it you?"

"The very same," he said, holding out his arms.

Lily flung herself towards him. "Oh, Tommy, it's so good to see you! We never thought we'd see you again!" She stepped back. "My goodness, how you've changed."

Gone was the gangly youth with limbs too long for his skinny body. Here was a tall, well-built young man, hard and strong. Even his face had changed. The boyish softness had gone. He was all hard planes and edges.

"Plenty of food, courtesy of His Majesty's navy, I suppose," she said, smiling.

"His Majesty certainly knows to feed his forces well," Tommy agreed. "Otherwise, they wouldn't be much good at fighting."

"You were wrong to run off, though," she admonished him. "No one knew where you were or what you were doing."

"John and I wanted to be involved and do our bit," he replied, adding, "We were too young and foolish to know any better."

She hugged him again. "I don't suppose you were the only foolish ones." She looked behind him. "Where's John? Is he with you?"

"It's a long story and not one to tell here," her brother replied.

"Then you must come home. I hope you're going to be able to stay," she said.

"I hope so too."

fifty-seven

Later, when they had settled into their rooms and enjoyed a meal together, they sat before the fire.

Lily said, "Tell me. Tell me everything. I need to know what happened to you and what happened to John."

Tommy took a deep breath and closed his eyes. Even for a young man, there were lines of strain around his eyes. "We had sort of settled with Aunt Polly," he began. "But we still weren't happy at being packed off with a stranger. The day we signed up, the army had come to town. They looked splendid in their uniforms. John and I were fascinated. We wanted to be part of the excitement, and to be honest, we knew that once we went back to Hope, we'd probably be sent down the mine. We dared each other to sign up. They knew we were too young, but they didn't seem to care. Before we knew it, we were on a train to Portsmouth.

"I don't quite know how we managed it, but we were sent to a naval base to train. They split us up. It's not good to have two brothers on the same ship, just in case. Anyway, John was taken to train as a radio operator, and I was sent to learn the basics of the engine room. It would seem, our Lily, that you weren't the only one in the family with brains. I started as a stoker, but they found I was interested and had a knack for engines, so that's how I served. To be honest, we lost men quickly, so progressing up the ranks was quicker than it should have been. Eventually, I became a sub-lieutenant, and John, the last time I heard of him, was a radio officer."

"What do you mean 'the last you heard of him'?" Lily asked, her eyes wide.

Tommy ran a hand through his hair. "I was on a dreadnought in the North Sea, keeping the German navy in port for most of the war. From what I gather, John was on escort duty in the Atlantic."

"Is that supposed to mean something?" Lily asked.

"They were defending the convoys bringing supplies to Britain. It was probably the most dangerous place in the navy. The convoys were under constant attacks from U-boats."

Lily shook her head. "I'm sorry, Tommy, but you'll have to excuse my ignorance. U-boats?"

"Submarines, craft that sail underneath the water and can fire almost at will, and that's what they did. Much shipping and many lives were lost."

"And that's what happened to John?"

"I believe so. The official story is 'missing, believed killed,' but to be honest with you, Lily, I can't see how he could have survived if they were attacked," he replied quietly.

"But surely they have life rafts?"

"If men can get to them, the sea surrounding them isn't a sea of fire, and they survived the explosion, there are so many things against survival."

"But we mustn't give up hope," Lily said firmly.

"If you say so," he replied.

"I do say so. If there's a way, John will find it," she said, thinking of her brother. He had always been the joker, the one to cheer everyone up when they were sad, the one to get into trouble for his high spirits, and the one to laugh trouble off. She couldn't and wouldn't believe she would never see him again. There was silence, broken only by the crackling of logs as father, brother, and sister thought and prayed for their missing son and brother.

Eventually, Lily's father spoke. "There's something else, lass," he began. "Two things, actually. How would you feel if Beryl and I wed?"

Lily smiled. "I think that would be a very good idea, Dad," she replied. No one could ever replace her mother. Beryl had made it clear when they had first met that she knew that. In his later years, why shouldn't her father have companionship? "What's the second thing?" she asked.

"That's not such good news," he admitted, lowering his head for a moment. "As yer know, our 'ouse is rented from Mr. Grove. Since I don't work for him now, 'e's put the rent up. I was wonderin' what yer think about Beryl and me comin' to live 'ere. We wouldn't be no trouble, and perhaps we can 'elp a bit with the kiddies. Beryl's very fond of kiddies."

There was no doubt in Lily's mind that Grove putting the rent up had less to do with her dad not working for him and more to do with his petty need for revenge against her. The sooner they were all away from his malign influence the better.

"Of course, you can move here, Dad, and I think there might be work at the factory for you," she said, smiling.

"If there's anything going for an engineer as well," Tommy put in, "I've a mind to settle down, find a nice girl to marry, and start my own family. Here's a better place than Hope to do it."

"As a matter of fact, we could do with an engineer to maintain the machinery." Lily smiled again. "So long as the other directors are happy, we will have solved several problems at one go."

Neither Ian nor Annis had any objections and were in fact both more than happy to have more hands in the business. Within the month, Tommy, her father, and Beryl had moved into a cottage on the edge of Hawes, and both men were working in the factory. Beryl was only too happy to look after the twins when Lily needed her, and she quickly became a familiar figure pushing them down the High Street in their pushchair. When she wrote to Aunt Polly to tell her of Tommy's return, she received a letter and photographs of Nora, Betty, and Vera, who were all young ladies now and all at grammar school. Betty hoped to go to university, Vera was keen to go to art school, and Nora had decided to take a secretarial course. Even baby Emily was at school and growing up fast. As soon as she could find the time, Lily decided she would drive down to visit them. Perhaps she and Ian could make the journey part of their honeymoon trip.

In the few weeks before the wedding, Ian appeared in her office at the end of lunchtime.

"I know you're free this afternoon." He grinned.

She consulted the diary on her desk. "No, I'm not. I have a meeting with a Mr. Ironside."

"That's me." He laughed. "There's something I want to show you, and if I don't schedule a meeting, I won't see you until you walk down the aisle, and I know you'll do that because it is in the diary."

fifty-eight

"Is this really necessary?" Lily asked as Ian led her down what she imagined was a street, Though she couldn't be sure due to the fact he had insisted she close her eyes as soon as she got in the car.

"I want it to be a surprise" was all he said, but she could hear the laughter in his voice. "To be honest, you surprised me by doing as you're told and keeping your eyes closed."

"Well, it had better be worth it," she replied. "How much further?"

"We're here. You can open your eyes now," he said.

They stood in front of a beautiful stone house with steps leading up to a front door and mullioned bay windows on both sides of the house, with additional mullioned windows on the first floor and, as far as Lily could see, attics at the top of the house. They stood at the base of the steps. What Lily had taken to be a winding road, was in fact, the tree-lined drive leading to the front of the house. She turned around to see the beautifully manicured lawns and flower beds stretching across the fields below.

"It's beautiful, but why are we here?" Lily said in awe.

"This is our house, Lily. Or it could be, if you want it to be," he replied.

"I don't understand."

"This house belonged to my great aunt. It's only recently that I found out about it. My great aunt didn't live here, and it was rented out. The tenants have moved, so it's empty and ready for us should we want to raise our family here."

"I'm still not sure I understand," she said. "Are you telling me you actually own this house?"

He nodded.

She looked from him to the house. "This isn't the sort of house a regular sort of person owns," she said, placing her hands on her hips. "Is there something you need to tell me before we get married?"

"It's not a big deal," he replied.

"Oh, I think it might be," she shot back. "You know about my family and circumstances, but now I come to think about it, I know very little about yours."

"There's really not much to tell," he replied. "But if you insist," he said, taking a key out of his pocket. "Let's at least go inside and talk in comfort."

The spacious hallway had a traditional black-and-white tiled floor with a light oak curved staircase rising from its centre. The walls were covered with rather old-fashioned, but clearly expensive, pale-blue-and-silver flocked wallpaper. Ian opened a door to the left and led Lily into a large, airy room— what she assumed to be the drawing room. The walls were covered in pale blue watered silk with drapes and carpets chosen to match. There was a large fireplace on one wall. The mullioned window she had seen from the outside stretched almost from floor to ceiling. The furniture was covered in dust sheets, one of which Ian whisked off so they could sit on a leather chesterfield.

"Well," he said, running a hand through his hair, "the fact

is that we both apparently have black sheep in our families. Your mother and mine seem to be one of a kind."

"Go on."

"I only fairly recently discovered that my mother came from a wealthy, landowning family. Apparently, like your mother's parents, they didn't approve of her marrying my father. Consequently, when she married my father, they cut her off, and she never had anything more to do with them. As far as I know, they didn't even know where she was living, which is ironic given the fact that this house is only just outside of Hawes."

"How did they trace you? We at least knew that Mum had contacted her sister, Polly."

He ran his hands through his hair again. "Apparently, my great aunt's solicitor hired some kind of private investigator. Otherwise, there was a chance the estate would go to the government or something. It seems I am the last of the family line. Mother's sister died in childbirth, and her brother was killed in a hunting accident, Mother died while I was at university. My great aunt had been married but was unable to have children."

"What a sad story," Lily said, placing her hand on Ian's arm.

"It came as something of a shock," he replied. "This isn't the only property. Apparently, Great Aunt Lucy was married to an American, so there's property there as well as others in Yorkshire and some in the south of England."

"You'll be telling me next you're a duke or something." Lily laughed.

"No, thank God. No title." He joined in her laughter before adding, "This means, between us, we have more than enough money to build our business, and our children will have security. The money you inherited from Jonathon was life-changing, as is this," he finished solemnly.

"Well, I can assure you I won't let it go to my head," she

replied, adding with a glint of laughter in her eyes. "I shall want a tiara, of course, and to bathe in ass's milk every day, but apart from that, it won't change my life."

"Whatever you desire," he said, taking her hand and bringing it to his lips. "It will be my honour and pleasure to give to you. I love you, Lily. That will never change."

"I know," she replied softly. "I love you, Ian. Now and always."

"Will you be happy to live here?"

"I will be happy to live in a tent with you." She laughed.

"When I think of the chances of us meeting at all, I begin to think that God or fate or whatever definitely had a hand in it." He drew her into his arms and kissed her.

It was some time before they drew apart. "I think we must stop now, my love," he whispered into her ear, causing her to shiver. "Our first visitors will arrive shortly."

"Visitors?" Her eyes widened.

"I invited Annis, Joey, Beryl, and Tom to come," he admitted, looking a little sheepish.

"Not that I'm not happy to see them, but why?"

"Well, there are several cottages on the estate. I thought they might like to move here as well. Annis isn't getting any younger. I thought she might agree to a cottage here where she's not so remote, and Joey and Beryl want to help with the twins and any other children we might have. As for Tom, he's already said he wants to settle down and have his own family."

She looked up at him. "You seem to have it all worked out."

He shook his head. "Not all of it, and none of it will happen if you don't want it to. As far as they know, they're just coming to see what I hope is to be our new home."

"Then let's see the rest of it," she said, standing up and taking his hand.

It was as close to perfect as a house could be. The kitchen

was large and airy and had recently been modernised. There was a small breakfast room as well as a formal dining room, morning room, library, and small study as well as the drawing room she had already seen. Upstairs, there were seven bedrooms. One bedroom even had its own bathroom, which the Groves hadn't even had in their home. There were four more rooms on the second floor, as well as attics and cellars. There were several fireplaces throughout the house, and each room had its own radiator. There would never be the issue of scraping ice from the inside of the windows on winter mornings.

"Most of the rooms seem to have been decorated fairly recently," she observed.

"I don't think the tenants were planning to move quite so quickly, but I believe there was talk of an overseas posting for the man. I think they'd decorated and modernised when they had to move and Aunt Lucy died," he explained, adding, "If you don't like it, we can redecorate."

"No," Lily replied. "I like it, but do you know what I like best?" she asked, moving toward the window and looking out. "It's the thought of waking up to that view of the dale every morning, whether it's green like today, or purple with heather, or yellow with gorse, or even covered with snow. I don't think I will ever tire of it."

"Even when the black clouds come and it's pelting down with rain?" he asked with a smile.

"Even then," she replied. "It's a reminder that life has days of clouds as well as sunshine."

"And what's today?" he asked, coming to stand beside her.

She turned into his arms. "Sunshine. Definitely sunshine."

Their conversation was halted by the sight of not one, but two cars coming down the drive and pulling up next to Ian's. Out stepped Annis, her father, and Beryl with the twins. From the second car, Tom and another man with thick dark hair and a bushy beard, whom she didn't recognise, stepped out. The mystery man walked with a slight limp. No doubt one of Tom's shipmates had decided to visit.

"Is this what yer wanted to show us?" her father was the first to speak.

While Ian was explaining his plans, Lily stole a glance at the stranger, waiting for her brother to introduce him. They had taken a tour of the house and were walking towards the cottages when the stranger caught up with her. "Is this any way to greet your brother, sis?" he said.

Lily stared at him. "Johnny? Is it really you?"

"In the flesh," he replied. "Well, what's left of it after the German navy and the medics took their pound of it."

She flew into his arms, stepping back slightly when she felt him wince. "Oh God, Johnny. We thought you were dead."

"Well, as you can see, I'm very much alive." He smiled.

"You're so different," she said.

"War changes a man," he replied. "I went away a boy, but war makes men out of the boys it spares."

"What happened?"

He shook his head. "That's a story for another day. I was lucky. I survived. A lot of men, good men, didn't. For now, I just want to be with my family and have some normality."

"Of course, and there's plenty of room here for you to rest and recuperate."

"Thanks, our Lily. I appreciate that, but will your new husband want all your relations hanging around?"

Lily laughed. "Having all my relations hanging around was actually his idea. One more won't make much of a difference."

"I'm not the person I was, Lily," he replied.

"I hope not," she teased, adding, "Neither am I. Both of us have changed, but what's important is the person you've become."

As she walked beside her newly found brother, she looked around at her family: her father and new stepmother, who seemed content with each other; her children, who clearly adored their grandparents; Annis, who had given her the opportunity to succeed as well as great friendship; her two brothers, who had miraculously been saved from the war and Ian; and the love of her life. As she approached a new stage in her life, she knew that everything she had experienced—from her life in Hope, to working for the Groves, to her relationship with Jonathon, to having the twins, and coming to Hawes— had all been part of the making of her.

Don't miss out on your next favorite book!

Join the Satin Romance mailing list
www.satinromance.com/mail.html

acknowledgments

Many thanks to all at Melange who have worked with me and made me a better writer.

about the author

Although born in Yorkshire, Anna now lives in a lovely village in Hampshire not far from the home of her literary heroine, Jane Austen. She lives with her husband and they have two grown up children. Anna spent many years teaching a range of subjects from religion to drama but has always been fascinated by history, and, although history frequently records the actions of men, she is interested in the lives of ordinary women who are often in the shadows. Away from Hampshire, Anna frequently enjoys walking in the beautiful Yorkshire Dales, not far from the home of her other literary heroines, the Brontes. She continues to play the piano, badly!

also by anna aysgarth

Unsuitable Brides

A Bride for Christmas

The Marquess Meets Miss Nobody

Never a Lady

Novels

The Making of Her

Printed in Great Britain
by Amazon

13715293R00195